ANDREW SCOTT

Andrew Scott is the author of seventeen books, most under his full name of Andrew Murray Scott, including biographies of Alex Trocchi and Graham of Claverhouse. Graduating with first class honours in English and History, he worked as freelance journalist, media lecturer, and for ten years as a parliamentary press officer, returning in 2016 to full-time writing. His novel, *Tumulus*, won the Dundee International Book Prize in 1999. He is a member of the Society of Authors and Scottish PEN, and registered in the Scottish Book Trust's Live Literature scheme. *Oblivion's Ghost* is his seventh published novel, the third in the Willie Morton Scottish political thriller series.

https://www.andrewmurrayscott.scot

Twitter: @andymurrayscott

Facebook/Andrew Murray Scott

Oblivion's Ghost

ANDREW SCOTT

– Twa Corbies Publishing –

First published in 2020 by Twa Corbies Publishing

© Andrew Scott 2020

Twa Corbies Publishing
twacorbiespublishing@gmail.com

The moral right of the author has been asserted in
accordance with the Copyright, Designs & Patents Act 1988.

British Library Cataloguing-in-Publication Data
A catalogue record for this book is available on request
from the British Library.

Typeset in Adobe Garamond Pro by Lumphanan Press
www.lumphananpress.co.uk

ebook version also available. ISBN: 978 0 9933840 9 7

ISBN: 978 0 9933840 8 0

1: VANISHING ACT

PROLOGUE

Luke Sangster was hard at work in the larger of the two empty bedrooms in the almost-derelict fifth floor flat in Marchmont Crescent, Edinburgh when his spy-cam buzzed. He switched screen and saw the two men in the ground floor hallway. He knew instantly what they were and that he had to get out. Police officers or spooks of some kind; hard-faced, dark-haired men in black coats, suits, black shoes. There was no time to lose. He leaped over to the door and turned the key. Setting the data file to download onto the portable hard-drive, he grabbed the satchel on the floor and began to stuff his laptop and notebooks into it. The room was a digital cave, a hacker's cell with two desktop PCs and a laptop connected with co-axial cables to a satellite dish on the wall outside and the broadband hub. He would have to leave it all. There was warm tea in the mug in the room and the computers were hot. He would not be able to do anything about the warm teabag in the galley kitchen. They would discover a kettle had recently boiled. There wasn't much for them to find elsewhere. In the smaller of the two bedrooms his sleeping bag on a pile of flattened cardboard boxes. The other rooms were empty, no furniture, no belongings, nothing. He had known this day would come but there was an unreality about it now it was actually happening. How had they got onto him?

On the spy-cam the men were racing up the stairs, turning

around the bannisters from flight to flight, first floor, second floor, third, starting up to the fourth. Sixteen flats in the building and they were heading straight to his. They'd been tipped off or was it just a lucky guess? The download was clocking round, now at sixty per cent – maddeningly slow. He watched it rocket to seventy-three then it seemed to stick… seventy-six, seventy-nine… *come on*! They were right outside now, on the fifth floor landing. A second spy-cam up there, in a tiny hole in the coving, showed them peering at the name on his neighbours' door. One was getting down on his knees… eighty-five…eighty-eight… ninety-three… he picked up the leather satchel… ninety-eight… hundred. He unplugged, but still had to delete the user account and reset the PC.

He heard the knock on the front door. He had to get out. He whipped out the hard-drive, stuck it in the satchel beside the laptop and looped the strap around his neck. The reset process would take an hour but could not be stopped and it would silently remove everything. He checked that it had started and now he could go.

He stepped onto the flimsy wooden shelf unit and lifted his left leg onto the top shelf. Balancing carefully, he stretched upwards to the attic hatch and flipped it with one hand, as he had practised. He reached up, catching hold of the wooden sill, jumped off the shelf unit, pulling himself up into the attic, the dead weight of the bag constricting his neck. He heard the first attack on the front door. They were booting it in!

In the musty attic, kneeling on thick foam insulation, he carefully rearranged the hatch behind him, sealing out the light from below. Crouching and blinking in the dim light, he stepped on beams between the piles of foam, to the ancient skylight. A rusted iron frame holding two narrow glass panes, one of which was cracked. Checking his pockets, adjusting the satchel he took a deep breath, lifted the skylight halfway and stood up in the open space. Holding up the heavy weight of the skylight frame, he climbed out, left foot onto the slate, left knee pressing inwards. He could feel the cold air at his forehead and cheeks. With the fingertips of both hands grasping the skylight frame, he drew his right foot out to find a toehold on the greasy slates. Let the skylight down with his right hand. He crouched close to the roof, took a breath. Behind him were the fifth floor windows and roofs of the tenements on the west side of Marchmont Crescent. He was high up but had no time to be anxious. Once, a friend, Gary, had tried to interest him in parkour or base-jumping. He often wished he'd given it a go. His boots had a good, thick tread, with Vibram soles. It wouldn't take them long to work out where he had gone. He should not have left the key in the lock. Smelling the moss and seagull guano there was nothing below him but the old lead guttering, then a sheer drop of nearly sixty feet onto concrete and tarmac. Gripping with the toes of his boots, knees and fingertips, he scrambled up the slates so that he could put his boots on top of the skylight frame. And use it to lever himself upwards to grasp the zinc ridge cap at the apex of the roof. He pulled himself up and over it. Swivelled around and slid feet first down into the lead gulley behind. It was a feature that only roofers would know existed, perfectly concealed to all but pigeons and seagulls. It ran the length of four blocks, a flat valley between the pitched roofs. At the far end, he would descend onto a roof where there was a roof terrace. It was an escape plan he had practised several times. He crouched as he ran along the lead gulley, dropped onto the roof terrace and moved to the door at the top of the stairwell. He was five tenements along from his own house now and had calculated that that would be enough. He knew that the door from the roof terrace into this building was not generally locked. There always was the possibility that someone might lock it, of course. But it was open. He got inside, pulled it shut behind him and sped down the four flights of stairs to the front door, meeting no-one on the way, hearing no sounds. He suspected they would soon discover he had escaped by way of the attic and maybe call in a helicopter, and try and block off the entire Crescent. So time was short.

At ground level, he opened the front door and peered at the street. Nothing unusual. They would pick him up on CCTV monitor screens once he left the building and was out in the open. Nothing he could do about that. He drew out the green woolly hat from his satchel, pulled it low over his ears and forehead.

It was a high-density housing area. Tenements, mostly sub-divided into student flats. He was thinking hard about where he could go. There were possibilities, options, some better than others. He looked at his watch: 10.30 a.m. Right! Out and go for it. He walked into Marchmont Crescent and, resisting the urge to look back at his own tenement, crossed over, walking swiftly onto the main road.

On two corners of the junction, there was a small knot of shops; on his side, a fresh fish shop, barbers, a flower shop and an internet cafe which he had often frequented. On the far side, a fish and chip shop, a cheesemongers and the Red Box Cafe. He saw that a red double-decker bus, the 24 to West Granton, was coming up the road. Its indicator was on. It was stopping. He sprinted between oncoming cars to the bus stop. The small queue seemed to take ages to get on and he had to assist an elderly lady in a mothball-smelling woollen coat onto the bus deck.

'Thank you, son,' she said toothlessly grateful to Luke,

slowly revealing her bus pass to the driver in a shaking hand. She began to totter unsteadily – blocking the aisle – towards the Priority seats for the elderly and disabled. The entire performance had taken about three minutes, Luke reckoned as he placed his Lothian Ridacard on the card-reader and sprinted up the stairs. The bus started. He kept his face turned away from the CCTV camera and sat with his hand partially covering his face, studying the Crescent as they passed. Through his fingers, he saw that a black Mondeo and a people carrier had arrived outside his tenement. The police or spooks had called in reinforcements. Then he realised that he had thoughtlessly used his Ridacard. Pointless to try to evade the cameras. They'd be checking all footage in the vicinity. He thought fast, visualising routes to his bolt-holes, trying to think of ways to get there that had no CCTV or were beyond the range of cameras on passing buses. Cameras on buses filmed the streets on either side of the bus as well as the interior. The spooks used them a lot to track a moving target, a dissident. And he was one of those alright, moving in plain sight – for now.

CHAPTER ONE

Life had returned to normal for Willie Morton. His front page exposure of the GB13 group – gained by putting himself at risk – was unlikely to lead to work offers. He was a marked man. He had briefly appeared before the public at large, or that diminishing band who still read printed newspapers like the *Scottish Standard*. Although no longer a person of interest to MI5 or Special Branch; the niggling feeling of being followed or spied upon seemed to have receded, he knew that surveillance is omnipresent, but it didn't feel as intrusive as it had been. The life of a modern citizen, as he was well aware, is a full-colour movie, available 24/7 for any spook that cares to watch. You just had to hope they had more interesting subjects to distract them. In a few days, it would be the spring teaching break of early April. He and his girlfriend, Professor Emily Louise McKechnie, were supposed to be going on a week's hillwalking holiday, although they had failed to arrange anything. They had not booked accommodation or a flight or even decided where to go and now it was too late. He was spending more time with Emily, often staying overnight at her place in Lochend Grove in Restalrig. Or walking from his flat in Keir Street to meet her for lunch near the university. Morton was, however, finding it difficult to settle down and commit to writing his monthly political commentary for *Der Ubergang* the German news journal or his four paragraph digest for Japanese press agency Taimuzu. The referendum, only six months ago, seemed a distant memory. In the wider world, a crisis was developing within the Cameron government over Europe, under pressure from UKIP and the frog-like chortlings of its leader, Nigel Farage. He had begun to read for pleasure again – which he had not done for years – and to visit the library. It was a rebirth of his inner soul. Emily said she thought he was becoming a more relaxed person.

'You can't see it,' she reiterated, sipping a glass of Chardonnay in the beer garden at Jablonkis in Bristo Place. 'But I can. You must have been under a lot of stress. No wonder.'

It was a sunny day in late-March, spring-like. The sun illuminated the rim of her glass as she raised it to her lips and made the wine look greenish and yet golden too. They had kept their coats on because of the cold wind funnelling between the tenements on the opposite side of the street. Jablonkis was one of many handy lunchtime haunts, more or less equidistant between the university, the *Scottish Standard* office and his flat. Morton was drinking St Miguel and had ordered spicy-sausage pasta salad and Emily, avocado on rye toast and wedges.

Morton toyed with his tall, slender beer glass, which he knew was called a stange, swirling anti-clockwise to re-invigorate the white froth, tracing with his finger in the sheen of condensation on the green bottle. He poured some more into the glass. 'There's still a lot of loose ends,' he murmured. 'But I don't suppose I can do anything about them.' He was trying to ignore the large TV screen flashing at him from inside an area protected by an awning. It was just at his eye level. Some kind of music concert, difficult to make out in the strong light. Luckily the sound was turned low in deference to the neighbouring properties.

Emily smiled indulgently, eyelashes flickering behind the lenses of her chic black specs. 'There will always be loose ends, dear. Life is a continuum. A spectrum of human activity of which we are part.'

'Very philosophical,' Morton observed. 'Things continuing. Like Lord Craile, ninety-seven and not out – wonder if he's still in that private hospital?'

'Maybe. But at least he's stopped sending brutes to try and kill you.' She laughed. 'That's progress!'

Morton sniffed. 'There is that, I suppose. I often think I should have preferred charges against him. I think the police wanted me to but it seemed pointless. People like him have no respect for the law.'

'Which is deeply ironic,' Emily said. 'Given he was a Sheriff on the bench for a while and a legislator in the House of Lords.'

'One law for them…'

'Talking of loose ends, Willie, I'm a little worried about Luke. You remember him? Luke Sangster.'

'Oh, yes,' Morton asserted dryly, 'my kidnapper.'

'Hardly a kidnap!'

'No, I suppose not. But anyway, what about old Luke?'

'You know he is an ethical hacker, doing stuff that might be dangerous? You know that, Willie? Well, he's not been seen for a while and he missed the meeting, which is unlike him. We're worried about him.'

'Really?' Morton squinted in the sun. 'You think, what? He's been…?'

Emily shrugged. 'He hasn't previously missed a meeting. He's important within the group, you know. There are others who are keen and committed but it's usually Luke who acquires the most valuable information. He's very bright. Brilliant at getting access to secure online sites, databases,' she laughed, 'or whatever hackers do. But he can do those things and not get caught, not leave a trail. People who know about such things say he's one of the best.' Emily looked around and her voice became conspiratorial. 'You know about the leak of Brian Treanor's financial dealings? He was a key player, *the* key funder of *Scottish Britons*, heard of it? No, me neither. It was a front organisation that popped up six weeks before the referendum, to leverage extra funds by avoiding Electoral Commission rules.'

'Tory gold?'

She rolled her eyes. 'It was Luke who got the stuff to Libby Hope at the *Guardian*. Turns out Treanor gave more than half of all the funds raised. And all of it came from people like him who didn't live in Scotland and didn't have a vote. Well, that never would have come to light without Luke. But he's a serious young man too, reliable.'

Morton nodded. 'Can't say I really formed an impression of him. Some of the time, he was wearing a pig-mask.'

'Goodness, yes,' Emily smiled. 'How weird. I'd forgotten that.'

'Yeah. And once he'd taken the thing off, he left after a few minutes.'

Emily looked up. 'Ah – our food, lovely!'

The waitress, a waif-like blonde in black jeggings and tee-shirt, put their plates in front of them. Morton wondered if she was Romanian or Slovakian though her accent sounded very Scottish. Her skin was chalky white. Maybe she was Italian and missing the sunshine? It was one of the things he loved most about Edinburgh; its diversity. That you couldn't say for certain where a person had come from originally. Edinburgh was changing and for the better, becoming more cosmopolitan, dragging its ancient corpus into the modern world. And he loved that the incomers often sounded more Scottish than indigenous folk.

They ate in silence for a while. The sausage was properly spicy, with plenty of basil and oregano.

'Avocado okay?' he asked, nicking a potato wedge on the sly.

'Oi, you! Yes. Mind you can't mess up an avocado. Yours?'

Morton tried to speak with his mouth full. 'Sausage… lovely.'

Emily sniffed. 'Carnivore! Slaughterer of beasts!'

Morton laughed and pulled a face. 'Sorry, Em, I'd forgotten you've gone vegan.' He grinned wickedly. 'Looking forward to your meeting?'

While Morton was contemplating the luxury of an afternoon of research in the Reference section of Edinburgh Central Library, poor Emily was scheduled to attend a staff meeting of the Politics and Constitutional Studies Department at 3 p.m. She gave him a sour look.

'I shouldn't have had this glass of wine. I'd better get peppermints on the way over there.

'Anyway,' Morton began, keen to change the subject, 'Did Luke work – or was he self-employed like me?'

Emily readjusted the spectacles on the bridge of her nose. 'Not sure. Luke keeps himself very much to himself. I don't know if he works or if he's married, or where he lives. He's a mystery.'

Morton pursed his lips and swigged the last of his beer. He put down his glass. 'Interesting. Is that because he keeps a low profile? I mean, for the type of work he does? He seemed fairly intense, not that I saw much of him.' He belched quietly into his hand. 'Um – he jokingly said to me… admitted to being… "the brains behind the gang." That's what he said. Alasdair and Marco were like his assistants.'

Emily looked up. 'How is Alasdair?'

'Huh, well.' Morton pulled a face. 'He has both feet well-planted under Celia's table. He's still living there.'

Emily shook her head in wonder. 'Amazing how that came about! They really get on, don't they?'

Morton nodded, shading his eyes. 'Who would have thought it? On the face of it, they have nothing in common. She's a sort of one-nation Tory, he's an utter pleb.'

'Opposites attract, perhaps?' Emily commented. 'He's a nice man. Okay, Mr M, I'll let you have that last wedge.'

'Thanks. I wonder if people would say that about us?'

'No. We've got a lot in common,' Emily said warmly. 'Books, hill-walking, getting out and about...'

'Yes, we must... must get ourselves organised.'

'For the summer vacation? We will. Anyway, we like some of the same music,' she grimaced, 'well, not the twangier country stuff obviously, but our political views are similar – we see things the same way, in general.'

'That's true.'

'You up for a dessert? Or a coffee?'

'Might have a coffee. Do you have the time?'

'Not really.'

'Well then, I won't either. I'm not fussed.' Morton stood up. 'I'll get this. My shout, I think.'

As they walked back to the David Hume Tower, Morton took Emily's hand. He was conscious that they didn't do the hand-holding thing often, or other signs of affection. They weren't very demonstrative but he was making an effort to change that.

'You can head off if you like,' she said as they entered George Square.

He grinned. 'Embarrassed to be seen with me in case any of your students are watching?'

'No! Course not! I just didn't want to hold you up.'

'You're the one with the meeting…'

'Think I'll text Marco this afternoon,' Emily murmured, as they reached the base of the tower. They walked over the wide area of concrete slabs and parted at the front entrance.

Morton's thoughts were elsewhere. 'Marco? Oh – about Luke?'

'Yes. Marco knows him a bit better than anyone else.'

'Right,' he said. He kissed her chastely on the cheek. 'Enjoy the meeting.' He smiled as Emily stuck out her tongue at him and waved as she entered the building.

CHAPTER TWO

Emily's meetings often over-ran until exhaustion, physical and mental, took its toll. As Head of Department, her descriptions of proceedings afforded Morton considerable amusement. There were those male members of staff who felt contractually obliged to contribute in equal measure to their inflated sense of self-importance. The meetings thrived on ego-fuel, intense hidden rivalries among the closest of colleagues. As a self-employed journalist, Morton thanked all the gods that he would never be required to attend Departmental meetings. It was one of the reasons why he turned down the offer when it was made – and it had been made on several occasions – by Hugh Leadbetter, of a fulltime staff position at the *Scottish Standard*. Emily's meetings seemed like a special circle of hell from which she could not escape.

Having spent a pleasant but rather unproductive afternoon in Edinburgh Central Library, he was glad to get out into the fresh air at 5 p.m. It was difficult to settle down to work when he'd had a beer at lunch. One beer made you want another, set up a restless craving to spend the afternoon in the pub. But he had persisted. He was working up a piece on the impending General Election. It was an interesting scenario in Scotland; a deeply unpopular Labour leader, Ed Miliband, seemingly unable to prevent the leaking of Labour support to the Nationalists against the usual background of yet another easy Tory victory at Westminster. Sturgeon's personal ratings were the highest of any politician in the UK. SNP membership had hit one hundred and five thousand. How many of Labour's forty-one Scottish seats would fall to them?

It was getting dark as he emerged onto the pavement of George IV Bridge. He planned to walk to Emily's, via the Sainsbury's at Meadowbank Shopping Park, a good couple of miles. He needed to pick up some wine and other items to concoct his unique version of spicy vegetable curry with dhal, rice and naan bread. He had found in his early forties that he liked cooking. It was a new thing for him, part of his relationship with Emily. He didn't seem to mind shopping these days either. He wondered if that too was a sign of aging. He was forty-three but forty-four was in sight, the grim reaper not far behind.

Sainsbury's was busy with the after-work crowd. It had the perfect ambience for de-stressing, he supposed. Orange colours, bright lights, subtle music hinted at, gorgeous displays of exotic fruits and vegetables. There was the luxury of choices, the decision-making empowerment of selection. Most of the prosperous middle-class now shopped at Lidl or Aldi, kidding themselves, as they disgorged from their gas-guzzling SUVs that they were saving a bob or two. Morton ambled about, fully absorbed, a zombie with a plastic basket. He queued at the checkout and loaded his purchases into the plastic bags he had brought with him.

When he got to Emily's ground-floor flat in Lochend Grove the central heating was on. He drew the curtains and switched on the TV in the living room, the radio in the kitchen. It was an ex-Council house and the scullery-kitchen had a door to the backyard where coloured bins stood in line, beside a shed in the tiny garden. It was a comfortable place and he often compared it to his own flat. Of course, while his flat was rented from a Housing Co-op, Emily owned hers. She had invited him to move in, but he couldn't decide what he felt about that.

He stood watching the TV news but there was little of interest so he returned to the kitchen, uncapped a bottle of Grolsch and swigged it, enjoying the cold yeasty taste. He began to organise the curry. As well as the spicy vegetables he was using Greek yoghurt, sultanas and unsalted cashews. He could take his time because he knew Emily would be late.

It was after 7 p.m. before he heard her at the front door. She would need a lot of pampering and attention to soothe her jangled nerves. All he had left to cook was the rice, everything else was done and keeping warm; the dhal in danger of going thick and crusty.

Although she had come home by bus, plugged in to her music, she was still stressing over what had been said, or not said, at the meeting and full of recriminations.

'What Madam needs,' Morton said, taking her briefcase from her and throwing it on the hall floor, 'is a nice cold glass of wine.'

'Ooh, lovely,' she exclaimed, kicking off her shoes. 'You're so right.'

'Come and sit on the sofa,' he instructed, leading her by the hand. 'I'll just put the sound off.'

An hour later, after the meal and more wine and a second glass of beer for Morton, she had sufficiently chilled-out that they could converse as normal, sprawled on the sofa in the living room.

'Did you contact Marco by the way?' he asked.

She turned her head slightly. 'Oh yes. And it's disturbing.

Marco says spooks – whether Special Branch or MI5 or whoever – raided his flat but he escaped, apparently, or at any rate they didn't arrest him – and then he disappeared. It doesn't look good. Poor Luke.'

Morton pulled himself up on the sofa and stretched his back. 'Ohh, ooh.' The sofa wasn't good for his spine and neck. He sighed. 'Well. Right, but why *did* they raid his flat? And where is his flat?'

Emily sighed. 'Don't know. Marco knows – I think. Well, he must.'

'The stuff about Brian Treanor was months ago. Why raid him now?'

Emily murmured: 'No idea.'

'So if he's done a vanishing act, how does Marco know? Has there been contact with Luke?'

'Again, I don't know. You'd be better to speak to Marco. In fact, yes, you definitely should. I can give you his mobile number.'

Morton thought about it. 'Okay. I could do that tomorrow.' He scented a story or the beginnings of one. 'I'm kind of fed-up of the piece I'm working on now, Em. I can easily leave it for a day or two.'

She smiled. 'I was so caught up in my day… didn't ask how you got on.'

He grunted. 'My heart's not in it. I'd be glad of a diversion. Where does Marco live?'

'By the Meadows, Marchmont, I think.'

The next day, after Emily had cycled to work, Morton sent a WhatsApp message to Marco. He was standing in the kitchen in his briefs wearing a velour towel robe of Emily's, looking out at the block of flats opposite and the driech-looking morning and feeling cold, when he heard his mobile ping. Marco could meet him at noon in the Red Box on Marchmont Road.

Morton dressed in black technical shirt, grey microfleece and grey/black walking trousers. In the hall, he zipped his shirt to the neck, laced up his heavy walking shoes and donned his Jack Wolfskin puffer jacket, beanie hat and gloves. He was changing, or adapting to circumstance. A few years ago he had gone over wholesale to functional, high-quality technical kit. He still favoured jeans and tee-shirts for lounging in his flat or going to the pub. Smart but casual style; jackets, shirts and ties had gone. Now everyone wore leisure-wear all the time and Morton was ready for any-thing; an urban warrior, equipped for whatever the weather or hostile forces might throw at him.

The Red Box in Spottiswoode Road at the junction with Marchmont Road was a quirky cafe and licensed restaurant, with huge windows and colourful plastic chairs on the pave-ment outside. Named for the reconditioned phone box that now served as a community information board, its exposed brick walls, shelves laden with books and an eclectic mix of species of tables and chairs, gave it a homely feel. It was lunch-time and busy, Morton saw, mostly young working people fiddling with smart phones or reading the complimentary copies of the *Herald, Scottish Standard* and *Evening News*. He tried to order a black coffee but had to accept a medium Americano instead, sign of the times, and found a table by the window. He had barely taken a sip of the coffee before Marco Vanetti arrived. He was looking smarter than the last time they'd met, a couple of months ago, Morton thought; in a raincoat, blue suit and open-necked shirt. Morton remembered the pale skin, blue-dark curly hair and heavy blueish growth around his cheeks and chin. He *looked* Italian,

Morton thought, if that was possible or just an example of stereotyping.

'Hi Wullie, good tae see you,' Marco said.

Morton rose to shake his hand. 'Enter the second kidnapper…' he said laughing.

Marco grinned sheepishly. 'Oh aye. Sorry about that. But we got there in the end. You had a kinda bad time of it.'

'I survived,' Morton concluded. 'Meanwhile, Emily is worried about Luke's disappearing act. I think I'm being recruited to start a search for him.'

Marco grunted. 'I'll just get masel a wee cappuchino.'

Morton waited, idly observing the other customers. He noticed that the professorial gent in the blue waxed jacket, whose silky white hair was needing the attentions of a barber, had developed from reading the *Scottish Standard*, to doing the crossword, filling in the boxes with a biro pen. Morton wondered if he would try to purloin it when he left. It was surely the restaurant's copy. What's yours is mine, what's mine's my own, he remembered his mother saying, and smiled inwardly.

Marco sat down opposite him. He had a mug of coffee and a large sticky Danish pastry. 'I'll tell you what I know, which isnae a lot. I knew him only from meetings – apart from the time in the static – where we took you. He was a mystery man, though I know where his flat is.'

'Emily thought you might.'

'I don't think he wanted me tae know, but… it isnae far from here. We could take a look, if ye want? Just two streets away.'

Morton nodded. 'That's probably a good starting point – if you have the time?'

'Oh aye. I've no to be at work for another hour yet. Oodles of time, man.'

'You work at the Uni as a… programmer, was it?'

'I.T. technician. The programming is something I dae as a hobby, you could call it.'

'Nearby? Luke's flat.'

Marco nodded. 'Aye, Marchmont Crescent, nearer this end, about five or six doors along.'

'Right.'

A shadow of doubt must have assailed Marco because he added: 'When I say he lives there, maybe it's mair like a flat he uses. I got the impression it wisnae a…' he frowned, 'um… a permanent home, like.'

Morton drained the dregs of his coffee. 'Did he give you the address or… how did you come to know it?'

Marco sniffed. 'Found out by accident really. There was a gadget he'd ordered in somebody else's name. Well – long story – he asked me tae deliver it. He never ordered anything in his own name.'

Morton stood up and pulled on his puffer jacket. 'No, I imagine he didn't. He seemed very careful. Fastidious, I seem to recall from those few minutes in the static. And what was this gadget?'

'A Zotac GTX,' Marco grinned. 'Well, you did ask!'

Morton pulled on his beanie and gloves. 'A what?'

They went out onto the street.

'What in the name of god or gods is a Zotac?'

'A cracking rig,' Marco said. 'Or at least a GPU chip that had been repurposed intae a cracking rig.'

'But what is a cracking rig?'

'It's used with Hashcat software.'

Morton shook his head as they stood on the pavement. 'No – don't tell me any more. And are these things legal?'

'Of course. Everything is legal, until somebody adapts it,

or as we say, repurposes it. The one he'd ordered was part of a dedicated brute-force machine he was building.'

They crossed the road into Marchmont Crescent. Morton was contemplating the concept of a brute-force machine. 'This is all above my head. What was it for?'

Marco pursed his lips and shrugged. 'What was it for – originally – or what was he going to use it for?'

'Well, both.'

'Initially, it's a chip to improve the processing speed of graphics images and to increase memory. There are small ones in most smartphones. This was a much bigger one – and he already had a few – to enable him to crack faster.'

'But crack what?'

Marco looked at him incredulously. 'WPAZ-PSK passwords, like. To get into secure sites.'

'I see. It doesn't sound legal.'

Marco grinned. 'Well, aye, maybe, but there are bigger ones you can buy on the internet. He had been building his own, like I say, but it was too slow. He needed more processing power. Anyway, this is it.'

They'd stopped in front of a tenement door.

Marco pointed. 'Service button,' he said. 'Press it.'

'Will it work?' Morton asked dubiously.

'Aye – it's for the posties, see. Mornings, but the buzzers usually work until about 2 p.m.'

'Ah, the posties,' Morton sighed. 'At least I know what *they* do.'

They entered the hallway. Marco pointed to the sixteen metal mailboxes, four by four, fastened to the wall. 'That was where I'd to leave the package. Flat 16 – top right. These mailboxes would have suited Luke,' he grinned. 'Posties and the annoying people who deliver junk mail would just tip their stuff in there, grateful no tae have to climb the stairs. That would mean a lot less folk going anywhere near his door.' He looked around, staring up at the walls and the ceiling. 'I bet he has a micro CCTV camera in here somewhere and probably more on the stairs.'

Morton looked around. The tenement was in need of redecoration but looked clean enough. There was evidence of Victorian tiling in places. 'He sounds a bit paranoid, Marco. But then again, I've no idea the kind of thing he was up to. I mean, whose secure sites was he trying to get into? Maybe, he had good reason to be paranoid?'

Marco started up the stairs. 'You know about Viroil, the trading company founded by Brian Treanor, who gave the No campaign more than half a million? He had a very dubious record of tax-avoidance. He had paid kickbacks to Arkan, a Serbian war-lord.'

'Heard of him,' Morton murmured.

'Aye, later convicted of war-crimes. Viroil also made a \$1m payment to Saddam Hussein's regime. He was convicted of that one – in New York – and fined \$17.5m.'

'Ouch,' said Morton.

'He had bunged the Tories half a million too, in order to get influence – dinners at Downing Street. That was where – allegedly – he fixed up some of his dirty deals, getting UK Government backing. Or at least, they were turning a blind eye to what he was doing.'

They had reached the top floor. 'This is his flat,' Marco said.

'Doesn't look like it is, anymore,' Morton remarked. 'Seems to have been kicked in, then nailed up. Hell of a mess.'

They examined the battered door which had been nailed secure with rough wooden battens on either side of it.

Marco knelt down to look through the letterbox. 'That's been nailed down too,' he said. 'From the inside. So it's not burglars – they wouldn't nail up a door.'

'And if it was the police…' Morton added, 'where's the crime scene tape, or official notices?'

'He could have done it himself?' Marco suggested.

Morton looked at him. 'How do you mean?'

'Well, the polis, or burglars or somebody kicked it in and he came back and boarded it up.'

They thought about that. Morton grinned. 'Naw, that's not credible. If he did it to protect his security… how's he getting in and out? And if he had decided to abandon the place, why take the trouble to board it up?'

'Aye, it's a wee bit odd. See what you mean.'

'Is this the only address you have for him? I assume this place is rented?'

'We really only had contact with him at meetings, or events, like, you know…?'

Morton grinned. 'Kidnappings?'

Marco laughed. 'Aye. That was just a one-off. Though we did do some other stuff, not illegal, what you could call investigative… jaunts. But I'll no go intae that just now. Of course, Luke may turn up at the next meeting.'

Morton nodded. 'He might. Could you let me know if he does? By the way, when is the next meeting?'

'Tuesday. Emily will be there of course.'

'Right. I expect so. Is there any other way of contacting Luke?'

'The meetings are set up on WhatsApp.'

'Oh. Of course. Now we're getting somewhere. Send him a message.'

'Ah, but the meeting contacts are in a group so we'd have

to send a message to all the group. And I did that anyway, two days ago. No answer – I mean I know it wasn't read by him. So he's not online.'

'Right. What about asking the next door neighbour? Mr or Mrs Costello.'

Marco shrugged. 'Very unlikely they'd know anything.'

'I'll try anyway,' Morton said, and knocked. There was no answer.

Marco sniffed. 'I'm no surprised. This is a pretty transient area, like. Students, shift-workers, flats let for a month at a time by employment agencies.'

'Okay, we'd better go.'

'Yes. Work calls.' Marco glanced at the mobile phone in his hand.

'Thanks for helping.' They walked down the stairs and stood in the front hall.

Marco asked: 'What will you dae now?'

'I'm not sure. By the way, do you have the WhatsApp address?'

Marco paused, hand on the door. 'I'll copy you in to the group.'

They went their separate ways, Morton back to his flat in Keir Street. He was starting to get a feeling that something wasn't right. Emily believed Luke was a very intelligent, dedicated, even inspired hacker. There was the successful hack of Treanor and Viroil's dodgy financial dealings. Maybe someone saw him as a real threat? Morton pondered that as he strolled across the Meadows, past the fenced-off old Edinburgh Infirmary and the front of George Heriot's school and into Keir Street. Was Luke simply lying low, or was he on the run? And if the latter, whose nose had he got up?

It had been agreed that Emily would come over to his flat for dinner after work, and he was making a Quorn lasagne. It was more unusual for her to come to his flat than he to hers and she rarely stayed the night there. It was true there was less space at his, though its central location made it better for going out of an evening. She just about tolerated Quorn.

'I don't want a meat substitute,' she complained, 'I want a life without meat.'

While they ate, he told her about their visit to Luke's flat, sitting on stools, at his breakfast bar in the kitchen.

'Marco's right,' Emily said, lifting a forkful of lasagne to her mouth, 'it's perfectly possible Luke will turn up at the meeting tomorrow. You should come.'

Morton raised an eyebrow. 'Me? Would that be okay? I thought I'd have to be invited?'

Emily laughed. 'Well, I'm inviting you. We could make you an honorary member – after your efforts a few months ago.' She smiled archly. 'Or our patron saint. Mind, I'm not sure St William sounds right.'

'No thanks,' Morton said. 'No honours, no medals, no sainthoods. Where is the meeting by the way?'

'Aha!' Emily smiled mysteriously and tapped the side of her nose.

'Come off it!' Morton exclaimed. 'I'm not going to put it in the papers, you know.'

'I know, but we haven't got formal permission to bring anyone. It's a closed meeting structure. But you will be very welcome as my guest.' She smiled sweetly, 'so you don't need to know. We'll go along together.'

'Good grief, Em. And will everybody be wearing masks and using codenames?'

'Masks?'

'Didn't I tell you – when Marco and Luke…?'

'The pig mask? Oh, yes, you mentioned it. But you could see why. We're just trying to maintain some elements of security to protect ourselves. I thought you'd be all in favour given your troubles with GB13?'

'Oh yes, I am, honestly.'

'It's not easy. Things are at fever-pitch now. Everybody second-guessing what's going to happen. There are high stakes on all sides. Well, you *know*!'

'Want any more?' Morton indicated the clay oven dish on the table.

'No thanks, I'm stuffed. It was actually very good. I'll take another glass of wine though.'

'Praise indeed! I'm not so sure about the Quorn. I think I see what you mean. Next time, I'll do it pure veggie.'

'Good boy!'

They took their glasses through to the living room and sank into the sofa. Morton powered on the TV set on the wall and began to scroll through the guide. 'As usual, nothing but crap,' he muttered. 'Could shove a DVD on, if you'd like?'

Emily shook her head. 'Isn't there a good documentary? Let me see… Oh, Alice Roberts is on Channel 4.'

'Okay,' he agreed. 'Or we could go out for a drink?'

'Not tonight. Let's watch Alice. She's always interesting. You know, I like this room, it has a pleasing shape.'

'It's too small.'

'I think it's just the right size.'

These discussions about his flat and hers only served to remind them both of the fact that after a year and half together they weren't, not fully. They were a couple and together some of the time but lived separately and each had a full existence apart from the other. And he was further reminded that whereas she owned her flat, he rented his from a housing co-operative. He had often thought about changing career or trying to find more lucrative employment for not only was his income low – sometimes so low that he paid no tax – he had no pension scheme either. A part of him gloried in these proletarian credentials but it was a source of occasional anxiety. As a journalist he had had some remarkable successes; big pay days and front page splashes. He was known for his professionalism, but there were frequent no-pay weeks and he was often frankly hard-up. These gloomy thoughts recurred after Emily had made her excuses and got a taxi home. He was due at his parents' house the next day. His father's ninety-second birthday, just a few family and friends, a cake. Two years before, they'd had a big blow-out in a local hotel, more than twenty family, friends and a few neighbours. When you were that old, you had few contemporaries left. Morton wasn't looking forward to it. His father was getting a bit deaf, although he was physically and mentally amazing for his age. He always seemed to manage to convey a sense of disappointment in his only son, which Morton found difficult to ignore.

CHAPTER THREE

When Luke Sangster escaped at a moment's notice from his flat in Marchmont Crescent, he was sticking to a plan he had perfected months before. He had known they would be coming for him. Even though he had taken care to ensure that the data he had hacked had been distributed to the media in the name of the group and not his own name. He had rehearsed the way out, into the attic, through the skylight and between the roof gulley onto the roof terrace. And had imagined the route from there to the first of his emergency shelters. If you tweak a tiger's tail, he's going to bite you and Luke knew he had tweaked the tiger's tail. He had used his time on the bus to remove the batteries from his mobile and his laptop and insert them into the zipped foil sleeve. It wasn't enough to simply switch them off.

As the bus trundled into Lothian Road, past sets of traffic lights, picking up and letting passengers off at bus stops, he felt he was relatively safe. Two large men sat in front of him, talking loudly about football and he knew that the CCTV cameras were in the front. He could bide his time, ten more minutes, for the bus to negotiate the end of Princes Street and Charlotte Square and enter Queensferry Street.

Luke got to his feet behind one of the large men and as he turned to descend the stairs put his hand up to shield his face from the cameras and did the same on the bottom deck where the cameras were in the middle and stepped off the bus. He walked along the street for fifty yards towards the bridge and slipped down Bells Brae to the footpath of the Water of Leith. He knew this path well; it wound its way through the city for twenty-two miles from Leith to the Pentlands. It was a rapid way to get around on foot, well away from CCTV cameras although there were places where cameras on a passing bus or from a takeaway might overlap with the footpath. There were dog walkers and hikers but they were few and he could be unobtrusive. He had two options; two places he could go – north west by Stockbridge and the Royal Botanical Gardens to Leith docks or south towards the Union Canal – but he had already decided to go south. It was four miles and he was in no hurry. It was warm in the places along the way where the sun shone and where, because of the high bank, there was no wind. He sat on a wooden bench near the weir and gazed out at the white water tumbling by the ivy-covered mill lade, part of long-demolished mills from previous centuries. There was only the faint hint here, through the trees, of roofs, buildings, the surrounding city. He drank from his water bottle and watched a kingfisher dart along the bank. He planned to sit for an hour or so and move on only when necessary. He had to kill some time. He wondered what they were doing now; the men who had come to his flat and kicked his door in. He hated to leave his equipment but the computers were ancient, they were no loss really. Some other stuff of more consequence he regretted but it couldn't be helped. He rummaged in his satchel and found the key ring and identified the key he needed, slipped it off the ring and pocketed it. It opened a basement room in a small block of flats at the end of a cul-de-sac off the Gorgie Road in Stenhouse and he would be safe there. He knew where to emerge from the footpath and how to navigate the streets to get to this place. It had a high brick wall on one side and a high security mesh fence from a neighbouring security warehouse on the other. Beyond the grey steel fencing was a morass of weeds and bushes gradually turning into a swamp over which winds had cast a variety of rotting detritus. The block of flats at the centre of this was modern, owned by an employment agency which used it for contract workers, though it was nearly always empty. It wasn't the kind of area people would choose to live in, if they had seen it by daylight. Luke's theory was that they never did see it by daylight. They would be bussed in and out in darkness, worker bees. There had been a caretaker living in the basement but the company had replaced him with a once-a-week concierge service and sent cleaners only when workers were using the place. And Luke knew that that was very rare and when it happened, they didn't bother with the basement at all. He had been given the keys and codes more than a year ago by somebody who had worked for the company and no longer did.

He turned into the lane, a solitary figure walking along a deserted pavement under a line of streetlights. In his satchel, the laptop, hard-drive and mobile phones, along with a small toilet bag, spare tee-shirt and change of briefs; his 'flight' kit. He was fairly confident that no-one could have tracked him here. He knew that rolling wall-to-wall surveillance linking CCTV networks and satellite imagery from films such as *Enemy of State* was a myth. In Edinburgh, which had more CCTV cameras per head than any other city in the UK, 226, most of them, eighty per cent, were old analogues and the system of inter-connection was shambolic. Some of the cameras took images of such low quality, so few frames per second, they were demonstrably useless as court evidence, others took up to twenty-five frames per second but required massive memory and therefore clogged up quickly. He had been closely following the wrangling in the Council about funding an upgrade of the system and building a new city-wide hub to co-ordinate all the static cameras. He knew there was, as yet, no agreement on it. And there was an even lower possibility of integrating moving cameras; on buses, cycles and bodycams into the network. That would come of course, but not without more investment. Nevertheless, he approached the building cautiously in the afternoon gloom. There were lights, corridor and stairwell lights, which remained on all day and night. There was a regular pattern to them; he didn't think there were lights on in any of the rooms. There were no vehicles parked in the large carpark. Nobody walked here. It was well off the beaten track. He approached the front entrance across the tarmac and although there was enough natural light, the security lights came on. He keyed in the six-digit code and was relieved to find that it still worked. The thick glass doors opened smoothly and he entered the foyer. It was warm, well-lit and deserted. It smelled deserted, empty – if that was possible. No human presence. He turned left to a small tiled staircase that led to the basement corridor; grey-painted brick walls with several doors marked Private. These were Storage, Laundry Room and finally, Caretaker. Inserting the Yale key into this, he smiled with satisfaction as it opened. He closed it behind him. He switched on the light, a harsh and glaring yellow light bulb set in the ceiling in the exact middle of the room. The door fitted well and little light would leak out into the corridor. He had tested that to make sure. No-one would know he was here even if anyone did come along. He had several bolt-holes like these in and around the city where he would be safe, anonymous and undetectable, though it was his strategy never to stay long in any one place. The downside was he couldn't get the internet here. It was a dead-zone. But that was a good thing, he felt instinctively.

The bedsit was a large, low-ceilinged room with a bed in the corner and several rugs on the red-painted concrete floor. There was one long narrow window high up on the wall, at the point where the wall met the ceiling, too high to see out of and on the outside it had a security grille fitted across it at ground level. Light from the room, he had previously confirmed, was undetectable from outside for the room was at the rear of the building, closest to the steel security fence that divided it from the neighbouring warehouse premises and obscured by thick bushes. It was a safe place, a real bolt-hole.

Sangster dropped the satchel and jacket on the bed. He lit a gas ring on the stove with the battery lighter. Filled the kettle at the sink and put it on to boil. On his most recent visit, six months previously, he had left a holdall of tins and packets, everything he would need to sustain himself for a week. He sat propped up on the bed, his head against the wall, drinking instant coffee and eating digestive biscuits and began to reflect on the events of the past four hours. He could not believe that the raid by the police or spooks was a random event. He had decided that they were acting on a tip-off; an informer. He'd been very careful with security. No-one should have known about it. Marco – but Marco was cool – he couldn't countenance that. Was there anyone else? He tried to think of everyone who had attended the last few meetings. Had anyone shown an abnormal interest? Had anyone followed him after-wards? Was there someone who'd stopped attending or started again after an absence? He visualised faces, names, but could not resolve the issue. What irked him most was the way the spooks had come right up to the top floor without hesitation. They clearly had that knowledge. There must be an informer – but who? He would have to lie low for a while. There was the question of the meeting. Should he attend? There were pros and cons. He could use the group as a support network if he had to stay dark for a while, by carefully managing what he told them. It would be difficult, though not impossible, to stay out on his own, completely off-grid. It could be done but at the expense of work. He would find it impossible to operate, to complete his work, and remain entirely off-grid. And he needed to use the group and their contacts to get an idea of who was after him and why.

Morton walked the pavements to Merchiston Crescent in the early afternoon sunshine, along tree-lined streets to the familiar two-storey detached house, modestly elegant behind its rowan trees and holly bushes. The front porch was open and as he came up the path, his mother bustled out, looking elegant in a summer dress and pearls, smart shoes, car keys in hand. She was off to collect the cake.

'Surprised you're not baking it yourself?'

'Oh no, dear, I'm far too busy!'

It was true. His mother, Margaret, was seventy-three but could pass for a decade younger. They had married in 1975 when she was thirty-three and his father, a divorcee, was fifty-two. Now she had a busy social life while he pottered around at home. They were blissfully happy. He found his father in the warm wooden-framed greenhouse, potting-up seedlings. Although it was his birthday, Stuart Erskine Morton was wearing an ancient pair of cream-brown flannels, a checked shirt frayed at the collar, tweed tie, a tatty dark red pullover and leather brogues, polished to within an inch of their life. The old man didn't hear him at first, then slowly turned and smiled.

'William! You came.'

Morton noted the white stubble on the flabby brown skin of his neck. 'Well, of course. Happy birthday! Petunias?'

His father frowned. 'Surfinias. Your mother has gone out to collect a cake.'

'Yes, I spoke to her as I came in.'

'First time she's not baked it herself. A bad omen.'

Morton laughed. 'I don't think so. She's so busy.'

'Yes, always gadding about. Anyway, I'm glad you could tear yourself away from your busy working life.'

Morton felt the barb of the remark. 'I know I disappoint you, dad.'

The old man methodically filled the last of his pots, scooping soil into each with a flick of the wrist. 'No. I would never say that. Of course not. I had always hoped you would be an engineer, like me. Not to be, ah well. But we gave you a good education and you're doing what you enjoy, I suppose. Each to their own. Though your working life seems to get you into an awful lot of trouble.'

Morton saw the light glint on the watery rheum in his father's eyes. 'Well, but that's not my fault, dad. I'm trying to get at information they'd rather keep secret. It's not easy.'

'I daresay. Seems a funny way to earn a living. Now, you can give me a hand here. These have to be taken over to the sunny beds.'

Over by the high wall, his father straightened up, his hand in the small of his back.

'Back pains?'

'No. The old war wounds, as they say. I'm fit – reasonably so, I'm happy to say. Ninety-two? There was a time when I thought I wouldn't make it past twenty-two.' A shadow slipped over his deeply tanned and creased face and the day's white stubble. 'Many didn't, poor souls.'

Morton and Emily walked to the meeting in the narrow lane – Lyon's Vennel –off the Royal Mile. By the time they arrived, the meeting was underway. A dozen people faced each other across a rough wooden table, sitting on wooden benches. A single bulb hanging from a low wooden rafter revealed an indescribably filthy cellar. Plaster rotted off brick walls, shadows moved on clumps of indeterminate garbage. There was a smell of – what? – Morton wondered. Earth or wet plaster? A smashed beer cask in one corner, dismantled metal cabinets of a filing cabinet, piles of bundles of newspaper covered with a uniform grey dust. Was this really the best place to have a meeting of the best minds of the nation? The walls had perhaps once been whitewashed or plastered or papered, or something. It wasn't cold but he couldn't see any means of heating.

Their arrival had suspended the meeting. Emily exchanged greetings around the room while Morton found the empty places at the end of one of the benches and sat. The bench wobbled a little as he sat down. He looked around and realised he knew one or two of them and nodded. Marco wasn't there. Morton presumed he was simply late. Emily squeezed up beside him on the end of the bench.

The meeting started quite organically when, into a gap in several conversations, an ascetic-looking man in an anorak was seen to be holding up his hands. He had the broad handsome face of an intellectual or an academic, with remnants of long silvery hair luminous under the light bulb. Morton knew him. He was Liam McLanders, a famous writer and broadcaster.

McLanders acknowledged the silence with a broad smile,

waggled his fingertips in benediction and the meeting restarted. When invited, Emily introduced Morton. McLanders smiled and nodded. 'William, you are very welcome to our little enclave. Emily had mentioned you as a potential member.' Morton marvelled at the familiar deep resonance of his voice. 'We have all been reading your work. Well done.'

Morton was mildly embarrassed. 'Right, thanks. I have a couple of your books.' There was some suppressed mirth and a few grins. He realised that everybody was aware that he and Emily were an item. 'Thank you for that, William,' McLanders responded amiably. 'But let's leave the literary backslapping for later, shall we?'

The meeting continued and Morton was surprised to hear of the range of activities being undertaken by the group. There was a media monitoring group, a social media group, liaison with pro-Independence media groups, *Bella Caledonia, Wings over Scotland, Newsnet, iScot, Radio IndyLive*, which had been forged before, during or after the referendum, created out of pure enthusiasm and crowdfunding. All of the speakers, he realised, shared an ambition to build better communication away from the inherent bias of the BBC. There were so many topics on the agenda Morton found himself drifting off. It wasn't so much the warmth, it was more the dead, passive air and the muted give and take of the conversation in the poor light.

He woke guiltily from a drowse when Emily nudged him sharply in the ribs. It was Any Other Competent Business and Emily was about to raise her anxieties about Luke.

McLanders said: 'But as yet you have no real evidence that anything untoward has happened?'

'True,' Emily admitted, 'but we know his flat was raided by the police or Special Branch. Since then he has not been in contact. We wondered if he might turn up tonight, but... Willie, do you want to say a few words?'

Morton cleared his throat and sat up straighter. 'Marco and I visited his flat,' he told the meeting. 'The door had been booted in and nailed up again, quite roughly. Was he working on anything?' He frowned. 'Anything particularly contentious?'

A woman at the other end with black and blue braided hair and a lip ring interrupted. 'We never knew what the genius was up to. Us ordinary mortals were never given access to his inner thoughts.'

'I see,' Morton said, wondering if there was personal history there. 'So no-one has any idea?'

The meeting split into a number of different conversations. The man directly opposite him, a red-haired man of about his own age, in a blue denim jacket over a grey hoodie, leaned forward. 'I wouldnae say that; he usually spoke at meetings. Tae gie us a wee report, like.'

McLanders called for silence. 'Come on, now! We're going to get nowhere if we talk amongst ourselves.' He glanced to his left. 'Ned is right. Luke usually put in a report if he was making any progress. The way we tended to work, Mr Morton, was... each group has its own remit and Luke often took his leads from them. For example, Cecilia there,' he pointed to the woman with black and blue braids. 'Cecilia leads the social media group. They monitor what's going on and specifically monitor key figures of interest to us. Then sometimes, Luke will take their report as a starting point for his, um, unique methods of research.'

'Right,' Morton nodded. 'But no-one knows what was his starting point, or the area he was...'

'We all have our views about Luke's usefulness,' McLanders

said.' I mean, we all agree he had done good work but he *was* a maverick. I think everyone here would agree with that?'

There were murmurs, a few nods and wry smiles.

'What I meant to say, Mr Morton, friends, is that no-one here really knows much about him. He deflected questions about himself, about his aims and beliefs, his background. I couldn't even tell you where he was from. I mean, city, or area.'

Emily cleared her throat. 'I suspect he had some bad experiences in his past. We all tried to find out more. Initially, of course we were concerned on the security aspect. He was after all, a volunteer. But we all are of course.'

'That's true,' said McLanders. 'If I remember, he was invited along by a former member of the group and we had no reason to distrust him.'

'When was that?' Morton asked.

McLanders frowned and looked around for advice. 'I couldn't exactly say. Anyone else know?'

'About six months before the referendum,' someone said. It was a student in jeans and cagoule, with wispy blond hair and a patchy beard. There was general agreement around the room.

The woman named Cecilia said: 'We were wary at first. Rightly so. We have always been very conscious of spies and informers. Although what we do is perfectly legal, we must protect our work.'

'Mnn,' Morton said, musing on that. 'So how could you be sure that he wasn't…?'

'We couldn't,' said McLanders, 'but soon he began to provide very interesting information – and we had it counter-checked – that gave us some media scoops. And of course, the Treanor material went very well for us. And much of that came directly from him.'

The red-haired man opposite said: 'Ah wouldnae like to think something's happened tae the boy. I dinnae like the sound of that, I mean his door being kicked in. I hope he's alright.'

'You and me both, Morton agreed and again he was thinking about Marco. Why had he not attended after saying he would?

CHAPTER FOUR

Although not an unduly anxious person, Luke Sangster found sleep difficult on his first night in the room in Stenhouse. Unexplained noises, undetectable in the daytime, had irked him and kept him awake. Pipes creaking, the on-off-on again electric humming from the adjacent laundry room, even wind noises from an unidentifiable hole or gap in the window frame. He was out of bed several times trying to identify the source of these sounds. And it was hot anyway, too hot for sleep, but there was nothing he could do about that. Finally, around 3 a.m., he slept.

He opened his eyes, drowsily wondering what had wakened him. He saw from his wristwatch it was 7.30 a.m. Noises at the window? He decided it was rain, good old Edinburgh rain. With that he got up, groggy, rubbing his eyes and moved over to the stove in his boxers. He lit the gas under the kettle. The rain was trickling in blurred lines down the window above his head, diverging off into other lines, merging together, under a grey overcast wet sky. He felt dull, flat, as if everything was hopeless. Yes, though he could control his destiny, evade capture, his was a lonely, almost pointless existence. But he must go on. Find a way out of this. He sat on the bed, waiting for the kettle to boil. It was like being underwater. Was prison like this? HMP Saughton was less than a mile away. And if he had not escaped from those men who had come to his door, would he now be in prison, he wondered? Or on remand, which was the same thing. But there were no grounds for him to be in prison. True, he had accessed private sites, had got around firewalls, forced his way through chinks in security software, gate-crashed secret data of wealthy arrogant people, but he had not done so for personal gain. It was probable that he had not even breached the Computer Misuse Act but the legislation was a catch-all, defined so loosely that even just switching on a computer could be used as grounds for arrest and jail. And there were a whole battery of other laws, the Serious Crime Act, the Police and Justice Act and worst of all, the Terrorism Act of 2000 with its new section of 'advancing a political cause'. The laws were loaded in their favour. Hackers working for Governments and the police could do anything they liked with impunity. Most hacking was state-sponsored but Governments didn't like it when individuals went snooping online. They could use any excuse to get him. Since he had first taken an interest, around the age of fourteen, in the online world, beyond the shoot-em-ups and one-on-one fighting games, he had seen how the powerful elites had developed ever more sophisticated systems to keep their business dealings private. Digital data had been a godsend to them, had made their activities invisible, not least from the tax authorities. And he knew that the worst of them could afford to pay for the best people to hide their secrets and cheat the system. Well, confidentiality was one thing: everybody wanted online security but the quasi-criminal activities of the wealthy were put beyond the reach of Government officials and yet the Law condoned their secrecy. Out of sight out of mind. Things only got heated when someone leaked something and then officials had to act. Centuries ago, the rich and powerful called out the Yeomanry to cudgel those expressing undue interest in their misdeeds. Now they paid fortunes to techies to cover up their thefts. The legislation was firmly on the side of the rich and mighty and against those who simply wanted to level the playing field and let light into the dark places and get constitutional change. The kettle boiled, its rasping breathy cry never quite developing into a whistle. He jumped to lift it off the gas ring.

Luke sat on the bed sipping instant coffee and eating a digestive biscuit, hearing the wind through that invisible gap in the window frame and the ticking sounds of rain on the glass. He had the vague feeling that he could yet achieve something remarkable, uncover some important information that might make the news. He would give himself another six months to try and if he didn't, he would go away, somewhere far, perhaps Australia where he had a friend, and make a new start. And there was something at once comforting now that he had a plan. Purpose and direction applied through schedules, timetables and planning appealed to him. It was something he knew about himself. If he was getting frustrated, or if the blackness came over him, he sat quietly and tried to plan his way out of it. Mapping his way out of the moods, as he thought of it. He had never wanted what others had wanted; the easy life, the familiar, comfortable routine, relationships, steady job. He needed only to prove to himself his creative ability. Assert his imaginative thinking and achieve the impossible by applying himself to a task. It was, in a way, a monastic vow to eschew the mundane things of life. The lonely path of the genius cum social isolate. Self-denial was his main instrument. The human body did not require as much food as most people imagined, for instance. Exercise, mental and physical was the thing. Avoid all that is unnecessary to the achievement of completion, creative perfection. So he had accumulated few clothes, few *things*. All he needed were the tools of his trade; laptop, a few gadgets, the capacity to hack in to mainframes, some notebooks to chart his work in progress. Driven by a sense of injustice, of the poverty of the many and the refulgent luxury of the few, he knew which side he was on.

He dressed in tee-shirt, denim shirt, jeans and hoodie. He needed fresh air; the room was too warm. He pulled on thick socks and laced his boots. Checked the pockets of his green Gore-Tex jacket and put all his belongings into the satchel. This was all he needed. His life was remarkably free of clutter. He checked the room. If anyone came here, they would see the tins and packets in the cupboard but there was nothing personal in the room. He saw that the rain drops on the window were static, not moving, not replaced. The rain had stopped, or lessened, but he was going to enjoy being out in it. He'd had an idea. A friend from University was working a year's contract in Devon and Luke had vaguely agreed to look in occasionally during the time they were away, to check on the flat. And Jed had even said he could use their computer. It was in Leith, about six miles from where he was but he could get to it by the Dean Water footpath and not once come out onto a public street. He pulled his beanie hat low over his ears and neck and hair and stepped out of the room into the tiled corridor. It was 9.07 a.m. There was no-one about and looking out from the front door, no vehicles in the carpark. He saw the pattern of shade cast by branches of trees swinging about in the damp wind. He exited the building into the cul-de-sac, enjoying the raw fresh air and almost at once joined the footpath that threaded the tree-covered river banks of the Water of Leith. He headed north, following the stream in a tight curve around the Saughton Rose Gardens. The best thing about the footpath was that it was obscured by mature trees, often in a culvert, where high verdant banks kept away prying eyes. On this stretch, dog-walkers were few. A few hundred yards further on, near a bowling green, it went under a railway bridge and intersected a cycle track. Lithe, lycra-clad cyclists buzzed past him, singly or in twos, concentrating on the wet surfaces of the twisty path and avoiding puddles where the tarmac had broken up. Up ahead was the high white concrete of Murrayfield rugby stadium. The water began twisting and turning past a weir and a pond known as The Cauldron, entering the stretch of woodland before Dean Village. He knew there would be more walkers soon at an open stretch without trees and also the risk of being captured by CCTV cameras on buses crossing Dean Bridge.

The peaceful murmuring waters enlivened by the sounds of birds muffled the noises of traffic of the busy city. He felt a residual irritation that he had had to suspend his work on Clive Kenton. He had come across the name out of nowhere, mentioned in passing in an online Hunt Sabs newsletter, barely any hits or mentions on the internet. He was an entrepreneur, virtually a byword, Luke believed, for dodgy dealings. There had been a fund-raising dinner in The Royal Windsor Club in Edinburgh, attended by one of the minor royals, to raise funds for court action to reverse the ban on hunting foxes with hounds in Scotland. The photograph had appeared somewhere – it looked like newsprint – grainy, blurred, and the version he had seen had been photocopied anyway. Kenton's face was in the back row, his name appeared among the names in the picture caption. All of the media interest at the time had concentrated on the fake outrage that a minor royal would be at such a 'political' event. That was humbug, Luke thought. Of course the royals would do such a thing. They were the lynchpin of the entire charade, apex of the hierarchy. Fox-hunting was part of their DNA. But the name Clive Kenton had escaped media attention at the time. Using that piece of information, Luke had discovered some interesting things about Kenton. His wife was a wealthy aristocrat and they lived in opulent Buckinghamshire. Among numerous commercial activities, he owned a company called Greenlane UK, which touted for environmental work. It exploited a niche in maintenance of green spaces left over by developers on new build housing projects. There were often bits of land inside or on the periphery of such developments which were, in theory, not owned by anybody and which the Councils were reluctant to maintain. For a flat fee, Greenlane UK had been buying up the ownership of such pieces of land and promising to maintain them. In practice, they barely bothered, unless residents complained. And Councils were happy to be rid of such awkward areas, so Greenlane collected fees for doing it and subsidies from Government for providing 'wildlife corridors' and maintaining 'pleasant natural spaces adjacent to new housing areas'. Since no-one ever bothered to check, and due to confusion amongst residents as to ownership, Greenlane was coining it in, for almost no effort. They had a land portfolio thousands of acres, in theory. What a scam! But Luke had discovered the astonishing fact that Greenlane UK didn't exist as an incorporated business. It had some kind of relationship with another company owned by Kenton called Meadowsgreen, but neither as far as he could see were listed as businesses paying tax to HM Revenue. And that was about as far as he had got when the men were kicking in his door. The tax position was crucial, and he couldn't be sure, yet, if he had the whole story. Someone needed to do a Freedom of Information request on it. And here he was, the weight of the laptop in his satchel bearing on his collarbone and he couldn't use it. Couldn't even switch it on. If he logged on as Jed in the flat in Leith and continued his investigation, he'd be rumbled pretty soon. How soon? Well, that was hard to say. Probably not till he hit an alarmed firewall or real-time security devices. Luke was within sight of the Colony houses of Stockbridge now. With their neat lines, matching stone stairs and iron railings, the regimented attic dormers, they were distinctive and pleasing to his eye. Originally built as miners' cottages, he had read that planning restrictions were tight about altering the historic exteriors. He was nearly at the Royal Botanic Gardens. He wondered about going off the path for a while and sitting in the warmth and serenity of the glasshouses there, maybe even having a coffee and a cake in the cafe, if it was open. His stomach was rumbling but he was only a mile and a half away now from Jed's flat, so he'd carry on. The footpath went under Inverleith Row and soon he was cutting between two parks; Warriston Cemetery and St Mark's Park. Only a few hundred yards to the weir and his destination. Cyclists in lines raced past him, and he saw a variety of dogs with owners clutching green doggy-poop bags. He left the footpath. Everything suddenly became louder as he re-joined the city; all kinds of noises, traffic, music, unknown discords, distant sirens. He crossed Ferry Road and quickly located Jed's tenement in Portland Street, the bottom end. Entering the warm, quiet, carpeted stairway, he sped up the five flights to the top. The key was where it was supposed to be. He turned it in the lock and got into Jed's neat and tidy attic flat. He felt like a voyager who had reached sanctuary, having covered six miles and spoken to no-one and he was pretty sure he had not been caught on any cameras. Now he wanted something to eat and a drink of water. He checked the fridge and larder. Jed had left tins, coffee, teabags and milk powder. The flat was warmed by sunlight flooding through Velux windows. It had a view of the top of the masthead of the Royal Yacht Britannia, about two hundred yards away. On the wooden table was Jed's dusty old Samsung PC. Just waiting for him.

CHAPTER FIVE

Morton was irritated and mostly at himself. Just as he was about to sit down to breakfast in his kitchen-diner, he went to answer a knock at his door and, standing on the doorstep, were two men. Why had he been so stupid? There was a General Election on, but the men in suits and coats were not political canvassers or even early shift Jehovah's Witnesses. The tall stooping man with short curly hair had a squint nose. The short chubby one who did all the talking said his name was Blenkinsop. They flashed him some kind of ID cards and the word 'police' was mentioned, but Morton stood his ground, cursing his own stupidity.

'We can't discuss it out here, Mr Morton,' Blenkinsop said.

Morton considered his options. Could he refuse to let them in? And if he did, what then? 'I'm busy,' he said at last. 'Can you come back later?'

'Not really,' said the tall one, who'd called himself Dunan, moving forward and Morton was literally pushed back into his own flat. He wondered if Dunan was Welsh.

'Hey! Who are you pushing?'

Dunan smiled down at him. 'Pushing? You misunderstand, Morton. We simply want to talk to you about a mutual friend.'

Blenkinsop closed the door. Morton looked at him and felt his heart leap. *Emily?*

'Any chance of a cuppa?' Blenkinsop asked cheerily. 'Saul here could be mother, eh?'

Dunan grinned. 'Oh ay, I can do that. Kitchen this way then, chum? Tidy little place you have, Morton.'

There was an intimidatory air about them despite the chumminess. Blenkinsop preceded him into the living room which was slightly musty in odour he realised. An inch of stale lager from last night remained in the bottle of Becks on the coffee table.

'Smart place,' Blenkinsop said. 'Central, very handy I imagine?' He sat down on the sofa.

'What is it that you want?' Morton asked petulantly, opening the curtains to let in the dim daylight. The pavement outside was wet he noticed. 'Who is this mutual friend?' He could hear the other one barging about in his kitchen. The ID cards they'd shown were not standard police cards, but he hadn't made any comment. And now he was getting intrigued as the irritation he felt with himself faded.

'Luke Sangster,' Blenkinsop said. 'The lad himsel, as they say around these parts. We want to speak to him.'

'I hardly know him. Only met him once, briefly.'

'We know you visited his flat two days ago.'

'No – I didn't,' Morton replied. 'I went to see his previous flat, which is now abandoned, or derelict… as you'd know. Perhaps it was you or your friends who kicked the door in?'

Dunan came in with a tray. Three mugs, a teabag in each and the milk carton. 'Milk?' he asked, stooping to place the tray on the smoked glass coffee table.

'Me?' Morton glared, irritated to be offered tea in his own flat. 'I don't want tea. I was just about to have my breakfast…'

'Milk, two sugars,' Blenkinsop said. 'And a choccy biccy – if there is one.'

'Ah, that's yours then, boss. It's got sugar in it.'

'No choccy biccys,' Morton stated. 'Not good for you anyway, even if I had one, which I don't.'

'Shame. If we had known, we would have brought some,' Blenkinsop said, 'ay, Tiger?'

'Right, boss,' Dunan grinned, dropping onto the sofa. They sat there like two overgrown schoolboys, smiling at him, enjoying his obvious discomfort.

'What do you want from me?' he asked, 'apart from choccy biccys of course?'

'Simple,' Blenkinsop said. 'A few minutes of your time, then we won't have to bother you again.'

'But I haven't seen Luke Sangster for weeks and I have only met him briefly.'

'But you know that he has disappeared?'

'Has he?' Morton asked.

'Come on, you know that much. Else why were you at his flat with Mr Vanetti, looking for him?'

'Legged it,' Dunan grinned, slurping his tea. 'Escaped over the rooftops like a great skinny bat.'

Blenkinsop looked at his colleague and frowned. 'That's right. Evaded us by minutes. We need to speak to him urgently. It's in his own interests.'

'What about?'

Blenkinsop made a deprecating sound like a suppressed laugh or a snort. 'Huh. An urgent matter, Morton, which we're not at liberty to discuss. But I can assure you it concerns illegalities. Quite a number of offences committed.'

'He's a hacker,' Morton concluded. 'So what? Hackers' activities are not always illegal. Hackers can be helpful...'

'Well, not his. Sangster is a devious and tricky criminal who thinks nothing of breaking the law. Serious offences.'

'Offences?' Morton scoffed. 'So there are charges? I mean, some rich scrote has complained?'

Dunan leaned forward, hugging his knees. 'Rich scrote, I like that.'

'He's a serial offender,' Blenkinsop said.' Flouts the law. But initially we simply want to speak to him. We have recovered some of his equipment. If he was working legitimately, why would he go on the run? What does he have to hide? Why risk his neck clambering about on high roofs? You know this. It's in all our interests, and his, to apprehend him. Before he comes to harm.'

Morton bristled. 'What do you mean… before he comes to harm? Who would harm him?'

Blenkinsop put down his mug on the glass table. 'Very nice tea, Saul. Who would harm him? Who indeed, Morton? Certainly not us. There are many nasty people in this world.'

Morton stood up and looked down at them. Blenkinsop, who was probably in his early thirties, had a pink area at the back of his head, premature thinning. He'd soon be bald. Morton felt a smirk developing. 'Having established that I have no knowledge of his whereabouts…'

'Sit down, Morton!' Blenkinsop said calmly. 'This interview is not yet completed. Some more questions.'

'Do I have to answer?' Morton asked, moving over to the door. 'I don't actually know if you are police. I wonder if I should phone my solicitor.'

'No need for that,' Blenkinsop sniffed. He looked at Dunan. 'Crikey, Saul – solicitor – ye Gods!'

'Rich tossers, solicitors,' Dunan said with feeling. Morton wondered about that remark.

'Not mine,' he said. 'Well – what? Get on with it!'

'Now, now, Morton. No need to lose the rag.'

'Well, come on!' he expostulated.

'Ardbuithne House.'

'Pardon?'

Blenkinsop smiled curtly. 'You heard. Home of Lord Ronald Craile.'

'Good grief! That was months ago. I went there to interview…'

'Some interview, Morton. His Lordship wasn't very co-operative, I heard.'

Morton rummaged in his hair. 'This is ridiculous. That matter has been exhaustively written about. The police…'

'Oh yes, we know all that. But what I want to know about concerns Ms Haldane.'

'Who?'

'Oh come on! It was Ms Haldane who came to your rescue when you were attacked by Craile's bulldog, MacGillicuddy.' He grimaced – 'Terrible name. Sounds like a donkey.'

'Mac-Gilli-cuddy,' Dunan said, pronouncing the word carefully. 'Cuddy being a sort of work horse in Scotland, ay?'

Morton stood at the living room door. What if he just went out and ignored them? 'I don't know what you're talking about. Or anyone called Haldane.'

Blenkinsop expressed incredulity. 'Really, Morton! You're useless as a liar and believe me, I've seen some good liars. You're not one of them. That is one great big stinking porky you just told me. She rescued you from MacGillicuddly-cuddy and spirited you away, most probably by boat…'

'Ay, boss, gotta be,' Dunan nodded, hugging his knees.

'Pure fantasy,' Morton smiled. 'And I am going to phone my solicitor right now.'

Blenkinsop got to his feet and sniffed. 'Oh well, we've learned the truth of that little encounter,' he said. 'Even though you didn't co-operate as we would have liked. I don't know what she told you, or who she pretended to be…'

Morton saw the traps and smirked. 'Who? This mythical Ms Haldane?'

'Oh, I can assure you she's anything but mythical. But, regretfully, we'll leave it there, for now. You know, you *know* that we will be keeping a very close eye on you and your associates.'

Morton raised his eyebrows. '*Really*? Is that a threat? Are you *threatening* me?'

Blenkinsop pouted. 'Solicitation for your future welfare, that's all.'

As they stood in the hallway, deliberately prolonging – enjoying – his discomfort, menace beneath the veneer of their smug affability, Morton wanted to push them out, to shout or kick at them. It was an effort to keep control.

Dunan stooped under the lintel. 'Better get them choccy biccys in, Morton,' he grinned. 'It's likely we'll be back soon.'

Blenkinsop held up his hands like a preacher. 'Oh, Morton, Morton, if only you'd spill the beans now, we could clear up this matter completely and you'd never see us again. What about it, old chap? You know we are very thorough, you know we could cause you a lot of grief… inconvenience, I should say. And all for want of a tiny *morceau* of information, an address, a suggestion, a hint.'

'Goodbye,' Morton said evenly, shutting the door on them. He watched them through the net curtains in the living room and noticed with glee that the rain had come on. They were forced to scurry to the corner of Lauriston Place, getting wet. He wanted to phone Emily right away but reasoned that there'd be some kind of intercept of his calls, his texts, his emails. Here we go again, he thought to himself. Would there never be an end to all this surveillance? Suddenly, a thought struck him. The kitchen?

He went through and began examining utensils and cupboards. He lifted up the kettle and looked underneath, ditto the toaster. He disconnected the microwave and studied it outside and in. He probed around among the tins in the cupboard, looked under the sink. Nothing.

He went back into the living room and felt around the sofa where they had been sitting. He had never seen a bugging device but imagined they could be pretty small, perhaps microscopic. And of course, he himself had... there was no guarantee that either of them were not using... spy-pens! He laughed aloud, remembering the spy-pen Sean Kermally had given him, when he had infiltrated the meeting of GB13 in the Houses of Parliament. 'Why can't I find the little buggers?' he asked himself and laughed.

His mood had suddenly changed. He began to laugh at the ridiculousness of it. All he really knew was that he had done nothing wrong, nothing remotely criminal. He was safe because he was innocent, a humble hard-working journalist. Not like in those other places under despotic regimes where torture and disappearances occurred every day. As he ate his cornflakes, he decided that the best idea was to go over to Emily's place. He knew she was working from home today, and tell her what had happened and reassure himself that she was safe. He could do with a walk. He liked walking in the rain. He fetched out his blue Berghaus cagoule.

CHAPTER SIX

MI5 have operated in Scotland for decades, investigating Scottish Nationalists and republicans in the 1950s and 60s and more serious groups involved in gun smuggling across the Irish Sea in the 1970s and 80s. After devolution, they began to formalise their presence, as part of a UK-wide effort to disperse officers from Thames House to the regions. Prior to 2005, MI5 agents in Scotland were hosted in temporary shared premises at One Pacific Quay on the Clyde but on completion of custom-built new premises nearby, set up the Scotland Station which presently comprises eleven desk officers and nearly thirty support staff. In 2015, a smaller office was opened at the New Waverley Centre in Edinburgh with two peripatetic desk officers and two permanent support staff. The Scotland Station should have meant better liaison between MI5 and Scottish Special Branch, the second-largest in the UK, which is heavily involved in counter-terrorism work in Glasgow among the largest Muslim population in Scotland. But there was a problem. The problem of two masters. MI5 has supreme authority throughout the UK on matters of national security. It answers only to the Westminster Government's Joint Intelligence Committee and, in theory at least, the Intelligence Security Committee of the House of Commons. However, Special Branch are in charge of all police matters, including domestic terrorist incidents, under the remit of the Scottish

Police Authority whose masters are a Scottish Government, run, since 2007, by the SNP. MI5 officers in Scotland have no official powers of arrest and depend upon Police Scotland, set up in 2013, and its various units, particularly Special Branch, for operational assistance. It is not therefore clear who has partial and who has complete oversight and who has final authority over certain types of operations in Scotland. The public remain unaware of this uneasy compromise or grey area.

The Scotland Station, as far as any pedestrian passing along the public footpath by the Clyde is aware, is simply one of many office blocks. On the ground floor operates a bona-fide commercial enterprise as cover for the activities on the first-floor. The two-storey building itself is nondescript, the windows blind. There are no obvious signs of any particularly intensive security measures. Many buildings in the area also have anti-burglar cactus fencing on their roofs. There are CCTV cameras on the perimeter but this is in keeping with most other premises on Pacific quay. Nor is an underground carpark for staff unusual. The main conference room was at the western corner of the upper floor. The metal slatted blinds, which could deflect machine gun rounds of up to 9 mm, and the smoked triple-glazing, afforded a partial view of the Clyde. You could see the blue glass cube of the BBC Scotland building and the steel armadillo roof of the SECC across the river. The city was changing, with vast tracts of land adjacent to the river demolished and ready for new construction.

Desmond Thorpe reluctantly turned from the window and took his seat. He opened his files and glanced over the notes he had prepared, while his left hand stroked at the sides of his cropped hair. Richard Blenkinsop and Saul Dunan were helping themselves to coffee from the percolator near to the potted plants. Four others were seated and he noted two were still to arrive.

'Miller and Donaghy still to come,' he observed. 'Anyone seen them?'

'Just late, probably,' someone told him. 'Donaghy was around earlier.'

'Maybe we can start. There's a lot on the agenda.' He looked up. 'If everybody's happy we can kick off.' He repositioned his thick tortoiseshell spectacles and drew a deep breath. 'As most of you know, I'm Desmond Thorpe. For the past three years I was Admins Officer at Millbank for all the desks dealing with Scotland. I think I know most of you all, except for… you, Shiasta is it?' His eye fell on a young woman, Shiasta Shaheen, who wore a head-scarf, cream blouse and jeans. She nodded, smiled. Sitting next to her was a woman in tee-shirt and hooded top.

'And Maureen… Brady? Hello. And Donaghy… but anyway, I've just heard that my secondment here is to be made permanent.' He paused, smiling self-consciously.'

'Bravo,' someone said. It was Saul Dunan.

'Thank you. So I'll be getting to know you all better. Anyway, my main role as Admin is to take on the new requirement for setting up think-aloud meetings such as this, on strategy. To direct our ops… on a more focussed basis.' He glanced down at his notes. The door opened and the missing two arrived.

'Miller… and you must be Donaghy. Hello. I'm Desmond Thorpe.'

The new men nodded and sat down.

Thorpe glanced around the room. All eight officers were in situ. He idly wondered what an onlooker would make of the meeting. The average age was probably about thirty, younger than your average board meeting. And there was a casualness in dress. Dunan and Blenkinsop looked like policemen. They were part of a new intake of officers who had, from the successful completion of their basic training, known only secondment to regional offices. Blenkinsop, who had a year's seniority, and Dunan, had been based in Leeds and moved to Scotland during the final weeks of the referendum, mostly working in Edinburgh. He knew they had worked in a back office in a Police Scotland station there and then the MI5 satellite office in the New Waverley Centre when it opened. They wore suits and ties as did Freddy Blake, whom he recalled had previously been a policeman in the PSNI. The others wore fleeces over open-necked shirts, and of the two women, Maureen Brady looked like she'd just been on a run.

'So this is a think-meeting,' Thorpe repeated. 'The rules are that there are no rules. Everyone can say what they want, express your views. Nothing is recorded. And then we'll try to come to an agreed conclusion at the end. But I'll introduce the topic. Okay?'

Heads nodded, there was a murmur of agreement.

'Lunch will be delivered at one. Let's get to it. You are expected to participate.' He laughed and adjusted his specs. 'To kick off, I see the main issue we face as one of legitimacy. Mandates. What is our mandate and what is theirs…? Oh, and I should have said. No Special Branch liaison with us today, as you see. We're free to speak without fear of it going over the wall.'

Blenkinsop interrupted. 'That's the way I like it. It's always a strain having to explain yourself, interpret, translate…'

Thorpe laughed. 'Yes, we don't have these tensions elsewhere. When I was at Millbank, the co-operation of Special Branch was assured. It just happened. It was a given. Here…'

'They feel they have to exercise control all the time. Report everything back,' Blake said phlegmatically. 'I saw that with the PSNI, fear of decision-making.'

Blenkinsop laughed. 'The crisis of having some power but not all power.'

'Exactly,' Thorpe agreed. 'So back to topic, we have to decide about this group codenamed Claymore or the name they use: EH41. Ethical Hackers for Independence. Yes, I know, it's an odd name. And we know that not many of them are hackers. What we have to decide is: do this group possess the potential to provide genuine alternative leadership and how much of a risk are they to us?'

Blenkinsop read off a page in the folder in front of him. 'Fifty-two known associates, many of whom are no longer involved. Only three are considered to be hackers. The rest are academics or journalists, none with any substantial track record.'

'Until William Morton turned up,' Dunan put in. 'He's a known agent. We have a big file on him. We rattled his cage just the other day.'

'Yes,' Thorpe agreed. 'I was previously involved in Millbank as Admin of that case. I should remind you that we do not, as a service, get involved in political activity.'

There was a shared laugh around the room.

'Of course!' Blenkinsop said. 'As if!'

'Seriously… some of what they are doing is innocuous, not of interest to us,' Thorpe said. 'Though some people think that now the referendum is over, the pressure will just go away and we can relax. But we – in this room – know that the daily fight goes on.' He glanced around the table. Nods, grim smiles.

'We have to combat it every day, ride the pressure, infiltrate and head-off any upsurge, stamp on any new leadership before it gets traction. But there's no problem with activity channelled through the SNP. That's being firmly controlled by their leadership and their highly-disciplined – I nearly called it a cult – of fanatical loyalty. Even their MPs are scared to speak out of turn in case they are accused of being disloyal. The SNP leadership is crucial to our mission here. Agreed?'

'Agreed.'

'Of course.'

'But when we get a nexus of independent agents like Morton, the hacker Sangster and others, there is a raised possibility of something nasty developing. And that's when we need to get in there and damp it down, disperse the main agents or direct the group into less productive or perhaps pointless activity, break links, cause miscommunications, etcetera, the usual.'

Freddy Blake snorted. 'Mostly these here are pussy-cats. Intellectuals.' He pronounced the word with disdain. 'The others fart around in the media, whatever that is. Leadership? I don't think they know the meaning of the word. Risk assessment? Practically zero.' He looked around the room. 'Sorry if that doesn't accord with your thinking.' Blake was the oldest man in the room at nearly fifty. His face bore the scars of active service and the flabby skin on it was like stale porridge with a couple of visible scars; bomb blast injury. Thorpe deferred to him. As a newcomer in his late twenties, he had yet to see the kind of trouble Blake had seen.

'Okay. That's one view,' Thorpe said. 'Now we can all go home!'

Everyone laughed. Even Freddy Blake managed a smirk.

'You could be right, Freddy. 'But if you add other agents into the mix, you're starting to see the problem we have – or we might have. There are half-a dozen media groups, and more than one hundred and twenty groups of individuals, at least three *Foundations* as they call themselves, which raise funding, other groups that do crowd-funding, popular demagogues who are not in the party hierarchy such as Brodagh Maddox... sorry, Murdoch, writers, union leaders, plus of course the rabble.'

'The flag-wavers at marches.'

'Correct. The foot soldiers. They're no problem of course. Agreed?'

'Oh, yes,' Blenkinsop said. 'Pointless activity. Must be fun though. Gets them out and about, waving their flags, convincing themselves they're doing valuable work for the cause.'

'When the opposite is the case,' Thorpe said with a benign smile. 'They're demonstrating their lack of support. They haven't cottoned on to that yet. The point of course,' Thorpe said with a wider smile. 'Is that it was *our* idea.' He nodded sagely. 'True. You know this. We got a man on the rock. He built a group and they're off, and soon they had thousands following them to every town annoying the locals, disrupting town centres.'

'Coming to a city centre near you!' Blenkinsop crowed. 'A pied-piper!'

'Oh they had plenty of pipers,' Maureen Brady said. 'And my ears haven't recovered yet! Plenty of pipers and lots of hot air.'

'Yup,' Thorpe agreed. 'You get the point. All good clean fun in the happy-clappy Yes movement. But maybe some of you didn't know it was our work?' He looked around the room, frowning. 'Yes? No? And what followed on naturally from it was that our man on the rock engineered a split. Just when things were starting to take off. He fell out with his committee and went off and formed a splinter group. So now there are two opposing groups doing the same thing. And boy do they hate each other! That's exactly the kind of clever work we specialise in. But I digress. More input please. Joe Miller – what's your take on Claymore?'

Miller was a good-looking blond man in his early thirties with a deep tan. 'Um, like, the hacker is the greatest risk in my opinion, yeah?' he said. Gingery hair showed at the open neck of the shirt. He splayed his hands out, so that his biceps flexed below his shirtsleeves. 'He could be dealt with quite easily as he is most likely breaking laws. And the most powerful of the academics also, by means of attracting them away to promotion opportunities elsewhere.'

'Aye, that's an ongoing task I'm working on masel,' Shiasta Shaheen said in a strong Glaswegian accent. 'My particular brief. See, through my contacts and liaison with the SFC we move on potential troublemakers, disperse them out of Scotland.'

'Yeah,' Miller agreed. 'I know you do that. 'I'm assuming…' he eased himself forwards in his chair, 'that the information on Claymore comes from inside?'

'Oh, yes,' Thorpe smiled modestly. 'We have a man on that rock too. Or should I say a woman. Although it's backed up by a lot of backroom work on the dear old Preston national database at Thames House and of course GCHQ. Wait, do I smell food? Fantastic, we'll just keep going though…'

CHAPTER SEVEN

Morton walked down the Vennel Steps to the Grassmarket for his lunch meeting with the writer Liam McLanders. Petit Paris was a familiar sight to Morton, its blue façade, the jaunty blue awning. The white lettering in the typeface font, its squiggles, curly tails and dots, was called AR Hermann. Funny how he knew something like that. As it was a blustery early spring day, no customers sat at the tables outside, or at those of the next door establishment, Made in Italy. *Quelle Douleur!* Morton murmured to himself. He'd always felt there should be a Belgian Brasserie or an Amsterdam cafe there instead of the green-painted White Hart Inn, a decent-enough pub. He'd been to all three and remembered an early date with Emily in Petit Paris. He'd had a steak with peppercorn sauce and could recall the rich cognac of it and Emily had salmon – she'd not even been a vegetarian then, far less a vegan. It was a jaunty place of whitewashed walls, red, white and blue checked table-cloths and patrons seeking their inner *moules-frites*.

They had arranged to meet at 1 p.m. and it was five past when Morton strolled in. Ten of the twelve or so tables were vacant. Two couples sat at tables under the large mirror and garish poster of the Cabaret Moulin Rouge. He was welcomed by a squat waiter in a white apron, whose sparse black hair was gelled back from his forehead.

'Bonjour, M'sieur, you have a table booking?'

'In the name of McLanders, I think.'

'Ah yes. We have this one.'

'Perfect.' Morton sat down. It was a good table for two, near the door and windows but out of the draught. The waiter placed a carafe of water with lemon slices and ice near a vase of delicate yellow flowers. Morton discreetly checked. Yes, real, but he'd no idea what kind of flowers they were. A few minutes later he looked up and McLanders was coming in, wearing an off-white suit and bright blue open-neck shirt. Suited the colour of his eyes and the silver hair, Morton noted, as he half-rose to shake hands.

'Grand,' McLanders said, rubbing his hands together. 'Been here before?'

'Oh yes, a couple of times. Nice lunch place. Gets a bit boisterous in the evenings, I'm told.'

'Ha – don't we all!'

Morton laughed. The waiter came over with the wine list and took their drinks order. 'The house white is excellent,' McLanders said, 'but feel free. This is on me, by the way. No – I insist. The invitation was mine.'

Morton had to concede. 'Okay. I'll have the house white,' he told the waiter.

'Bring the bottle,' McLanders instructed.

'Okay,' Morton said when the waiter had gone, 'I'll write up some kind of an interview – if we can call it that – and find some way to get it out there.'

'Nice,' McLanders smiled. 'Useful publicity for my new book, thank you. But of course, that's not the reason for this meeting. We were going to discuss Luke Sangster and this trouble that seems to have come your way.'

A party of six was arriving and being shown to their table – three tables put together. This proved an entertaining diversion before their wine arrived with a basket of rustic bread and a dish of butter.

'Slainthe!' McLanders said.

'Salud!'

The restaurant was getting noisy and some clientele were taking some of the tables outside.

'Bit brisk for sitting out, I'd say,' McLanders commented. He'd put on a narrow pair of reading spectacles which made him look like a boffin. Morton loved the word that conveyed disrespect and at the same time a sense of awe... *boffin*. It was tabloid-speak for any scientist. He wondered at the origin of the word. English public school slang? It had a 1940s flavour to it.

'I'll have the pan-fried salmon in saffron, crayfish and parsley sauce,' Morton said, reading out from the menu. 'Comes with *salade verte* and sautéed potatoes. Sounds ideal.'

'I'm a fan of the *cocotte traditionelle*... they do their own,' McLanders sniffed, dabbing his nostrils with a clean folded linen handkerchief. 'Meat stew, if your French is not up to it.'

'Right. The prices are pretty reasonable. Getting busy here isn't it?' He counted only two tables vacant.

'What about entrees? Come on, you're at your Auntie's,' invited McLanders with a smile.

Morton spread a chunk of bread with butter. 'Wasn't going to bother but I could try the soup.'

'Good man. You get two courses you see, for about thirteen quid. Not bad at all. I'm going for the steamed mussels in creamy blue cheese sauce.'

'*C'est merveilleux, mon ami*,' Morton approved, recycling his best Hercule Poirot-speak.

'Now tell me about your unwelcome visitors. What did they want?'

Morton outlined the encounter with Blenkinsop and Dunan. The author listened attentively and at the end commented: 'So now we know that Luke is not in custody or in their hands. That's something.'

Morton nodded. 'But there is still a mystery. What on earth do they think he has been up to?'

'Offences,' McLanders repeated, drawing his long fingers over the wavy surface of his silver hair. 'Presumably infringements of the Computer Misuse Act or… something like that?'

The waiter came over and refilled their glasses with wine.

'Well, but even so,' Morton argued. 'Seemed a little heavy-handed to me. There must be something more going on that we're unaware of. I have to say I am a little worried for his safety.'

'You could be right. Some of the other hackers and media researchers in our group have been aware of being under… not overt surveillance, just perhaps they've been a bit exposed, you could say: since the Treanor and Viroil media storm. Maybe a journalist talked and revealed the source? Well, anyway, others in the group have felt that what we are doing is a little risky. There are many who would prefer we did not continue.' He pulled a sad face and shrugged, 'and no doubt some in the Nationalist camp would prefer that too, but it is essential work, you know. There is little enough independent investigation going on. Well, Morton, I don't have to tell you.' He laughed abruptly. 'But as to the matter of Luke, I'm not sure what we can do. He could be anywhere.'

The waiter brought their entrees. Morton's soup was an intensely leek affair, with cream cheese and chives. He didn't like the look of McLander's dark and threatening bowl of mussels. As they waited for their main courses, the conversation drifted off to other subjects; writing, books, writers, the difficulties of making a living, the prospect of independence, the General Election now only fifteen days away.

'A year ago, I was considering putting my name forward as a candidate,' McLanders told him. 'I wasn't awfully keen and anyway they selected a very good candidate. She'll make an excellent MP. She's every chance of being elected, even here in Edinburgh. Changed days.'

'That's something I've never fancied – politics – too much toe-ing of party lines.'

McLanders smiled. 'Loyalty is the nature of the game these days. That's why the SNP has got where it is – discipline. And talent. Bags of that. But there is a difficulty for writers and journalists in being involved directly. As combatants. Affects the neutral space where you do your thinking. At least, for me personally, I prefer to be an onlooker close to, with a ringside seat view of' – he gestured – 'but not *at*, the battlefield.'

Morton had flipped out a small notebook and jotted down an occasional line or quote for his interview piece. McLanders had promised to email him some material he could use as background. They'd established that the hook would be McLanders' forthcoming book. For Morton it was as good as money in the bank. It would take him half an hour or less to put all the paragraphs in the right order.

'I'll make sure Hugh places it in the Saturday supplement with a couple of stock pictures. We'll get a jpeg of your book jacket. I'll just take a pic now, too, if you don't mind?'

'No problem,' McLanders smiled as Morton took out his mobile. 'But try to keep the wine bottle and glasses out of shot… if you see what I mean. You know how rumours start?'

'No problem. These phone cameras are pretty nifty. Ideal for Twitter and social media.'

'Whatever did we do without them?' McLanders smiled. 'So how did you and Emily meet?'

Morton put down his glass. 'I was at an event at the University to do an interview with a colleague of hers, for the *Scotsman*. A group of us went to the pub and we got talking... and...'

'Very nice,' McLanders remarked. 'A bit of good old-fashioned romance. You can't beat it. My wife Krystyna and I met at an opera in Tallinn. *La Boheme*. Not that I'm a big opera fan.'

'You could try high-heels.'

'Sorry?' McLanders raised an eyebrow.

'Then you'd be a bigger... opera fan.'

'Very funny,' McLanders smiled dutifully. 'You wrote a book didn't you, Willie? About the death of Angus McBain? I've got it somewhere.'

Morton savoured a mouthful of the crisp and fruity Sauvignon. 'You've got a copy? Really? It did well,' he recalled, 'got to number five in the Waterstones' Scottish charts, then dropped out of sight. Sold quite a few thousand though. I have a couple of yours. I don't know how you do it. I've no aspirations to write more. Hard work.'

'Ah well, Willie, one sentence prepares the ground for the inevitability of the next. You could say that each sentence gives birth to the next, if that didn't sound a bit...'

'That's one way of putting it.'

'So – Willie – will you be coming regularly to our meetings?'

Morton considered this. 'I don't want to get *too* involved. I'm a bit of a one-man band, but now I have a stake in finding Luke, I'll come to the next meeting. If only to share news about him.'

'Fair enough.'

Morton smiled wryly. 'Each meeting gives birth to the inevitability of the next!'

McLanders laughed delightedly and ran his fingers into the silky hair above his forehead. 'Touché!'

The bottle was finished and as neither wanted dessert, they ordered coffee. Morton checked his notebook and was surprised to find that he had filled nearly three sides of paper. The restaurant was empty as 3 p.m. approached, the waiters clearing up the dishes as customers drifted off. Morton and McLanders lingered in the doorway, chatting, under the awning which lifted with each gust of wind, then went their separate ways.

When he got home, he found he needed a nap. His head was clouded with wine and the living room had warmed in the afternoon sunlight. He opened the window and stretched out on the sofa and let the inflowing fresh air do the trick.

He was awoken a couple of hours later by the cooling breeze on his face. He got up, shut the window and made himself a coffee. And while he had slept, his thoughts had been interrogating themselves and he found that sentences had been silently forming. He set up his laptop on the breakfast bar and rapidly composed his interview piece on McLanders' new book. He read it through. It was fine, complete and unimpeachable. He emailed it to McLanders and to Hugh Leadbetter. If the author had some startling material to add, well, he would consider it, but the piece didn't need anything more. Then he began to compose another piece, based on the premise that Luke Sangster was missing. He added paragraphs about the tale of his flight across the rooftops from police for offences or contraventions of some kind which the police had not specified, probably related to his work as an ethical hacker. Morton strongly hinted that these might relate to Luke's part in the exposure of Viroil billionaire Brian Treanor.

He drained the cold dregs of the coffee. But Luke must have family, relations somewhere? He hadn't officially been reported as missing. So, not a missing person yet nor a fugitive from the law.

He phoned Hugh Leadbetter's mobile number. His boss was gruffer than usual. 'Ah, okay Willie, hold on a wee mo… Kiddies' bath time.' Morton heard vigorous splashing and gleeful toddler sounds. 'Right, what's up?'

Morton explained the situation.

'Can't see a problem, Willie. Go ahead but ye ken to leave out the polis' names. Were they polis though? Detectives or Special Branch? Mind – it disnae matter. We can use it. Have ye got a photie of the boy?'

'Maybe, I'll need to ask around.'

'Do that. Needs the photie, if it's to be used. Come in to the office tomorrow, Willie, we'll talk about it.'

'Okay.'

'Right – urgent business calls. Oi, you, Tammy, don't do that! Look what ye've done now! Mummy will no be pleased…'

Morton rang off, chuckling at the image of his bearded boss struggling with a pair of exuberant toddlers.

CHAPTER EIGHT

Morton sprawled full-length on Emily's couch, feet up, reaching occasionally down to the glass of lager on the carpet. He was hearing sounds of Emily in the kitchen preparing their tea, catching intermittent words or phrases from the evening news on TV. He wasn't sure what she was making; it was more usual for him to do the cooking, but he heard the sounds of a knife on a chopping board. He had told Liam McLanders that he would attend the next meeting to resolve the situation of Luke Sangster. Given the difficulties he had encountered in the past with agents of the British state while investigating the death of anti-nuclear activist Angus McBain: and his more recent troubles with GB13 and their MI5-backed thugs, it was no surprise that there was a clandestine group on the other side. Many campaigning groups had forged new existences after the referendum as media organisations or media-monitoring groups, bloggers or vloggers. Some had set-up foodbanks or charities for the homeless or welfare of refugees. There was a burning desire to remake Scottish society – and a deepening mistrust in the British institutions that had failed over decades to effectively tackle these issues. Intransigent problems like drug addiction, homelessness, poverty and social inequality had been given a new prominence during the two year referendum campaign and some Yes activists had thrown themselves into the breach with a newly-found zeal. The group chaired by Liam McLanders was no different. It had formed after a few members of the Academics for Yes group at Edinburgh University learned of the certification of a new course in ethical hacking at Abertay University in Dundee and that some of the new course intake lived in Edinburgh. A third section of the membership were Yes-supporting postgraduate students from Napier University's media courses. The combined group had not agreed on a name. In fact, they had decided that having no name was an advantage. It was, in essence, three groups, or one group with three distinct aims. Security was maintained by an informal vetting process of any potential new member. But what held the group together was the idea of acquiring high-quality information to underpin their political aims; the 'facts' as opposed to the political ping-pong that constituted the 'news'. It aspired to being an alternative intelligence-gathering service for the Yes movement. In the twelve months of its existence, its membership had come and gone several times over. Morton had learned most of what he knew from Emily but even she was not able to enlighten him about who – or what – was Cerberus: The name of the three-headed dog that guarded the entrance to Hades. Was it just a name or a cryptonym? Or did it have a deeper meaning? Was there something, or someone that needed protection? And what was the connection to the underworld?

He took his empty glass to the kitchen. It still amazed him that he was in a proper relationship. It had happened so casually, incrementally, over months. And now here he was, with Emily, at her place in Restalrig. She had chopped celery, onions and spinach and was pressing a roll of pastry into a pastry dish. 'Another beer in the fridge – if you want,' she offered. 'I'm on fruit smoothie. Could make you one if you want.'

'Beer is fine.' He reached into the fridge and uncapped the bottle on the wall gadget. 'What's it going to be?'

'Vegetable quiche.'

'Homemade quiche, by jings. How do you do it?'

Emily snorted. 'It's pretty basic, I'm sure even you could do it!'

'Hmn, the Co-op ones are okay. Not a patch on yours I'm sure, but it's a lot of effort…'

She glanced at him. 'I like to keep my hand in, now and then. Don't want to lose my cooking skills.'

He took a swig of beer. 'Em, I forgot to ask earlier… about the group. How did it start? Were you at the first meeting?'

'I wasn't actually. But I know how it started. Don't quote me on this, but the idea was that the group intended on doing intensive investigations to find out stuff, so we needed a secure repository and not just a storage function but someone, some group, to analyse it independent of the researchers and provide an overview to redirect the efforts accordingly.'

'A team leader perhaps?' Morton suggested with a grin.

'Yes, well, fill in the gaps, resolve anomalies, etcetera.'

'I get that. But what is the linking mechanism between the whole group and Cerberus?'

'There's a liaison person who carries messages.'

'Ah. And that is Luke Sangster?'

Emily put on oven gloves and slid the quiche into the oven on a baking tray. She stood up. 'It used to be someone else but about three months ago, Luke announced at a meeting that he was the new liaison.'

Morton took a swig from his Peroni bottle. 'What did the group think of that?'

'They never questioned it. Particularly since the announcement coincided with the previous liaison person no longer attending the meetings.'

'So Luke was in a strong position? He had access to all the information that was being collated. Was that his main value or was he actually responsible for acquiring new information too? You see what I'm getting at, Emily? This information – presumably of some value…?'

Emily tossed lettuce leaves, spinach and rocket into a salad spinner. 'I think you're asking was Luke more than he seemed. But I can't believe that. I – we – trust him completely. No – initially he supplied information. No doubt about it; he was the source of some of the best material – then and only then he evolved into *also* being the group's liaison.'

'Okay, Em, I'm being devil's advocate. But if MI5 had come to know of the group – and I would be surprised if they didn't – this structure where all the information is channelled through one person could be the weak point.'

'Yes, but there may be other security checks we don't know about. Anyway, Cerberus must trust Luke.'

'Which is puzzling,' Morton mused. 'How could Cerberus be sure of that?' He thought about it for a moment. Then a thought came to him. 'Unless Cerberus is already involved in the group incognito?'

Emily stopped spinning the salad. 'That is a possibility, Willie. In fact, I've thought about that before a few times. Because there must be other channels of communication between the group and Cerberus. Must be. But I'm not aware of them.'

In the warmth of the attic flat in Portland Street, Leith, Luke Sangster was working hard but not very successfully. He had logged on to The Onion Router VPN to enable him to hide the search history on Jed's PC. He was testing vulnerabilities all around the social, industrial and commercial existence of Brian Treanor and Viroil using spelling variations on URL addresses, personnel files and even family members. There were several houses in the UK used by Treanor and his family and key associates such as Clive Kenton and these had online traces. A daughter with horse riding interests in a local stables, a private school attended by two sons, all of the family including apparently Treanor himself had online purchasing records. He was building up background; the comings and goings, but not getting closer to major financial transactions. He could see the gates of the important company websites but couldn't find a design vulnerability or any kind of glitch to allow him inside. The most tantalising was Viroil's main website, based, as far as he could see in Nassau in the Bahamas, according to the origin of the Jpeg images used in the public gallery on its Home page. But every other section of the site was locked down. He had spent several hours testing the security at this point of connection between the Home Page and the rest of the site. He was fairly sure personnel and possibly Treanor himself would log in for remote access but there were no obvious log in plugs. In most such cases, Luke knew, there was evidence of third party access – the administrator – who entered the site to update information and that was the vulnerable spot, his attack point. But he couldn't find it.

The sun had heated the room through the Velux windows. He stood up and stretched. It was a great flat, a real eyrie in the sky and Jed and Susan were very lucky. It was quiet too, the noise and bustle of Leith dockyards muffled by the triple glazing. He went over and opened the window and stood under it, gazing out at the dockyard scene, the Western harbour and the cold blue Firth of Forth. He wondered if it was too late to return to the normal nine to five world. Get a good job, settle down, find a partner, buy a flat like this. He sighed. He doubted whether it would deflate his restless urge to make a difference, his conception of himself as a crusading idealist. He closed the window and shut off the noise. He padded on the soft carpet to the kitchen-diner and made more coffee. And anyway, maybe he'd make his own job, pay his own way, by getting better at what he was doing? In a world of wall-to-wall surveillance and secrecy, there was going to be an ever greater need for spies.

CHAPTER NINE

Morton had pre-conceived notions as to what a survival expert would look like based on TV survivalists such as Ray Mears and Bear Grylls. He imagined Ross Mackie as a wiry, bearded figure in camouflage gear and hiking boots, or Scoutmaster shorts and rugged sandals. His anticipation was heightened when he received a text message an hour after his intended arrival time. *Sorry, held up, with you soon, RM.* Finally, half an hour later, Morton heard a motorbike growling up the cobbles of Keir Street. He went to the window to see a bulky black-leather-clad figure dismounting from a powerful machine. He frowned. Not very eco-friendly, with its two chrome-plated exhausts; a real gas-guzzler, surely? A short time later, he heard his doorbell ring.

The man filled the doorframe, well over six feet tall, holding a shiny white helmet. 'Willie?'

'Yes. Come on in.' He stepped aside to let him in then had to precede him into the living room due to lack of space in the hall.

'Where'll I dump the skid-lid?' he inquired. 'Alright here?' He gestured to the hall floor.

Morton nodded. 'No problem.'

Mackie placed the helmet on the carpet. 'Better get the boots off too,' he grunted, bending to unhook the Velcro tabs. 'I keep forgetting to buy new socks,' he admitted, as his toes appeared through holes in the thick woollen socks. 'Would you mind if I dump the trousers? Don't worry, I have long johns underneath, if that's what's bothering you.' He began to remove his thick leather one-piece suit. 'If you want,' Morton laughed. 'Christ, it's like a burlesque show.' Mackie grinned good-humouredly. 'Aye, well these leather breeks are great for the road but this flat's awfy warm. I cannae wear them indoors.'

'Okay, I'll get the coffee on, while you…' He cast a glance at the now-cluttered hallway. The huge helmet, the biker boots, black heap of leather, lots of kit. He went into the kitchen diner and spooned coffee into the filter machine. He found two mugs in the cupboard above the fridge.

'Right, that's me,' Mackie announced, coming into the kitchen. 'Reporting for duty.'

Morton suppressed a laugh. The big man looked like he was auditioning for a ballet; tight grey long johns, bare toes protruding from woolly socks. There was something hapless about him, disarmingly so. Morton had always associated bikers with some form of arrested development in men; big boys blundering about, good with machinery, less good with human relationships. He knew that was a subjective and possibly completely wrong idea. 'Take milk?' he asked.

'Aye, and two sugars.'

Morton handed him the mug and sat down at the breakfast bar. 'Sorry for being late. Had a wee problem with the fuel line but I sorted it. So it's tracking a misper – the job, I mean?'

'Only advice,' Morton told him, putting his feet on the foot rail and his elbows on the counter. 'I'm going to be doing the actual investigation. I just want your advice on possibilities. Basically, it's a colleague whose flat was raided by Special Branch. Or MI5, we're not clear on that yet. And he's gone to ground.'

Mackie squatted down onto the high stool. Morton could tell it wasn't too comfortable for him. It also meant their faces were a bit too close for comfort. Everything about him was expansive, his hands; thick fingers, his shoulders and neck. 'Been a naughty boy, has he?' Mackie grinned. 'Ruffled a few feathers.'

Morton looked up at him and frowned. 'That's exactly the position. We're not clear that he has done anything illegal. He was investigating financial dealings of some… establishment figures.'

'So, not the ordinary plod? He's not facing charges, just that they want him to answer some questions? I could ask around.'

Morton was alarmed. 'What do you mean, *ask around*?'

Mackie leaned back and held up his hands. 'Woah! No need to bite ma head off… I just meant discreet inquiries with former colleagues.'

Morton noted the heavy steel divers' watch on his wrist. 'I don't understand. Former colleagues? I called you in for your advice as a survivalist, an expert on off-grid living.'

'Of course,' Mackie nodded. 'And I am. But I learned all my stuff with Special Forces. The sass, boat squad, Commanchios, the Arctic training and so on.'

'The sass?'

'SAS. You name it, I've been there and done it. Most of those guys have training regimes that consist of survival exercises, living off-grid and the training is the best in the world. It's done for real, Willie,' he grinned. 'No mod-cons, no home comforts, and for extensive periods too, in hostile terrain.' His hands gestured expansively. 'Guys die on the training. Well, not often, but it happens.'

'I see. It didn't occur to me there'd be a military connection.'

'Inevitable.' Mackie grinned wolfishly. 'Good word that.'

He slurped his coffee. 'Nice place,' he said looking around. 'Not that I'd want to live in a city, me.'

'You're in Angus?' Morton asked.

'Aye, near Friockheim, about halfway between Arbroath and Stonehaven. Cottage. Bit of a ramshackle place. I'm doing it up.' He grinned. 'Not off-grid, if that's what you were thinking?'

Morton laughed politely. 'And is there a Mrs Mackie?'

'There is. But nowhere near Friockheim, thank god. Divorced. You?'

'I'm divorced too.'

'Right, well – you ken.'

'I ken,' Morton said, 'I think.'

'So – basically you want to track down your friend and you're going to do that yourself. But you want my help, how?' He placed his hands on the table top. 'You're going to pay me a fee, so how do I earn it? I presume you don't just want a load of verbal guff?'

Morton leaned his chin in his hand. 'I'm not exactly sure. It's been eight days since he went on the run. I've been to his former flat – door kicked in and nailed up again – and spoken to the few friends we're aware of. We think he had an escape plan ready in case he was raided. And he escaped by climbing out of an attic and away over the rooftops.'

'What age is he?'

'About thirty, we think. Maybe a year or two younger.'

'A reporter?'

'Well, sort-of, a computer geek, a hacker.'

'Hats off to the boy. I'm struggling just using a mobile phone.'

'When you said earlier, you could ask around, what did you mean?'

Mackie sniffed and rubbed at the stubble on his chin. 'I'm still in touch with a few lads I used to serve with, in various units. They might have heard…?'

'You have connections with Special Branch?'

Mackie laughed. 'Christ, no! That shower of shite! I just meant, you know, word gets around. I didn't mean any specific…'

'It's just that I've had trouble in the past. Crossed swords you could say, with various…'

'Spooks is the word you're searching for I think,' Mackie grinned. 'Aye the world is full of them, especially here in Scotland the way things are.'

'A few years ago, I had trouble with a man called McGinley who worked for the nuclear police squad. Sadly, he died. Although… it could have been me. Then – more recently…' He stopped. Mackie had more or less admitted he had continuing connections with serving forces personnel. How many of them might be spooks? Even he might be a spook? 'Well, let's just say, my activities as a reporter have been interfered with in the past by people I'm not keen to have dealings with again.'

'Ha! That's a good way of putting it. And anyway that's none of my business. I'm not under the Official Secrets Act any more. I'm freelance. Free to offer my services and my skills to folks who need my help. I've done a bit of everything since leaving the forces, Willie. Mountain-guiding, expedition-leading, some security work, that sort of thing. This job could be right up my street. Interesting and out of the ordinary. That's the kind of work I like. Outdoors, not regular hours. Ideal.'

'Okay, but this is not big bucks. We could discuss a fee but it isn't likely to be huge. And I'd need to discuss that with others.'

'Fair enough. And as I said, this consultation is free. What I suggest is you put down on paper the details, his friends, contacts, and what you want me to do and I'll have a think about how much time it's going to take up and email you an estimate. I won't get involved until I hear the get-go from you.'

Morton had been feeling a little apprehensive about giving out information and now saw the possibility that he could back-out of any arrangement. He nodded thoughtfully. He liked Mackie, there was something open about him and equally he was quite sure he was full of bluster and boasting. But there was the ambiguity of his connection to the military. He'd had the Queen's shilling for a long time, and god knows what he had done in that time and to whom. 'Okay, Mr Mackie, I'll do that in the next day or two. And I'll look into the fee possibilities.'

Mackie stood up and stretched. 'That's good – and it's Ross, by the way – I'm sure I can help. Thanks for the coffee. Now I'll have to get back into my kit.' He grinned. 'A reverse-striptease.'

'Going back to Friockheim?'

'Not immediately. There's a bike-run with some pals in East Lothian this afternoon, then a couple of pints. I'll stay over at a chum's, home tomorrow morning.'

'Nice. Well, thanks for coming.'

Mackie kitted himself up like a modern Knight in his leather equivalent of a suit of armour, added his incongruously-large helmet and then, zipped and strapped and entirely encased, he was away. Morton watched him from the window throw his leg over the modern steed and, sitting astride, back the bike out over the cobbles, kick it into life and sway out of Keir Street with a gutsy growl and off. He'd felt a little exposed during their conversation, uncomfortable. Perhaps some of his anxiety was due to an unconscious comparison of Mackie to his former nemesis McGinley. There was a difference between what Mackie said and how he was. Very Scottish in personality but perhaps working for the enemy. Morton wondered if Mackie was all he seemed and if there was a way to check up on him and he was also glad he had not mentioned Luke's name.

CHAPTER TEN

Morton switched on the radio in the kitchen, listening to commentary on the Madrid Open. Andy Murray was outplaying Rafael Nadal in twenty degree heat. He heard his doorbell ring and winced in annoyance. What now?

Two uniformed officers stood at the door. A male and a female, fresh-faced and almost exactly the same height as each other.

'Mr William Morton?' asked the PC.

'Yes, that's me. What's this about?'

'Mr Luke Sangster. He's a friend of yours?'

Morton sighed wearily. 'Ah, well, I wouldn't go that far. I know of him. You'd better come in.'

'Thank you, sir. I'm PC McKenna and this is WPC Webster. We won't take up much of your time.'

'Come through to the living room. Cup of tea or coffee?'

'Not unless you're making one yourself.'

'No, I've had one. I'll just switch the radio off.'

'Okay. Mr Morton, we're trying to trace Luke Sangster and looking for information on his whereabouts.'

The WPC interjected, seating herself on the sofa. 'So we're visiting all of the people who know him.'

They were both young, in their twenties and fit-looking. Police uniforms had changed over the last decade. Gone were the blue serge jackets, shirts and ties, now it was lycra, tight-fitting trousers and headgear similar to baseball caps. Also, male and female uniforms were now essentially the same.

'As I said, I met Luke a couple of times but I know very little about him. In fact, I'm trying to find him myself.'

'Oh,' WPC Webster said, 'any luck?'

'No. He seems to have completely disappeared. And I'm becoming aware of how few people seem to know anything about him.'

'Yes, we're finding that,' PC McKenna said. 'A mystery man. But the focus of our inquiries is a complaint by a former landlord of unpaid rent to the tune of more than three hundred pounds.'

'I see. And how did my name crop up in your inquiry?'

PC McKenna coughed behind his hand. 'Ah, we're not at liberty to say. I think yours was just a name on a list, really.'

'But why are *you* looking for him?' WPC Webster asked, reaching up to her shoulder to pluck off the mobile phone which had started to ping. She glanced at the screen, pressed the mute and clipped it back into the holster. 'On whose behalf? If you are not a friend, I mean, what motive have you got?' Morton took a deep breath. 'Well – that's a little difficult to explain without mentioning the context which would take too long. I'll just say some friends noted his absence and somehow or other, I've got involved. I don't really want to mention names.'

PC McKenna nodded. 'We understand. But if I say that we have already spoken to Professor McKechnie, would that make it easier?'

'You've spoken to Emily? She knew him when he was a student.'

'Correct. But like you, she says she knows little about

his home life. Do you happen to have a photograph of Mr Sangster?'

Morton frowned. 'I don't.'

'We've not been able to find one either, though there will be one on record at Edinburgh University and we're checking that.'

'Do you think there is a likelihood that Luke could be listed as a Missing Person?' Morton said, adding, 'the door to his flat had clearly been kicked in, as you might be aware?'

'We are aware.'

'And those were the premises where the rent was owed?'

'No,' PC McKenna told him.

'No? Really?' Morton was surprised. 'So there's no unpaid rent on that flat?'

'Not as far as we know. He seems to have used various addresses. As I said, a mystery man. We're quite interested to find out just what he has been up to.'

WPC Webster smiled. She had a little rosebud mouth. 'What started as a simple complaint about rent arrears is developing into... well, something else. Complicated fellow, our Mr Sangster, not that we have any grounds, as yet, for thinking he may be associated with criminality – apart from rent arrears, which as you know, is a civil matter.'

'So you don't know anything that might help us, Mr Morton?' PC McKenna concluded, rising.

'I'm afraid not. But, as I said, I'll be looking into things on behalf of our group. I'll certainly keep you informed if I find anything, or indeed, Luke – the lad himself – as they say in these parts.' He was astonished to find himself quoting the spook Blenkinsop and let out a little laugh.

The female police officer smiled at him expectantly. 'Something struck you?'

'Just something someone said,' Morton said. 'Nothing important. I'll see you out.'

After they had gone, Morton caught the end of the tennis. Murray had just won a double break in the second set to go 4-1 up and took the set with ease at 6-3; his first victory on clay against Nadal.

'Well done Andy boy!' Morton said aloud, clenching his fist in exultation. He switched the radio off and decided on a whim to phone his old school friend and solicitor Archie MacDonald. It was possible he was still in his office. He was, and answered the phone almost directly.

'Willie! It's yourself? Was just on the way out. The secretaries have buggered off. You just caught me. What's up?'

'Nothing specific. Just thought I'd give you a call. Was listening to the tennis just now, you know? Andy Murray. He did well. I'm thinking of heading down to the pub. Don't suppose...?'

'No can do, old chap. Confined to barracks.'

'How are you placed for a pint later in the week?'

'Should be possible. In fact, I'm having a day off tomorrow,' the solicitor said, 'if that might suit? Very rare occurrence a day off, in this establishment. It's been a long time since we raised a jar or two.'

'It is,' Morton agreed.

'Ahem,' the solicitor coughed discreetly. 'Presume there's nothing amiss and this is simply a catch-up? What I'm trying to say, Willie... you're not phoning me from the nick?'

Morton laughed uneasily. 'Of course not.'

'Not out on remand?'

'No.'

'Well, that makes a pleasant change. No recent convictions or unexpired sentences. Unpaid fines?'

'If there had been, you'd know about it.'

'Good point. So, been keeping your nose clean? Splendid! Well, name your licenced establishment of choice.'

'Okay,' Morton barely paused. 'Frankenstein's.'

'Frankie–what? Good grief, is that a hostelry now?'

'The former Elim Pentacostal church on George IV Bridge, directly opposite Chambers Street. Twelve?'

'Well, if you must. I presume this is a fully licenced and taxed... shebeen?'

But Morton cut him off with a curt, 'See you then.' And was still smirking five minutes later. Frankenstein's was a pub Emily had taken him to, because of its proximity to the University. He remembered a wan-faced barmaid there, profuse purple tresses clashing with scarlet lipstick and fake bloodstains on her chin. He looked forward to enjoying his friend's discomfiture.

He had received email replies from an acquaintance in Blackwell's Bookshop to his query about books on off-grid living. It seemed a number of high-profile experts had published books on the subject. He made another coffee, standing beside the filter machine till its process was completed, and took a mug through to the living room and opened his laptop. To his surprise, he found several Facebook groups about off-grid living and began to browse the posts. He became fascinated in the intricacies of the hut movement in Scotland and comparisons with Scandinavia. There was a lot of earnest discussion and advice about 'going dark' and topics related to surveillance; several diatribes about the increasing 'Big Brother' powers of the state. Other conversations agonised over the risks of online banking, online shopping, online activity in general, which struck Morton as a little hypocritical, given the context. After a bit of thought, Morton joined the group and put up a post announcing himself as a journalist seeking personal experiences about how, or whether, someone in Scotland could live off-grid. Within minutes, six people had liked the post and two had shared it. Someone commented: 'better just pay your debts and stay put lol.' Morton clicked his tongue in annoyance. He had an intrinsic dislike of social media. Another comment popped up: 'Wife kicking you out? If she's nice, I could swap.' That summed it up, really, he thought. People out there see it as entertainment. The modern way of ringing a doorbell and running away. He un-joined the site, clicked out of Facebook and realised he hadn't finished his coffee, which was cold. He put the mug in the microwave. He couldn't decide what to do about Ross Mackie.

Frankenstein's is a themed pub, bistro and night spot glorying to the full in its gothic credentials. A B-listed former Lutheran church, it has bars on three levels and all kinds of gory displays and dramatisations throughout the building. The basement is a genuine recreation of a Bier Keller, complete with barmen in lederhosen, fetching barmaids in low-cut frilly dresses and huge steins of foaming lager. Morton quickly checked the interiors and came out again into the glorious evening sunshine to wait outside on the steps. It was the third sunny day in a row, the thermometer hitting the giddy heights of sixteen degrees Centigrade. Archie was late and he wasn't inside. Finally, Willie saw him approaching and smiled. Even although he said he'd had the day off, Archie wore a grey lounge suit and black shoes. No tie – that was his concession to having a day off in warm weather. He came up the steps cautiously.

'No cape?' he enquired,' I thought that'd be *de rigeur* for a place like this.' Morton grunted, 'Huh! Thought you were on a day off?'

'My other suit's at the dhobi-wallah.'

'No, what I meant was… ach, never mind.'

'After you, old chap. Well – let's join the congregation.' They trooped down into the gloomy interior, checking to see which bar was quietest and found a corner table lit only by a wavering candle. The interior was dark, like a ramshackle crypt and no expense had been spared to keep up the conceit. Goths mingled with pale youths though there were a number of men in suits.

Archie narrowed his eyes. 'What will you have, Willie, name your poison, or perhaps I should say, potion.'

'Lager. And crisps – ready salted.'

'Absolutely, old chap.'

When they had settled, Morton cleared his throat. 'Been a while since we caught up.'

'Indeed.'

'How's Halbron, Finlay & MacDonald?' he inquired.

'Dead, senile and fair to middling, in that order,' Archie smiled.

'I see. Sorry to bring you to this place,' Morton said. 'I admit I did it maliciously.' The solicitor raised an eyebrow. Morton continued. 'All your cracks about my difficulties with the police, etcetera.' He grinned. 'You needed punishment.'

'As the actress said to the bishop. No, no, Willie, I'm enjoying this place. Very restful. Not as busy as I imagined but I suppose it's dead by midnight. Or perhaps – undead by midnight!'

'Ha!' Morton frowned. 'At least we don't have to face the Monster Show. That happens here you know, but not on a midweek night maybe. Anyway, I was going to ask your advice on something. And I thought, in a pub… I might get away with it on an old school tie basis: no charge.'

Archie laughed. 'And I left my tie at home! Well, fire away, old bean. Knew there was a reason I wore mufti today.'

'I'm helping to find someone who seems to have disappeared.'

'Oho,' said Archie.

'Not been seen since the police raided his flat.'

'Aha,' said Archie. 'A criminal acquaintance?'

'Not at all. A fine, upstanding young man. As far as I can see, he's not done anything wrong, not committed any crimes.'

'A tale of police blundering? Gone to the wrong address?'

'Could be. Can't rule that out. But I don't think so. He's a hacker.' Archie leaned back in his pew, miming deep shock. The heavy dark wood seats were from the original church. He scoffed. 'Good grief, they're arresting *golfers*?'

'No… ah, you're kidding?'

'Bit of a hacker myself,' Archie deadpanned, 'especially in the bunkers.'

'Seriously. He may have got up some people's noses. He uncovered money laundering by big business backers of the No campaign – ruffled more than a few feathers. Anyway, that's background.'

'A marked scorecard, so to speak.'

'Archie – will you please knock off the jesting. Let me tell the story.'

'Fire away, old bean. Tee-off.'

Morton gave him a withering glance. 'Right. So there's no trace. No-one has a photograph of him, he has few friends apparently. Then the police are knocking at my door. I mean I barely know this chap, whose name is Luke Sangster by the way.'

'Oh!' Archie grinned. 'Heard of him. Sangster the gangster?'

'Will you give it a rest! The police claimed to me that he, Sangster…'

'The aforementioned…'

'… is due rent to his landlord and they think, or thought, that I know where he is.'

'And you don't?'

'No. As I said, I barely met him. The police said that my name had come up as a friend of his. I have no idea how they would suggest that.'

'Ah, wait a minute, William. This Sangster fellow was one of the chaps who kidnapped you a few months ago?'

Morton was surprised. 'Archie, that's amazing. How did you remember that? But you're correct.'

'Well that's the answer to your question. They'll be aware of your connections.'

'I don't see that at all. Luke is very careful to keep himself incognito. He's paranoid about surveillance. I've been trying to find someone who knew him but all I've found is people who know him very slightly. The man is practically a ghost.'

Archie studied the remnants of his drink. 'Sounds dodgy to me, old chap. Just the type to run off without paying his rent.'

'Well, it's possible. Like I said, I barely know him.'

Archie finished his drink. 'So, to sum-up, a man you barely know possibly owes rent and has done a bunk. Hold the front page!'

'When you put it like that…'

'No other way to put it, Willie. You're just a bit miffed because the confounded Gendarmerie have had the sheer efficiency – or effrontery – to drag you into it.' Willie shrugged. 'Maybe, I'm just over-sensitive after my previous troubles. Anyway – another?'

'Certainly.' The solicitor grinned warmly. 'Dear Sarah's

lunching with friends. Chinwag circle. Has her car with her. Therefore, one might be chauffeured home, so indeed, I can stay for a couple more.'

A few days later, General Election day dawned bright and sunny. A few clouds, not many. Should be a good voter turnout, Morton mused looking out the window towards Castle Terrace. He glanced at his mobile and saw a text from Emily. *Don't forget to vote xx* After his coffee, he put on a jacket and strolled down to the Lauriston Halls, nodding to the two ladies with rosettes standing outside. He handed over his polling card to the clerk in the hall. In the wooden partitioned cubicle, he saw seven candidates listed on the ballot paper and swiftly made his cross against the sixth, a former Labour official and comedy club promoter who was the SNP candidate. When he came out into the spring sunshine, he wondered what to do with the rest of the day. He didn't feel like working and there was nothing he could usefully do to move the Sangster case on. He felt the pangs of hunger and went in to Doctors pub at the corner of Teviot Place and Forrest Road. It was almost empty. He sat up at the bar and had a pint of Belhaven Best, a tasty Scotch pie, and crisps; an early and well-deserved lunch.

2: ASSYNT

CHAPTER ELEVEN

After more than half an hour, Morton was beginning to get used to the various creaks and rattles of the VW Trident campervan. With Ross Mackie at the wheel they were heading north.

'It's no very environmentally-friendly, I suppose,' Mackie was saying against the drone of the engine, staring at the M90 snaking ahead of them, low-lying farmland on either side. 'Diesel, see. I'm lucky if I can get thirty miles a gallon.' He'd been talking about the van and his other vehicles since they set off. Half an hour gone, five and a half to go, Morton was thinking. He forced himself to concentrate and find something positive to say.

'Compact though. You've got everything here. Perfect for just taking off and going somewhere.'

Mackie grinned. 'Wild camping. That's my preference, Willie. When I get the time.' He glanced at his passenger who was studying the GB Road Atlas. 'Getting closer to nature.'

Morton nodded. 'It's good of you to take the time to drive me up. A heck of a long way.'

'No problem. Glad to help. Good to give the van a wee run.'

Morton looked out of the window. He felt high up, or higher than he would be in a car seat. They were in that no-man's land between Fife and Perth & Kinross. Signs for Kelty,

Lochgelly and Ballingry (Fife) and Kinross, Milnathort and Glenfarg (Perthshire) with Loch Leven coming up on the right.

'I always think of Mary Queen of Scots when I see Loch Leven,' he mused.

Mackie glanced at him.

'She was imprisoned there – in that castle on the island – and I remember reading that the key to the castle was found in the Loch. Much later, in the twentieth century, I think, a whacking great thing it was too, about a foot long.'

'No kidding? I ken sod-all about Scottish history.'

Morton frowned and looked again at his watch. It was going to be a long afternoon. He squirmed in his seat. All he had to do was relax. Mackie was a competent driver, if a little macho. The drive would take them through the very best of Scottish scenery. He thought back over what Marco had told him about the tip-off and how it had come about. He'd phoned and come round to Keir Street without giving anything away.

And when Morton opened his front door, he could tell from the look on Marco's face that he had news to tell.

'Ah didnae want to discuss it over the phone,' he said in Morton's scullery. 'Your phone could be bugged. Anyway, it's best done face-to-face. In fact, that's what he wanted.'

'Who?' Morton asked, putting a fresh filter paper into the coffee machine.

'Luke. He phoned me.'

Morton paused, spoon in the coffee packet. 'Luke phoned?'

Marco nodded. 'I could hardly hear him. Like he was phoning frae Mars. Anyway, he tellt me to speak tae you.'

Morton switched on the coffee machine. 'I see. Maybe he'd heard I was looking for him. You'd think he'd just phone me directly.'

Marco grunted. 'Probably remembered the trouble you

were in last time, maybe thought your line would no be safe? Or maybe he disnae even have your number?'

'Mnn. What exactly did he say?'

'Well, when I picked up, I didn't think there was anyone there, then he says: "Marco? This is Luke. I'm going to make it quick" or maybe he said: "I haven't got much time" something like that. So I asked if he was alright and he said: "I'm at Clachtoll, tell Willie," and he rang off. It sounded like Clack-toll, you know, with his accent, but I'm sure it was Clachtoll. I've looked it up, it's…'

'Yes,' Morton nodded. 'Up in Assynt. I've been there. And that was it? He rang off?'

'Aye, the whole call must have taken, like, twenty seconds.'

'Probably to reduce the chances of surveillance,' Morton said. 'On the other hand, he used my name, which might have tripped their electronic detectors or whatever.'

'Only your first name though and it's a very common one.'

'Well, yes, I suppose it is.'

They sat opposite each other at the breakfast bar. Marco rubbed the dark stubble on his chin. 'He must need help otherwise he widnae have phoned.'

'You're right. But Clachtoll's a long way to go, well off the beaten track.'

Just then the doorbell went. 'Who's that?' Morton sighed in exasperation. 'I'm not expecting anyone. This flat's getting like Picadilly Circus. Better go and see, get rid of them.'

Ross Mackie stood on the doorstep, grinning. Morton was amazed. Had he seen Marco and followed him? Did he even know Marco? Or was it pure coincidence? The big man ran a hand through his dishevelled blond hair. 'Willie. No heard anything from you. Thought I'd drop in see if there's anything happening. With your search, I mean.'

'Right,' Morton said, holding the door. 'Well, I've got someone here at the moment, can you call back? Or I could meet you in the pub later?'

'Aw, no can do. I'm on the way home. Just thought I'd call in on the off-chance. If it's no convenient, I'll be heading up the road.'

'Well,' Morton prevaricated, 'I don't want to be rude.'

'Actually man, any chance of a slash before I head off?'

Morton stepped aside. 'You'd better come in.'

'Unless it's a burd,' he chuckled. 'Ah widnae want to be a gooseberry.'

'It's not a *burd*,' Morton said. 'Just a mate. Come in.'

Without his biker leather gear, Mackie seemed less bulky and imposing.

'Where's the bike?'

'Bike? Oh aye. No, I'm in the van. Parked round the corner. There was a space. I dived into it.'

Marco looked up as they entered the kitchen. Morton could see that they didn't know each other and made the introductions, trying to make eye contact with Marco to alert him.

'Ah, you're the survival expert? Willie mentioned you.'

'Aye, any news about your misper?'

Morton was making urgent signals behind Mackie's back.

'Any coffee left?' Mackie grinned. 'Well, go on, Willie. Two sugars. I'm watching my figure.'

'Misper?' Marco frowned. 'You mean Luke?'

Morton's heart sank.

'We think we know where he is,' Marco said, blithely unaware of Morton's furious head shaking.

'Aw well, no need for me then,' Mackie said. He pulled a comic face. 'Nae cheques in the post. Still, it's a mystery solved.'

'Maybe it is,' Morton prevaricated. 'Thanks for offering your experience.' He turned to Marco. 'Ross here had offered to give me a few pointers about living off-grid.'

'Aye,' Marco enthused, 'see, we thought Luke would be living out in the wild somewhere, which, it turns out, he is doing.'

'We don't know that... do we, Marco. Don't jump the gun.'

'Oh, right?' Marco was giving him a funny look. 'But he phoned me. And asked me to tell Willie. I think he needs us to go there,' he hesitated, catching Morton's glare, 'there... to where he is.'

Mackie grinned. 'Good show. Wee trip oot tae the boondocks.'

'I thought you were needing the toilet?' Morton asked pointedly.

'Busting. Second left, if I remember.'

As soon as he was out of the room, Morton hissed: 'For god's sake, Marco. You just blurted it all out! I'm not sure we can trust...'

At first, they'd listened to the news headlines on the radio. Commentators discussing Cameron's majority and the un-precedented result in Scotland where Nicola Sturgeon's SNP had won fifty-six out of fifty-nine seats, leaving Labour, Lib-Dems and Tories one apiece.

'Amazing,' Morton mumbled. 'Totally unreal.'

'I didnae reckon to any of them,' Mackie said casually. 'Didnae vote, me.'

'No?' Morton remarked. 'You didn't *vote*?' And he began to wonder about the man. Later, as the conversation drifted, he had to listen to some long-winded story about life as a squaddie in Bosnia. Morton couldn't see the point of it. Mackie was an enigma. Full of bonhomie, but there was something missing. And where did his loyalties lie?

'I've always liked Arbroath,' he said. 'My kind of town. Lots of the guys run it down, say it's a one-horse kinda place, but for me, it's ideal. No too big, no too small.'

'Right,' Morton grunted. *Arbroath*?

Mackie drove on, northwards, dispensing contradictory comments and baffling remarks that might turn out to be clues to his character. He wasn't a guarded sort of person, or maybe it was all an act? Who was he? What was he?

On the east coast near Arbroath, RM Condor, a large military base, built in 1938, is home to 45 Commando of the Royal Marines, 3 Commando Brigade and 7 Battery of the Royal Artillery. It's a sprawling site, a mish-mash of green hangars, concrete huts, old runways and housing blocks. From the A933 road between Arbroath and Brechin, it's almost invisible in the gently undulating landscape, among arable fields and polytunnels, remote farmhouses, drystone dykes and ancient oaks at the junction of tiny backroads. Passing the front gates, on the A933, you'd notice a security box, a boom gate, an armed sentry and a stretch of high mesh fencing that runs for miles mitigated in places by thick hedge. You wouldn't imagine hundreds of some of the toughest marine commandos in the world living behind them.

Despite his best intentions, Ross Mackie had struggled for nearly a year with the training and operational regime after his posting to RM Condor. The problem was his weight which had ballooned over the year. Eventually, he was called in by the CO. Colonel Innes Duguid was sympathetic, a fair man, quietly-spoken. Due to retire in six months, he viewed his final command as a winding-down from a long career. Mackie knew that he had seen action from the Falklands War in 1982 to the Gulf War in 1990 and the wars in Bosnia and Kosovo thereafter but he had been kicked upstairs at the millennium and so had missed the start of the Afghan campaigns. He wondered if Duguid had been glad to be withdrawn from active combat in his mid-forties?

Colonel Duguid sat back in his chair, hands palms-down on the metal desk, facing him in the cramped, whitewashed office. Mackie could see through the window, beyond the CO's head, one of the many runways that were now rarely used and beyond it, a small triangle of the North Sea. The CO was a small, chunky man, whose pink and fleshy face registered a calm expression. His receding hair was cut very short. Mackie wondered how old he was. He must be in his sixties. A long career. He was a decent man. He was looking down at Mackie's personnel file.

'I have tried, sir,' Mackie said. 'I guess I'm just big-boned.'

Duguid smiled benignly. 'I'm sure you have, Corporal. Well, don't worry, your record is exemplary. You served in Afghanistan and Iraq and saw a fair bit of action. As I have myself.' He frowned. 'It says here you were up for a medal. In Helmand?'

'Yes.'

'But didn't get it? What happened?'

Mackie squirmed in his seat. 'I was part of… a joint effort. Task Force Helmand, in June 2007. Other lads,' he petered out and was surprised that he felt embarrassed. 'I couldn't really say.'

'Couldn't say, or don't want to say?'

'It's not my place, sir.'

'So the gong went to someone else?'

Mackie was unconsciously wringing his hands. 'The Lieutenant got it,' he said at last.

'But you were the one who got your hands dirty?'

'Aye. It got pretty hairy.'

'Who was the Lieutenant?'

'Pardon, sir?'

'Who…?'

'Lieutenant Jeremy Purce-Bowden, sir.'

'He still in the service?'

'No, sir.' Mackie felt a smile flicker on his face. But the CO must have noticed because he frowned.

'So *he* got promotion?'

'Captain, sir.'

'And then left the service? Any idea what he is doing now?'

'MP for Hendon South. Tory. Of course.'

'I see.' The CO's mouth tightened with distaste. 'Well, nevertheless, your record is a good one and I'm sure we can find the right secondment for you. Something more interesting.' He sat up straight and closed the file, then scrutinised Mackie. 'You've leave coming up? Two weeks? Right – take it and I'll look into the matter meantime. I've been around a long time and I'm sure I can come up with some ideas.' He lowered his voice and tapped on the file. 'And don't tell anyone – that's important, Corporal.'

Ross Mackie twiddled his thumbs for a week around the base and the town, using the mess in the evenings for a pint or two. He might as well be on duty. Then he got an offer of a day's work through an old chum, Roderick, who now worked on the Invercreighan Estate in the Cairngorms. A day's shooting, he was told, 'but you'll get paid.' Cash in hand. He had nothing better to do. He was collected from the sentry post by Roderick in a Shogun 4x4 with bull bars and two sheep dogs prowling around in the open back. The big foreign SUV could go some lick and soon they were past Brechin and heading up into the hills. The road got narrower as the heather moors undulated on either side, the mountains rising ever higher in front of them. Roderick parked at last by a ford where two tracks met in the heather. Ahead were a line of vehicles, quad bikes, 4x4s, SUVs and Land Rovers and a dozen men in an assortment of camouflage gear and heavy jackets. Some had balaclava masks on, others full military webbing kit.

They got out and joined the group. Roderick lit a cigarette in his cupped palm as introductions were made. Mackie spotted the crate of guns in the back of a Land Rover.

'Two groups,' Roderick instructed, 'one goes north, the other south, along the ridge and into Creaghan Dhu. And mind and only fire downhill. When you get to the end, use the walkie-talkie and we'll wait a wee while and come back.' There were grunts and nods. 'You're with me, Ross, aye? We'll get you a weapon.'

The man Roderick had referred to as Stew, lifted a weapon out of the crate and handed it to Mackie, with a box of shells. He was astonished to see it was a sub-machine gun.

'What the fuck?' Mackie said. 'An SA80? What the hell are we shooting here?'

Roderick threw down his cigarette. 'Did I no tell you? We're culling the mountain hares.'

Mackie was incredulous. 'Hares? With an SA80?'

'Aye, we've two of them. You get one because you're experienced. I mean, you've used one before, I assume?'

Mackie cleared the chamber of the weapon. 'Of course, I trained with one of these. Make a hell of a mess of a wee bunny though. Is this legal?' he asked dubiously.

One of the others laughed. 'Maybe, but no this time of year.'

Roderick quelled the discussion. 'Of course it is, orders of the big Laird himself. And he's a fucking Sheriff. He should ken.'

'Right,' Mackie said. It seemed like overkill. He saw the other men had a variety of pump-action shotguns, even a few semi-automatic rifles.

The weather was fine and dry if a bit windy as they ascended the long ridge in the back of the Shogun. The dogs had been turfed out and followed on behind. Their task was to collect up the kill. To leave no evidence, Mackie guessed. Bosnia it wasn't. The hares were not the VRS. In their white winter fur, they were visible for miles on the dark heather, easy targets. They were small and fast but he soon got his eye in. It was amazing how easy it became, anticipating their movements, but it left a bad taste in his mouth seeing the dogs gathering the bloodied hares into a pile for disposal. Hundreds of them. Roderick had explained how they competed with the grouse for the young heather shoots and had to be culled.

'The Laird has it in for them,' Roderick grinned. 'He believes – and give him his due there's some evidence – that less heather shoots for the sacred grouse means they have less young. That's where the money is, see. This is a shooting estate.'

At the end of the fortnight, Mackie was glad to get back into uniform and report to the CO as arranged.

'At ease, Mackie,' the CO said. He looked up. 'Have a good leave?'

'Yes sir.'

'Take a seat,' the CO motioned. 'I've been looking for a secondment for you and I think I've got something.' He opened a folder on top of a pile on the table and glanced quickly through the papers in it. 'Yes, as we discussed, your service record is a good one. You were born in Stonehaven. That's nearby?'

Mackie, surprised by the question, merely nodded.

'And for a while, when you were first posted here, to this base, you were in a relationship with a woman who later turned out to be in the Scottish National Party?'

'Ailsa Meldrum, yes. That all ended a long time ago. Two years or so. I knew her from school.'

'Yes,' the CO said, reading the papers in front of him. 'And then she got herself elected,' he looked up, frowning, 'elected onto Angus Council and was, or is, pushing for a position on the SNP's National Council. Ambitious?' He waited for Mackie's response. There was none.

'Wouldn't you say? Is that your impression?'

'Ailsa? Not really.'

'Are you still in contact with her?'

'No.' Mackie hesitated. 'Wait a minute, I bumped into her a month or so ago… but not really.'

'So you're still on amicable terms.'

'I suppose.'

The CO looked directly at him for a long moment. 'That might be useful.'

He'd wondered what the CO was getting at but put it out of his mind. Ailsa Meldrum wasn't a friend in high places, or even low places, she was just someone he used to know from school, just an ordinary woman he had liked back in the day.

Mackie put these thoughts out of his head. 'The B869,' he said, above the rattle of the van and the gear change. 'We're getting there, Morton. Hey – you sleeping again? We turn off here.' He grinned. 'The roads get narrower and bumpier.'

'Right,' Morton said warily, blinking out of a doze. 'On the map it's a dotted brown and white single track road.'

'Bugger – a cattle grid,' Mackie grunted, changing down to second gear. 'We're right in the boonies now, William.' From the head of Loch Assynt, they had crossed an endlessly low-lying lunar landscape, leaving the peak of Quinag behind, and seeing ahead, the distinctive bulges of Suilven and Canisp to the south. 'Only another five miles, but it'll be slower going.'

'Well, let's hope he's there after all this,' Morton said, as they drove the winding roads through thick woods that mostly obscured the shoreline.

'Amen,' agreed Ross Mackie. 'I'll sleep well tonight, at any event.'

CHAPTER TWELVE

Morton glanced down at the few vans and caravans on the machair and the sea beyond. He wondered how he was going to make contact with Luke. If he *was* here on the campsite or in one of the half dozen houses in the vicinity. It occurred to him that the presence of Ross Mackie might be inconvenient to the process of making contact. He wasn't sure of Mackie's loyalties. It was good of him to volunteer his services, but to what end? What was in it for him? Morton had made it clear that there was no payment, other than petrol money and subsistence. Marco had to work and as neither of them had a vehicle, he hadn't been able to come up with any reason not to take up Mackie's offer. Maybe he'd be able to locate Luke and keep Mackie out of it?

Oblivious to his doubts, Mackie slowed the vehicle as it approached another cattle grid at the bottom of the hill. 'We'd better get in to the campsite. Ten to one your man is there, in one of those vans.'

'Maybe,' Morton mumbled.

'Well, there's bugger-all else round here. No even a pub by the look of it.'

Morton grunted. 'True.'

'And what are we going to do when we find him?'

Morton looked at him. 'Talk to him. Find out if he's okay.'

'Right. I'll drive in. Book for one night.'

'Yeah, I'll pay,' Morton said.

'Okay, and we need electric. Hard-standing too if we can get it, though there doesn't seem to be much of that about.'

Mackie slowly bumped the Trident off the road onto a track, through some low wooden gates, a cattle grid, and into the grassy site itself, up to a wooden ranch-like building with a sign: *Ranger's Hut*. He shut off the engine and they got out, stretching and easing their cramped limbs. A gaggle of curious hens rushed in their direction, watched warily by an orange-maned collie dog lying on the decking of the hut with its paws over the edge. It looked like it was grinning at them.

Morton went up the wooden steps. The collie glanced round at him, disinterested, its tongue out. Morton looked out at the sea, the calm waters of the Bay of Clachtoll, the odd rock sticking up on the headland. As a hiding place, not bad, he was thinking. Few trees. A stranger here would be seen miles away. He wondered if Luke was watching him, from wherever he was.

Mackie followed him inside. A rangy fit-looking man in a black wetsuit leaned against the counter of the office. Maps and notices pinned to a corkboard around him, shelves of tinned provisions, and a large fridge occupying one wall. It also served as a campsite shop, Morton observed.

'Good evening, gents,' the man said amiably. Morton detected a hint of Canadian or eastern American in his voice. 'As you can see we're not fully booked.'

'Popular place in the summer though,' Morton said. 'I was here once in mid-July.'

'Ah, yes,' the man smiled. 'We have the best midges in Scotland.'

'Any hard standing?' Mackie asked.

'Sorry, no, this is a machair site. We have removable plastic matting down; we try not to impact too much on the land-scape. You probably saw the recycling area round the back? We have electric hook-up, if you need.'

'We do,' Morton told him. 'Just one night, though if we need longer, I'll let you know.'

'That's no problem, gents. Watch out for the hens. They'll try to get inside your unit. Just curiosity but they do make a mess if they get in. Leave your windows closed at all times.'

'That's a good tip,' Mackie said. 'Chicken shit is the devil in a van.'

Morton paid and waited, pretending to study local maps, until Mackie had wandered outside. 'I'm up here looking for a friend of mine,' he said quietly. 'Would have been here for a week or maybe more. Young chap, English, tall, wiry, long hair.'

The warden frowned. 'We don't have many tourers on site at the moment as you can see and none answering that description. Some of the statics are in use, but they're elderly folks. Wait a minute, there's the guy in the shack.'

'Shack?'

'Just around the headland a ways, by the Memorial, there's a shack built onto the rock face. Only about ten minutes' walk from here. It's the ruin of a clearances house but was made water-tight years ago and actually it's quite comfortable. Belongs to no-one and occasionally you see folks coming and going, usually bird-watchers or itinerant types, beachcombers. They stay but not for very long: it's a cute spot. I heard there was a young chap. Could be him. Haven't seen for myself. I live a few miles up the road. You could check it out. Might be your friend.'

'Thanks. That's helpful.'

'Remember now, keep your windows closed.'

Morton went back to the van, where Ross Mackie had connected up the electricity and had the gas kettle on. The interior of the van was surprisingly spacious. Everything was multi-purpose, folded over or into something else. Storage lockers became sofas and the kitchen, two rings and a grill underneath the side window, appeared if you lifted up the melamine table top. Morton stretched out on the sofa and looked out at the bay where the light was fading. The kettle began to whistle. Mackie bustled about making cups of tea. 'Cosy in here,' Morton commented. The blue gas ring cast shadows on the walls of the van. Mackie was skilfully peeling potatoes.

'Corned beef, mash and baked beans do you for tea?' he asked.

'Grand, I'm pretty hungry.'

'Peach slices and custard – custard's tinned, I'm afraid – for afters.'

'Okay. We'd better wait till tomorrow to try to find Luke.'

'Yeah. I'm bushed. Amazing how tiring it is driving these single-track roads.'

'Not much else we can do. No street lighting. I suppose we could take a torch.'

'You'll be on your own, Willie. I'll be keen to get my head down pretty early after our scran.'

Morton knew 'scran' was a word used by soldiers. He knew Mackie had been in the army. He wondered what a military career serving Queen and Country under the Union flag, hearing 'God Save the Queen' morning, noon and night, did to ideas about Scotland and Scottish nationhood. But he knew plenty of ex-squaddies were SNP supporters. Out of the window, in the gathering dark, he saw sparse, weak lights in the caravans spread over the site and wondered if Luke was in one of them. He'd take a stroll around the beach tomorrow and investigate the shack. He'd have to find an excuse to go on his own. It was inevitable that if Luke was here, Mackie would meet him, but he'd prefer to have a quiet word with him before that, to warn him. He puzzled how he was going to do that, but the hot tea and warmth of the van...

'Oi, matey, wake up!' Mackie said jovially. 'Scran's up.'

'Right.' He opened his eyes. 'Must have dropped off.'

'I just left you to it. Here's the grub.' He handed Morton a blue mellerware plate piled with steaming mashed potato, slices of corned beef and a sea of baked beans. The window was opaque with steam. He sat up.

'Lovely. Thanks. This looks good.'

'Wish we'd some music. There's a radio up front but I can't be bothered just now.'

'What kind of music do you like?' Morton asked, piling the food into his mouth. They hadn't talked about music so far.

'Mixture,' Mackie said, with his mouth full. 'Some punk stuff. Meatloaf, Foo Fighters.'

'Right.'

'Metallica, Firehouse, ach, most things. I like big noise guitar bands.'

Morton pondered that for clues. It was a macho list.

'So what sort of stuff do you...?'

'Not that sort, to be honest. I like loads of stuff, David Gray, Sheryl Crow, The Stone Roses, traditional folk, loads of old stuff too.'

'Right. Sheryl Crow. She's Gwyneth Paltrow's pal, isn't she? Quite like some of her stuff.'

Morton finished his food and lifted the plate onto the kitchen counter past Mackie's head, then stretched out. 'Comfortable van,' he remarked. 'Warm enough.'

'I had extra insulation put in when I bought it.'

'What's the sleeping arrangements?'

Mackie looked at him in the dim LED light. 'Eh? You have that side, I'll make this one up. We leave the side door unlocked in case one of us needs a pish in the night. The site toilets are open all the time. You've got your sleeping bag?'

Sometime in the middle of the night, Morton awoke from deep sleep and wondered where he was. He could hear loud snoring nearby, then he remembered: Mackie, the campervan. A pale light filled the campervan as he swung his legs over the couch and found his shoes. He needed the toilet and after a bit of scrabbling, found the door catch and stepped out onto the grass which was already dewy or perhaps it was the gleam of chicken shit? He saw the lights of the toilet block and moved across the undulating grass towards it, still half asleep.

When he came out, a few minutes later, into the dark, he chanced to look up and stopped in amazement. The entire sky was a heaving mass of millions of stars, like thick purple velvet or diamante, millions, possibly billions. It was amazing. He couldn't remember ever seeing so many stars before. He felt privileged, as if he stood on the edge of the planet looking out into space, with a ring-side seat at the corner of the universe. After a few moments, he felt the cold air on his neck, ankles and arms, shivered and returned to the warm sleeping bag in the van and fell instantly asleep.

Next morning, they woke to a bright sunny day and drank their coffee outside the van, sitting in canvas folding chairs, watching hens scrabbling around and occasionally chasing each other.

'Any bright ideas?' Mackie said. 'I mean, about the misper?'

'Well, if he's here, maybe he's spooked because there are two of us.'

'Would he recognise you?'

'I think so. Anyway, he was expecting me to show up.'

'So your plan is just to hang around and wait for him to come forward?'

Morton sipped his coffee. 'I think so. Can't see what else we can do.'

Mackie stood up. 'Okay, but while we wait I'm going for a shower.'

'I might take a stroll down to that rock, fifteen minutes.'

'Okay.'

As soon as he saw Mackie head for the amenities block, he donned his jacket and headed quickly north around the machair. There was a line of rocks that followed the shoreline and below it a narrow sheep track. Morton was quickly beyond view of the campsite. Ahead of him, low rocks on the coastline, the tide booming underneath jagged promontories. He saw the shack built out from rock, well-hidden inside a great pile of stones. It could have been overlooked, except for the timber roof, composed of logs and pieces of wood which jutted out from the rocks. On top of the rocks was machair and some wildflowers growing. But there was a window and it was this, reflecting sunlight, which drew the eye. Nearer, Morton saw the rough wooden door. His shoes clinked through the heavy shifting pebbles. He could see nobody about. That window would have a view of the Minch and Lewis in the distance. He wondered how far away that was, perhaps thirty-five or forty miles of open sea.

He approached the window and peered in. He was fairly sure there would be no-one there. If there had been someone, they would have come out to meet him. He examined the window. It was a double-glazed unit, whose PVC frame was jammed into a line of rough mortar. Gaps were filled with what looked like scrunched up polythene bags. He tried the door; open. Inside, as expected, there was little of interest, some wooden chairs on wooden pallets that acted as the floor. And a rucksack.

'Aha.'

But where was he? He began to scout around. He climbed the pile of stones onto the roof of the shack and looked around. He could not see the campsite, hidden by the bend in the shoreline and intervening rocks. Ahead, on the shoreline at the bend of Stoer Bay, was a vast pile of rocks, a ship made of stone lying on its side. He knew from his study of the map it was the collapsed ruins of a broch; an ancient circular stone tower. He could the silhouette of a figure, a man, sitting on top, looking out to sea.

Morton made fast progress across the machair, dropped down to the beach and approached the edge of the broch. The man turned to look down at him. Morton waved. The man stepped carefully down from his viewpoint.

'Luke?' Morton shouted. The man came on and waved.

When he got nearer, Morton began to wonder if he had made a mistake. The man was young, about the right age, slim, but somehow, Morton thought, a little shorter than he remembered Luke to be. He was wearing sunglasses and he had shorter hair. He must have cut it.

'Willie?' the man said. It *was* Luke, Morton realised, even though he did not look familiar. He wore a blue fleece jacket over a white tee-shirt and jeans and trainers. He had at least a weeks' growth of beard and looked unkempt.

'Yes. Marco told me you were here. We know what happened.'

They shook hands. Luke looked rueful. 'I had to leg it. Marco not with you, then?'

'He had to work. I've come with someone you don't know, who doesn't know you.'

The sunglasses turned in his direction. 'Right, and what did you tell him... that person?'

Morton kicked at a pebble. 'Nothing – just that you've gone missing. Not why, none of the details, just your name.'

'Okay.' Luke seemed relieved. 'That's good.'

'Did you come here right away?'

'No – I stayed for a few days in some other places I know.'

Morton looked him up and down. 'You look a bit... rough.'

'Of course. I've not had the benefits of home comforts for more than a week. What did you expect? Anyway, thank you for coming. Is your car nearby?'

'How did *you* get here?'

Luke looked out to sea. 'Don't bother about that. Why I wanted you to come is because I'm going crazy out here. I need to get to a safer place.'

Morton looked at him in surprise. '*Safer*? This place looks pretty safe to me. Here you can spot a stranger a mile off.' He laughed. 'Like you saw me.'

They stood looking out at the sea. The tide was coming in fast, with a rushing noise, then silence, then the sudden roar, then the shifting and sifting of pebbles. Morton squinted as the sun picked out a million flashing points on the blue silver water, dazzling him.

'What I want,' Luke said at last, 'is to find a place where I can carry on my work. I need to get back to it, that's important.'

Morton mused. 'I didn't know if I would remember you, Luke. Having only met you once under... well, unusual... circumstances. And some of the time you were wearing a mask.'

Luke looked at him. 'Oh yes. But I thought Marco would be with you. Or maybe Emily. They know me better.'

'Well. A little,' Morton said dubiously, 'but nobody really seems to know you. For example, I couldn't find a picture of you.'

Luke laughed, a little nervously, Morton thought. The accent was familiar, just a tinge of Geordie that he remembered from the interrogation in the static caravan on the outskirts of Bo'ness. 'I've worked hard to keep it that way. That's why I'm so good at what I do.'

'Anyway, what do we do now? How can I help?'

'The first thing is to get in touch with Cerberus?' He looked straight at Morton, his eyes obscured. 'Do you know who I mean?'

'Cerberus? I know what that is, but not who… or anything.'

'I need to make contact. But I can't do it in person. Someone needs to alert them.'

'Them? It's more than one person?'

'No – slip of the tongue, Morton.'

'But I thought you were liaison?'

'Yes. I was. But I can't be, up here.'

'Well, I could help. But you'd need to tell me how, I mean – who.'

'But I don't know who.'

Morton did a double take. 'Whaa-at? Well, who *does* know? You were the person who collected instructions and delivered them to the group.'

'Yes. But I've never *met* Cerberus. We had a dead-letter drop arrangement.'

'Someone told me you knew all about him – or her.'

'Well, I've no idea why. Who told you that?'

'Liam McLanders, or Emily? Someone told me.'

Morton couldn't see Luke's eyes and yet felt his nervousness. This wasn't what he had expected. 'Where did the name come from anyway? Cerberus – a three-headed dog guarding the entrance to Hades? Should be easy to spot.'

They laughed and Morton felt the tension ease a little. They began to walk along the shingle back to the shack.

'Are you at the campsite?' Luke asked.

'Yeah.'

'With this other person?'

'Ross, his name is. And I'm not sure I entirely trust him.'

'No?' he stopped. 'Why did you bring him then?'

'Ah, he offered. He had a vehicle.'

'A volunteer? Never trust a volunteer.'

As they walked towards the large upstanding rock on the shore, the campsite and its parked vehicles came into view. Luke stopped. 'We're going to have to involve him. Trust him a little. Do you know Brodagh Murdoch?'

'I know *of* her, of course,' Morton replied. 'I've read some of her books and seen some of her TV programmes. Even went to one of her talks once. But I've never met her. She's heavily involved in the Yes movement. I know that much.'

'A powerhouse. And she has no ego. She's doing it because it has to be done. Amazing woman.'

Morton stood and wondered. 'Are you telling me, trying to tell me that she is Cerberus?'

Luke laughed. 'God no. At least, I don't know. I think it unlikely. But she'd help if I could speak to her, or someone spoke to her on my behalf.'

'Well, making contact with her can't be too difficult. She's probably on Twitter and Facebook and she does public talks all the time. She has an office. Galavant Media, I think, in Glasgow.'

'Emily probably knows the best way to contact her.'

'In the meantime, what are we going to do?'

'Well, introduce me. Let's not arouse his suspicions. If he's keen to help, let's accept it at face value. I need to get out of here, to somewhere there is WiFi, Broadband. Tell me as much as you know of this man.'

As they walked slowly in to the campsite, Morton told him everything he knew about Ross Mackie, which wasn't much but was at least a little more than he knew about Luke Sangster.

CHAPTER THIRTEEN

Luke Sangster was bored. His work on Clive Kenton had failed to keep his interest. It was going nowhere. In the nasty world of corporate finance, the Tory backwaters of corrupt dealings in and around Westminster government, there were hundreds of Clive Kentons and Brian Treanors large and small, sharks, cannibal sharks, great whites disguised as porpoises or pretending to be basking sharks. The media were uncritical, interested only in the bloodied flesh they might procure when there was a big killing in their vicinity. And in Jed's overheated attic flat in Portland Street, Leith, he'd lost focus. More often he'd wasted the day in front of Jed's forty-eight inch plasma screen consuming hours of daytime TV. Trash, meaningless, but easy on the eyeballs and the mind. He got to know all the minor celebrities, the C and D-listers, all the nuances of game shows about antiques or country houses, hosted by smug, plump little people so pleased with themselves. Shows that featured actors pretending to be couples with budgets looking for houses to buy, in the Cotswolds, Wales, Greece or the Costas. TV chefs by the dozen, interchangeable and self-regarding, faces fluorescent orange: too much pancake makeup. Luke took it all in, eating junk, getting fatter and more sluggish. In his now infrequent online activity he had to be circumspect; he was using Jed's computer and didn't want to raise suspicions. Even using VPN software he wasn't able to visit certain sites he knew were security protected because Jed's IP address might be tracked. His only relief was to wrap a scarf around his face, pull his beanie down over his ears and take long walks. He could walk around to Granton and look at the yacht harbour or out by Newhaven Harbour onto the West Breakwater, cast an eye around the building sites that jutted into the Firth of Forth, walk out as far as the disused Lighthouse and then round and back by the Cruise Liner Terminal. There was one cruise liner berthed; gleaming white with red and blue funnels and elaborate gold lettering. He couldn't quite make out the name of the ship. There was the Ocean Terminal. He definitely couldn't go in there. It was a lively place with over seventy busy retail outlets. Plenty of state of the art CCTV cameras too, inside and out. He could walk across Ocean Drive to the swing bridges and into Leith Docks. He kept to the backstreets of Leith where he knew he could evade Facial Recognition scans. He knew it would be unwise to try to make contact with anyone from the group or go further into town. But the enforced idleness and above all, the isolation was starting to get to him. He knew he couldn't stay incommunicado forever. He needed a change of scene. Jed and Susan weren't coming back for another six months but Jed had left his passport in the bedroom, in the middle drawer of the bedside table. Luke had studied it, and wondered. He didn't look like Jed but there was some similarity in their appearance; long faces with pointed chins and straight noses. Jed's eyes were brown, Luke's grey-blue, and where Jed's hair was short, blond and spiky, punkish, Luke's was long, dark and straggly. Jed wore steel-framed specs but Luke knew there was a spare pair in a drawer in the kitchen. They were exactly the same height: 1.67m. If he cut and dyed his hair, wore Jed's clothes and specs, could he get through Passport Control? He knew that passports were barely, if at all, scrutinised at internal borders within the EU, in the Schengen travel area. The UK was not in the Schengen area. The problem was getting in and out of the UK. Luke had thought a lot about his flight from the spooks in Marchmont Crescent. He was surprised that they – whoever they were – had not tracked him to Portland Street. He had to assume that they hadn't, that he was not under surveillance. He had made mistakes in getting away, of course, but not many. He had been careful about using natural cover on his trip to Leith from Stenhouse. It was unlikely cameras in passing buses had glimpsed him and he knew he had evaded static cameras. He spent a lot of time thinking about where he could go and what he should do. He needed a new plan. He had been thinking about his close friend from Uni, Mariette Jansen. Although he hadn't seen her for years, he had her home address in Haarlem. It would be quite natural to write her a friendly letter, see what her response was. Of course, she might be married or in a relationship, in fact that was very likely, given that she was sociable and attractive.

On his daily exercise route one day, he went in to the small Post Office on Ferry Road, a few minutes' walk away, and posted the letter. He remembered her tanned shoulders and toned arms. She did weight-training and a lot of running. He remembered her black crop tops and leggings and yellow or white polo shirts with olive cargo pants she often wore tucked into green Doc Martens. She might not reply. Might have moved, might be on holiday, might be married and think it inappropriate to respond. He walked unobtrusively up Ferry Road, adopting the head-down generic slouch of teenagers, hood pulled over, hands in pockets. He went in to the Library. No cameras here. He loved the place, its quiet calm, its unusual semi-circular interior. The astonishing skylights set round in a giant half-wheel, cast light onto the tables and study carrels. Using Jed's library card, he borrowed several books. In his letter to Mariette, he had appended his temporary address and a new google mail address he had created. Not many people under thirty used snail mail these days. And of course, it gave him an excuse to check the new inbox every couple of hours, just in case, even although he knew she couldn't possibly have received his letter. Apart from these diversions, life for Luke Sangster was a repetitive, under-stimulating and increasingly lonely routine.

They got into the campervan. Ross Mackie started the engine while Luke stretched out on top of the sleeping bags and cushions on the floor in the back. Morton lay back in the passenger seat and prepared to let the unique landscape of Assynt and the Coigach roll past, with the familiar grinding of the VW engine as Mackie rolled over the cattle grid and started up the hill.

Half an hour later, Mackie looked in his mirror. 'He's asleep, I think.'

Morton glanced round. 'I think you're right.'

'How long had he been missing?' Mackie asked, navigating the tight turns of the narrow road through the woods between Achmelvich and the junction above Lochinver. He pulled into a passing place to allow an oncoming delivery van to pass.

'About a week,' Morton lied. 'Not much more…'

'Thought it would be longer. Bit of a rum fella,' Mackie commented, after glancing in his mirror to check Luke was asleep. 'Does he do this a lot?'

Morton shrugged. 'Not that I know. I was asked to look for him on behalf of a friend.'

'That chap Marco?'

'No. My friend Emily.'

'Emily,' Mackie repeated slowly. 'Okay. It's none of my business. I'll just drop you in Glasgow if that's okay. Then I'll be off back to my place.' He laughed abruptly. 'Haven't been there for near two weeks. No doubt there'll be bills to pay and other things to deal with.'

About half an hour later, as they travelled down Strath Oykel heading due east for Tain, Morton tried to probe more deeply into Mackie's character. At first, he'd suspected him of trying to snoop, now it seemed that he had no interest at all. But it seemed a little too generous for him to drive all this way north and now all the way to Glasgow without so much as even a slight interest in who Luke was, or what he had done. The weather was closing down around them, grey skies spitting a dispiriting drizzle. Mackie put on the windscreen wipers.

'I'll give you money for petrol,' Morton said. 'That's only fair. Maybe you can stop at the next service station, wherever that is?'

Mackie grunted: 'Still quarter full. These babies have large tanks. I'll find somewhere nearer the city. Then you could pay if you want. Cost a bit though.'

'It's only fair. So – got any jobs on at the moment?'

Mackie glanced at him but didn't speak for a while. He turned down the gears ahead of a sharp bend. 'No much to be honest. I like to keep busy. I'm doing up my cottage when there's nothing else on. It was semi-derelict when I got it. Got it for a song, as they say.' He grinned. 'It'll be a wee palace when I'm finished.'

'Right.' Morton realised he'd been neatly diverted from his question. 'There can't be much money in the survival skills business?'

'Ach, that's not all I do,' Mackie smirked. 'I'm a gun for

hire so to speak. Can turn my hand to a lot of things. Little of this and that.'

'Crikey. A man of many jobs.'

'Well you have to, don't you?' Mackie stated. Morton wondered if he'd touched upon a raw nerve. There was a little defensiveness there. Was he unemployed, or under-employed and feeling guilty about it? Maybe the Services had dispensed with his services?

'I suppose ex-service people have lots of useful skills. I mean, for a variety of occupations.'

Mackie squinted in the afternoon sun emerging from the clouds. 'Aye, that's it, Morton. You hit the fucking nail on the head.'

After that, Morton began to doze, lying back upon the headrest. He was no further forward in finding out what made him tick. Curiously, Mackie elected to continue south on the A82 after the Kessock Bridge instead of joining the A9, which Morton would have done. Instead they set off around the western bank of Loch Ness. It reminded Morton of his difficulties back in 2007 when he'd tried to interview Dr Reginald Matthews of AtomTech with Danny Stark. They passed several driveways but Morton couldn't recognise the house where Matthews had lived, or perhaps still lived. He saw a sign for Dochgarroch. Wasn't that where…? But it was long ago. No point in thinking about it. He wondered where Danny Stark was these days. Was he still with the *Guardian*?

The A82 trunk road is a narrow, fast, dangerous road, often wet with rainfall pouring from the mountainside, while on the passenger side, the loch is obscured by thickets of bushes and stunted trees at the water's edge. In several weeks' time, in summer high season, it would be clogged with traffic crawling along but Mackie was able to achieve decent speeds on the long straights before bends when not dazzled by sudden glimpses of the low sun. They passed Drumnadrochit, Urquhart Castle on its promontory overlooking Loch Ness, Invermoriston, Fort Augustus, the forested bend at Invergarry and crossed the bridge to run down the eastern edge of Loch Lochy to Spean Bridge. Then a long run down through thick forestry plantations to Fort William at the junction of Loch Linnhe with Loch Eil.

'I'm going to stop,' Mackie said, nudging Morton. 'Got to have a break. There's a snack bar a little further down, on the shore. I know this road well. I'm up here a lot on the bike. Nice wee run.'

Mackie pulled off across the road into a parking area behind a ranch-type wooden building: *Mac's Burger Barn*, a flashing red neon sign. It had a corrugated iron roof and enough decking overhanging the shore of the loch for tables and chairs.

'We're stopping?' Morton asked. 'Or just a toilet stop?'

'I'll go to the Gents,' Mackie said. 'Then I'm going to have a coffee and something hot to eat. Here's the keys. One press locks it.'

'Right, well, me too. See you in there. Luke? Are you awake?'

There was a grunt from the rear. 'Where are we?'

'Fort William. Coming in for a coffee?'

'Okay.'

The car park was busy as they locked the van and sauntered into the place. 'I feel hungry,' Morton said. 'When did you last eat, Luke?'

'Ages. I'm starving.'

Morton got a table with a view across the wide Loch

Linnhe. It had become quite warm in the sunshine. One of those days that couldn't make up its mind. On the opposite shore, the vast wilderness called the Ardgour peninsular was almost entirely unpopulated, he knew, although he could see a few white dots of houses at the shoreline, linked by a narrow A road with passing places.

Mackie joined them at the table. Their food order was delivered on a tray by a bustling middle-aged woman with an orange tan and bottle-blonde hair. Each of them had selected cheese burger and chips.

'Tomato sauce?' Morton offered.

'Give it here,' Mackie said, splodging it over his chips. 'Nice looking woman, eh?' he indicated the waitress, now at the cash-register dealing with customers. 'Good figure.'

Neither Morton nor Luke made any comment. There was a motorboat, Morton noticed, at the far shore of the loch, trailing a white ribbon of water. He remembered that the loch widened out to become the estuarine Firth of Lorn, so it was sea water.

They ate in silence. The burger was home-made, the orange-coloured cheese slice melting around the edges, red onion and gherkin slices.

'Good scran,' Mackie said. 'Been here a few times.'

'How long till we get to Glasgow?' Luke said sleepily.

'God knows,' Mackie said. 'Hours yet. I think I'm going through Glencoe to Tyndrum. What do you think, Willie? Much more direct than the coast road. Then Crianlarich, Loch Lomond tae Balloch and then I'll decide which route to take into the city.'

'Yeah,' Morton agreed. 'The coast road is much slower. There's holdups at the Connel Bridge, not to mention having to go through the Pass of Brander.'

'Aye. That's a great route on a motor bike. Scenic.'

They set off down the shore of the loch, climbing to view-points and through thick forest to North Ballachulish. The tiredness and monotony of the road dropped Morton into a doze. He woke to find the van racing past the glint of water with misty mountains all around.

'Glen Coe?' he muttered.

'Away past that, chum, we're nearly at Bridge of Orchy. Had a good sleep?' Mackie chuckled. 'You've been out for nearly an hour. I was tempted to stick in a CD of Metallica Live! But I'm not that nasty.'

'Thank god, you didn't.' He stretched and inhaled deeply. 'How are you doing? Want me to do a stint of driving?'

'Aw, you're alright. I enjoy it. Another two hours and we'll be in Glasgow. Just relax. Luke is sleeping.'

'There's a surprise.'

'Don't worry Willie, we're getting there.'

Morton gratefully rested his head on the armrest and drifted back to sleep lulled by the wet blur of oncoming lights and the regularity of the engine noise.

Ross Mackie had been surprised by Colonel Duguid's proposal and at first, a little disappointed. He'd spent his career in the ranks and now was being asked to leave, seconded to some civvie outfit and some hush-hush operation.

'I think you'll find the new unit much more interesting than what you are doing here,' the CO said, coughing discreetly 'You'll be playing a much more important role and of course,' he coughed again, 'your salary will increase commensurately.'

Mackie frowned. 'Comm…?'

A trace of a smile crossed the CO's face. 'The money will be better. It's true you will be working in plain-clothes, unconventionally, undercover, I should say. But your particular abilities make you eminently suitable for the work.'

'Right. That's good. What…?'

The CO put down the file and looked him straight in the eye. 'These are your qualifications for the work. Firstly, you have a strong record of keeping your head in action. Secondly, you can distance yourself from the military, appear to be someone who is no longer in the service.'

'But I will be, won't I?'

'Technically yes. But your money will be paid through a third party. Your new unit will fill you in about that. Broadly, you'll be liaising with people from a variety of units, Special Branch and Police Scotland and perhaps some military connection there too. You'll have an HQ but will work mostly from home. That's really all I can tell you, for now. Your new section chief will be coming here tomorrow, to speak to you and get you up to speed.'

'He's coming here?' Mackie exclaimed. 'To see me?'

'Yes, Mackie, you're so important that they're coming to you! There will be the formalising of the secondment and you'll be given all the information you need to get an understanding of how it is going to work. All that remains, Mackie, is for me to say thank you for your work here at Condor, and to wish you luck in your new posting.'

'Right, I'm still not getting the picture really,' Mackie said reluctantly. 'What happens about my pension…?'

'Everything will be explained tomorrow at fourteen hundred hours. Ask all the questions you need then.'

'Right.' Mackie stood up.

The CO stood up and offered his hand. 'Well done, Mackie and good luck.'

He found he was a little apprehensive about the new posting. The details were vague. He'd seen the same thing over the years. People found they liked the familiar regularity of being on a base, got a little squitty when they were to be moved on. Fear of the unknown. He went into the mess to see if anyone would chum him into town for a drink. He was mindful that he couldn't tell anyone. He supposed it'd be okay to say he was getting a transfer. That much would surely be okay. He wanted to get bladdered. But there was no-one. No-one whose company he could bear for an hour or two, so he got the bus into the Westport. Mooched around the High Street, looking into the black bow-fronted windows of the Pageant on Kirk Square. Dead as a cemetery. He saw the same wooden tables and chairs, edges worn and scuffed, the beeping puggie machines, the bald middle-aged barman reading the *Courier*. Further down the street, he tried the Rampant Lion. There was no-one there he knew but he caught the eye of a woman in the snug as he was walking by. He bought a pint. There were two of them sitting together at a semi-circular table by the exposed brick feature wall beneath framed black and white photographs. Sure enough, one of the women came over to check him out. He'd never seen her before. If they were interested, it was likely there'd have to be money involved and he wasn't up for that.

'Don't remember me, do you?' she said. He looked at her.

'I don't think so,' he smiled. 'Should I?'

'It's Dawn,' she said helpfully. 'Dawn McAdam. We were at school together.'

'Fuck me – Dawn McAdam!' He looked at her, the red hair, the pasty skin, lipstick making more of her thin lips, but had no recollection of her at all. 'Who would have thought? You live here now?'

'No. Visiting my sister.'

He glanced over. 'Right. Fancy a drink?'

Dawn glanced back at her sister and grinned. 'Vodka and coke and Nicole is on Bacardi and blackcurrant. Thanks.'

'Okay. Mind if I join you?'

'Of course. I'm just off to the Ladies.'

It didn't take him long to realise he'd been had. He had known really before he even sat down. Their accents were West-of-Scotland somewhere. He didn't mind their company on a quiet night in Arbroath but there was no way he was going back to some house in the backstreets, or worse, up against a wall somewhere while the 'sister' kept watch. Those days were long gone, for him.

Four days later, Luke heard the tiny 'ping' notification that the inbox of his new google mail account had received its first email. It was from Mariette and it was brief. 'Lovely to hear from him... she was working, teaching IT in a college, living with a man called Kris... but would be happy to see him again, if he was anywhere near Haarlem.' She appended her mobile number. He did a Google Map search for her flat and explored the nearby city centre. Haarlem was on the coast and had a river running through it. Twenty minutes or less on the train from Amsterdam Central. Sounded ideal. He recalled Mariette's strawberry blonde hair and piercing blue eyes. Of course he had fancied her; everyone in his year had. He wondered what special charms Kris had. Maybe just being Dutch was enough? Maybe she'd known him before she went to Scotland, but he couldn't remember her talking about a boyfriend. Anyway, it was ideal. Nicely out of the way. Mariette might know of cheap accommodation? He hit reply and told her he was planning to be in Amsterdam soon and would come over by train. He looked at what he had written. He didn't want to be too pushy, but… it had to be said. 'Know of any cheap accommodation in the area for a few weeks, month even?' he typed. Then he typed his name added kisses and clicked *send*.

CHAPTER FOURTEEN

The main problem which Richard Blenkinsop and Saul Dunan faced was not the lack of information on the missing hacker, Luke Sangster, it was the need to evade harassment from Chief-Inspector Colin McLennan, their Special Branch Liaison officer. He was entitled to a weekly report and insisted on it being provided in writing and in person. But was also quite likely to turn up suddenly at Pacific Quay and start sniffing around their desks. They had a theory, or many theories, about him. They had, at first, imagined McLennan trying to push his way onto the attention of MI5 for career reasons, then the theory mutated that he hoped to catch them out, and get promotion through Special Branch by using their misdeeds, real or imagined. McLennan was ex-army and had seen a lot of military service. A short, squat Highlander with thick grey sideburns, he favoured an old-fashioned leather blousson jacket and covered his thinning brown hair with a grey tweed bunnet. It was known he had a Rampant Lion tattoo on his shoulder. They had a private nickname for him and it wasn't polite. The weekly meeting was held on neutral territory, often in the staff canteen of the Police Scotland station in Baird Street, a fortress-like conglomeration of four-storey sandstone buildings beyond a spaghetti junction of roads and the motorway. The canteen was in the basement where perspiration or condensation streamed down yellow painted walls. No matter how busy the canteen was, McLennan always managed to be there before them and he was usually tucking into a mince pie, chips and beans or similar, his grey bunnet beside him on the table.

'Here they come,' he muttered, 'Dampsey and Makepiss. Get me another mug of tea, if you're going.'

'How's Colin?' Blenkinsop asked politely, sliding into the seat opposite him. They were trying to overwhelm him with love. It wasn't working.

McLennan ignored the remark, extricating a piece of gristle from his pie and flicking it at the backs of the uniformed officers at the next table.

'Charming!' Blenkinsop remarked. And they sat in silence as McLennan finished eating and shoved his plate aside. Dunan weaved towards them with a heavy tray.

'What took you so long,' McLennan grumped, lifting the mug of tea off the tray.

'Careful!' Dunan warned. He laid Blenkinsop's cling-film-wrapped cheese and pickle roll and mug of black coffee in front of him, the ham and tomato sandwich and tea at his own place and went off to deposit the tray.

'So? Where's the report?' McLennan said, dropping four sugar cubes into the mug and stirring. 'What's going on?'

Blenkinsop reached into his inside pocket and removed some folded pages. 'I've emailed it, but I know you don't hold with email,' he said, rolling his eyes at Dunan, who smirked as he sat down.

'Fuckin internet,' McLennan opined, smoothing out the pages. 'What have we got here then?'

'As you can see, we're no further forward on Sangster. He's gone to ground completely since he triggered cameras in Charlotte Square. No Facial Recognition Scans, no nothing.'

'I could have told you that. I see the same scans you do. It's like he's not using ID or moving around. Not anywhere we can see, anyway.'

'Armoury is on the move,' Blenkinsop said.

McLennan looked up suspiciously. 'Morton, the journalist? Where's he off tae? Ah, yes, up north.' He sat upright, hands on the formica table-top and a grin appeared on his face. 'Which means I need tae tell you. In the circumstances, I've nae other option.' His tongue probed for morsels of food in his teeth. 'Aye. I've tae tell ye. See, I've been bringing on a new boy. I think he shows potential. Ex-army. Has some useful friends and contacts. Anyway he's a contractor and is now part of our joint operation.' He sniffed. He needed a cigarette and it was raining outside. He felt in his pockets for his fags. 'Back in a wee mo. You just keep eating your sarnies, boys.'

They watched him picking his way between crowded tables of uniforms.

Dunan frowned. 'What the fuck does he mean, part of our joint operation?'

'There's no knowing with him,' Blenkinsop muttered. 'It wouldn't surprise me, if he's recruited Armoury.'

'What a fucking disaster that'd be!'

When McLennan returned and sat down heavily on the seat, he seemed in a better mood. 'Right, where was I? My new boy. Codenamed Condor for the purposes of the files. Real name, Ross Mackie.' He grinned and nodded. 'Aye, he's presently with our target, Armoury, up north. In fact, he's doing the driving. Not so much a ring-side seat, as in the *driving* seat!' He laughed abruptly. There was something about that laugh that the other two disliked. It was glottal, mired in phlegm, unnaturally moist.

As they drove back in the light rain, they laughed about

the older man's foibles and imitated that horrible noise that passed for mirth.

'I'm glad we don't have to see that tosser for maybe a week,' Dunan concluded.

'Although Condor is a good piece of work,' Blenkinsop admitted grudgingly. 'Fits in with things very well. In fact it may help to stand up our man's credentials. As long as the tweedy tosser doesn't get wind of our little gambit.'

'We'll have to tell him. Next week. The miraculous re-appearance of the missing hacker.'

'I've a feeling, Saul, that he'll know that before we tell him!'

And they laughed as they drove down the Broomielaw, heading back to the office.

CHAPTER FIFTEEN

The buzzing of the mobile phone in his jacket pocket woke Morton. Blinking, he found that it was nearly dark. It was raining, the windscreen wipers thrummed. They were in a built-up area under the ghostly glow of streetlights. All the vehicles had their full beams on, illuminating rain falling in long diagonal lines. 'Are we there?'

Mackie grunted. 'Nearly, Willie. Going through Milngavie. The evening rush hour but we shouldn't be long now.'

'Thank the lord. I'll be glad to stretch my legs. Luke...?'

'He's out for the count, I think,' Mackie said, looking in the mirror. 'I've never seen somebody sleep so much. Where am I going to drop you?'

'Anywhere in the centre will do.' He looked at his mobile phone. There was an unread new email from Brodagh Murdoch: *Not sure what this is about, though I'm aware of your work. I can meet you briefly at 6:30 in cafe at Central Station. Brodagh x* 'Anywhere near Central Station. We're meeting Brodagh there.'

'Brodagh Murdoch? I've seen her on telly. Funny she's getting involved. What's that about?'

Morton frowned. 'She's a friend of Luke's,' he said, and wondered if that was true. 'She'll help me,' Luke had claimed. 'All we have to do is contact her,' he'd said, and expected Morton to have her contact details.

'Why would I? I don't even know her!'

'You could get them from Emily.'

'Well, I could but, I'm not wanting to get her involved. You're the one with all the contacts, supposedly.'

'Willie – you forget I'm on the run. I don't have all my stuff. I had to leave it all.'

'Okay. I'll text Emily.' He wasn't happy about having to do it. Mackie had made no comment at the time, he remembered, hands on the steering wheel, disinterested.

'Central Station, okay,' Mackie said now. 'She talks a lot of sense, for a woman. That Brodagh… didn't she used to be with the BBC?'

'She's been around for a long time. What do you mean, *for a woman*? Sexist git!'

Mackie just laughed. 'Whoops!'

Morton's plan was simple. Enlist Brodagh's help to find Luke somewhere to stay. Get the next train back to Edinburgh. Dark thoughts had been coming to the fore about Luke since they had left Clachtoll. Was he really on the run from spooks because of his hacking activity? Morton felt like telling him to turn himself in to the police and pay his rent arrears. Who would be interested in what he had been doing online? Even if he had accessed a few restricted sites, who could prove it? Maybe the landlord was the only person after him? Maybe the whole trip north was one big diversion, waste of time, some kind of charade… whatever it was, he was losing patience with it. He wanted to see Emily. They needed to make bookings for their summer vacation holiday. He was determined that they could finally get away together. They needed to move things on and he was becoming more convinced that moving in together was the answer.

'Luke – did you hear? Brodagh can meet us at 6:30. We'll just make it.'

'Great,' Luke said behind him, without much enthusiasm. 'I'll be glad to get out of this van, no offence.'

Mackie laughed good-humouredly. The traffic was heavy as they came through the wet streets of Bearsden, queuing from one set of traffic lights to the next. The wipers pushed away rain drops, blurring red-amber-green, casting rainbows at the concave edges of the windscreen. It was fully dark now, pulsating with lights of shop premises, bars, hotels, traffic lights.

'Argyle Street. I can get you quite close to the station. The Heilanman's Umbrella. If you're quick. You'll have to jump out. I can't hang around. I'm heading for the M8.'

'Heading home?'

'Yeah,' Mackie grunted. 'Loads of work to do.'

A line of buses stopping for passengers in front of the glass-walled railway bridge gave them the opportunity. Mackie pulled in behind the buses.

'Right, lads,' he said. 'Out, out!'

'Thanks.'

'Don't mention it. Slam that side door hard. Cheers!'

Luke and Morton were on the wet pavement with their rucksacks. The van moved away. He felt a sense of gratitude to Mackie for all the driving and he was glad to be back in the city. The rain was slight, little more than drizzle. 'Good to get the legs moving again,' Morton said. 'You must be feeling quite rested, Luke. You seem to have slept all the way.'

'I think so. I need a coffee.'

'We're not bad for time.' Morton looked at his watch. 'Ten minutes early.'

Central Station was noisy with announcements and

commuters hurrying for trains although the main rush-hour was mostly passed. He saw the black minute hand on the large white clock face move over the V.

'I'll just nip to the loo,' Luke said.

Morton frowned. 'But you could go in the cafe?' Too late, Luke was off. Morton took out his mobile and dialled Emily. She answered almost at once.

'Thanks for sending me Brodagh's contacts,' he told her. 'We're about to meet her.'

'Yeah. I would have assumed that Luke had her details.'

Morton scoffed. 'Claimed to have lost them when he escaped from his flat.'

'Fair enough. What did she say?'

'Well, she's meeting us. We're at Glasgow Central.'

'How is Luke?'

'He's alright. Where are you?'

'I'm just home, Willie,' she said brightly. 'Getting a cup of tea.'

'Long day you had.'

'Tell me about it. Well, hopefully Brodagh can help.'

Morton glanced around carefully. 'He's gone to the toilet, Em, so we can talk. I'm hoping to get back to Edinburgh on the next train. I have to say, he's not quite... he's different from what I expected. And it was odd, that business of not having her contacts.'

'I always thought Luke was a close confidante of hers. Maybe I got that wrong. And that other chap, Ross Mackie, has gone?'

'Yes, dropped us off.'

'He didn't want to hang around? He drives you all the way up and back and then just goes away? That's a bit odd, isn't it?'

Morton saw Luke emerge from the Gents at the far end of

the concourse. 'Have to go now, Em. We'll see what Brodagh says. Far as I'm concerned, Luke has to do all the talking. Then I'm heading home – I hope – so I'll see you later.' He pocketed his mobile.

'Alright?' he inquired as Luke came up to him. 'You were a while?'

Luke just laughed. 'Who were you phoning?'

'Eh?' Morton was surprised that Luke had seen him, a little embarrassed. 'Mind your own business.'

'No. I just wondered if it was Brodagh.'

Morton coloured. 'Oh, I see what you mean. No.'

The snack bar was practically deserted, a pattern of red plastic chairs yoked together in facing pairs across melamine table-tops. Two members of staff were mopping the floors and collecting rubbish bags. Only four customers, an elderly couple and two single persons. Depositing their rucksacks, they ambled over to the counter. A young Asian woman in a uniform emerged from the backroom, stripping off yellow rubber gloves.

'Still open?' Morton enquired.

'Aw aye. Till seven, but. What ur ye wantin, love?'

'Coffee – Americano.'

'Any milk with that?'

'No thanks, and I'll have a piece of this fly cemetery.'

'Awright, love,'

They sat at a table near the glass door, with a partial view of the station concourse. Garbled announcements continued. 'Before Brodagh comes,' he began. 'What is it that you are trying to achieve? What do you want from her?'

Luke brushed the damp tousled hair back from his eyes. 'I need some safe place to stay for a while where I can work.'

'Yes, but I don't see how Brodagh fits in to that? Who is

after you anyway? If it is MI5 say, well, then you'll simply get her embroiled in it. What have you actually *done*?'

'You know the answer to that,' Luke said, with – it seemed to Morton – a lack of enthusiasm. 'My hack of Viroil.'

'Really? That was a while ago. And you passed all that information into the public domain. What more do you know, or what more do they *think* you know?'

'I have some new material, but it's rough. I need to work on it.'

Morton sighed. 'And is this really such strong stuff, that they're still hunting you, all this time later?'

Luke peered into his latte, scooped up froth with a teaspoon and ate it. 'They know my potential as a hacker. They know I'm not planning to give up. They fear me. I know that sounds silly, but they know I can get more, penetrate their defences. They probably have a record of where I've been probing, or firewalls I've breached.'

'So it's not just a landlord that's after you for rent arrears?' Morton laughed nervously.

Luke flared up. 'Of course not, Willie!'

'Here's Brodagh now, I think.'

'Thought you didn't know her?'

Morton started. 'I told you, I don't. We've never met. I know her by sight.'

'Okay.'

'You're doing the talking,' Morton said emphatically. 'It's your gig.'

Brodagh Murdoch entered the snack bar. Morton saw the few other customers look up. She was a 'well-kenned face,' from frequent appearances on TV politics and current affairs programmes. Tall and slender, she wore a full-length blue woollen coat, her long dark hair visible under a white fur hat.

She came straight over to their table, laid down a small folded umbrella and took off black gloves. They shook hands.

'Nice to meet you, Willie. And this must be Luke?'

Morton flinched. Didn't she *know* Luke?

'I'll get a green tea.' She put her hat and gloves on the table.

'How come she doesn't know you?' Morton whispered to Luke. 'I thought…?'

Luke shrugged. 'She's so busy… must have forgotten.'

There was a series of strangulated tannoy announcements about services to Gourock. Platform 11R, next train… Largs…Ardrossan.

Brodagh returned and sat down facing him, next to Luke.

'It's a surprise we've not met before, Willie. I've read some of your pieces of course.'

Morton smiled. 'Thanks.'

'And this is Luke. We finally meet. I've heard about your work too.'

Morton frowned and sipped his coffee. Something wasn't right. Here, in Glasgow Central Station, CCTV cameras would be recording, the footage would be instantly available to anyone in the security and intelligence community. But Luke didn't seem to be nervous or exhibit any of the symptoms that you'd expect from a fugitive. He was self-contained, defensive even. Morton couldn't put his finger on what was irking him, but something was not right.

'So what can I do for you boys?' Brodagh asked.

Morton shrugged. 'It's Luke that's needing help. You know the background presumably?'

Brodagh sipped her green tea. 'Not really, Willie. I have no association with the group, although I meet Liam from time to time.' She smiled faintly. 'It's not that I don't share your aims. Believe me, I do, but for me, it's important that I retain my flexibility, my distance.' She fluffed the fur hat and set it upright on top of the gloves and the folded umbrella on the table-top and shook out her hair. 'I'm fully in support, but need to be able to retain my broadcast credibility. I feel that's what I can most usefully provide, as a sort of media outrider, do you see? Although If I can ever help specifically, well, I'll do that when I can.'

'I understand. I'm in a broadly similar position, I suppose. Although my pieces usually appear in the *Standard*, I aspire to an objective neutrality. We have our political views of course, but this is work, for me, anyway.'

'That's a good way of putting it.'

'So – Luke is wondering if you can assist him…' Morton prompted, gesturing at Luke who sat as if stupefied, fiddling with his coffee mug.

'With his hacking activity?' Brodagh queried.

'With accommodation.' Morton said.

'Oh? Well, I'm not sure.' She looked at Luke. 'How have you managed thus far?'

Luke stared gloomily into the distance. Like a surly teenager, Morton thought, although he knew he was thirty or more. He didn't look like a threat to anyone's financial empire. 'I try to move around a bit,' he said in a monotone. 'Vary my routine.' He looked up blankly, disinterested, Morton thought. 'And of course there's methods I can use, when I'm online, to disguise my trail.' Morton felt almost sorry for him. He was clearly not enjoying having to ask for help. Maybe that was the problem?

'Brodagh nodded. 'Yes. Very sensible. But if I was to help you – and I would like to – I would have to be able to keep myself clear of your activities. What you are doing is commendable no doubt; revealing hidden information that perhaps should be in the public domain. But if I was to assist you I could be held liable if any of the activities crossed a line into illegality… or could be construed as doing so. My reputation would be at risk. Such things can be easily trashed.'

Morton nodded. 'Emily thought you would say that. You know Emily?'

Brodagh put down her mug. 'Of course. Professor McKechnie. Haven't seen her for a month or two. And you and she are…?'

Morton coloured. 'Um, yes, we're…'

'Give her my regards, will you.'

'Of course.'

'Anyway, back to this problem. What was it, Luke, that made you think of seeking my help?'

Luke sniffed and didn't answer. Morton was outraged. He wanted to get the Edinburgh train and leave him to his own devices. 'I think he thought that you were Cerberus,' he prompted, nodding at Luke.

Brodagh looked startled. Her eyelashes flickered. 'Thought I was… what?'

'Cerberus.'

'Oh.' She looked at him and then turned to Luke. 'I'm sorry, I have absolutely no idea what you're talking about. *Cerberus?*'

Morton's expression of alarm must have registered with her because she continued in a whisper. 'Has there been a misunderstanding?'

'I think so,' Morton said, in a quiet voice. 'This is difficult for me. All I know is what Emily and Liam McLanders have told me. I'm not a member, although I attended one meeting. Luke is the liaison with Cerberus.'

'But who…?'

'Luke,' Morton said, getting irritated, 'will you bloody well explain what your role was, or is... or I'm going to walk away now!'

'There's a group.' Luke said.

'We know that!' Morton interrupted. 'About Cerberus.' He glanced around quickly. One of the customers had left, the couple were ignoring each other in silence and the young man on his own seemed to be absorbed in his mobile phone. None were listening, as far as he could discern. 'How exactly did you act as liaison?'

Luke sighed. 'The group collects data from various projects and that is collated and passed on to Cerberus, whoever he, she or it is. I've no idea. I simply leave the material at an agreed place and later, I collect instructions from the same place. I've never met the person. I got the details of where to collect and deliver from the previous liaison person. It's a dead-letter drop.'

'What a stupid idea!' Brodagh commented. 'A gift to the secret police. All they'd have to do is follow you around and find the dead-letter drop. How long has this been going on?'

'I don't know. Maybe a year.'

Brodagh expressed incredulity. 'All these bright people... and this is how it works. Inept, to say the least. Willie, what do *you* think?'

'It does seem a bit daft. I thought the idea was to disseminate the information widely. Instead, it's all put into a bag and left god knows where. In a cistern in a public toilet?'

Brodagh laughed, a melodious sound, and finished her tea. 'Ludicrous. I mean, Luke, if you were needing help, why didn't you simply put a note in the bag.'

'And leave it in the cistern,' Morton grinned.

'And ask this Cerberus fella to help?' Brodagh said.

'I did!' Luke said quietly.

'Ah,' Brodagh said. 'Now we get somewhere.'

'You didn't tell me about that,' Morton said. He felt that they were going round in circles. 'So what happened?'

'Nothing. The note was gone but there was no response. And I went back several times.'

'All very cloak and dagger,' Morton grumbled. 'I don't see why there needs to be such mysteries about it. As far as I could see, the group's activities were perfectly legal. Why have all this ducking and diving, as if there is something to hide?'

'I'm in agreement with you, Willie,' Brodagh said. 'Everything should be kept in plain sight and shared as widely as possible. Anything else is just asking for problems.'

'I've had problems in the past myself,' Morton told them, 'as you might be aware. Doing investigations for the paper, all perfectly legal, but we live in highly-politicised times. The security intelligence services have carte-blanche to do what they want. They can close down political dissent where it might affect members of the establishment. Well, I don't have to tell you. The only way to guard against it is never to have any secrets or anything that could be loosely interpreted as a secret. If you stumble on one – immediately reveal it as widely as possible to the media. That's what saved me when I discovered the GB13 data-file. We made many copies, got it to the media, made it a story that many people quickly knew about. And then I was safe.'

'I played my part,' Luke put in. 'I know all this. But someone has to acquire the information first of all. That's what I do.'

'That's certainly the dangerous part,' Brodagh agreed. 'We must never be naive enough to believe that someone can simply be allowed both to acquire information *and* disseminate it. Even although both parts of that sentence relate to legal means and methods. If the information is sensitive enough it doesn't actually matter to them how you acquired it.'

There was a silence as they pondered what Brodagh had said.

'And do you have – or might they believe you have – that kind of material?' Brodagh asked quietly. 'Whether you do or not doesn't matter either, only if they *believe* that you do.'

Luke's hand rubbed at the stubble on his cheek. 'Not yet. Potentially. But I need time to complete, to check it and I can't do that till I feel safe.'

'Well, best to steer clear of dead-letter drops and that kind of play-acting,' Brodagh suggested. 'Wouldn't it be better if you went abroad somewhere, where you weren't known?'

'Yes. As long as I have internet access, fast broadband, I can work anywhere.'

'I'll need to have a think.' Brodagh mused. 'Where are you staying tonight?'

'I was planning to head home to Edinburgh,' Morton said. Then it suddenly occurred to him that Luke might expect to come and stay at his flat in Keir Street. 'But probably, we'll need to stay overnight in a hotel,' he added quickly.

Brodagh stood up. 'I'll speak to a few folk, see if I can come up with something. I'll text you tomorrow, Willie. Right, I'm off. I'll see what I can do.'

After she had gone they sat in gloomy silence.

'Doesn't look too hopeful,' Luke said.

'Let's wait and see. We need to find a hotel for tonight. Come on.'

CHAPTER SIXTEEN

It was dark, wet and getting cold as they trudged the streets. Morton did a Google search on his phone in a shop doorway. They were relieved to find the two-star Montrose hotel in Cathedral Street not far from Queen Street station. It was 7.30 p.m. On street level, the facade looked like that of any budget hotel chain. An impressive glass-fronted reception area, smart reception staff, but no lift, no breakfast included. The hotel did not have catering facilities other than a half-empty vending machine. WiFi was available, at a price. TVs in the rooms were coin-operated. The rooms were not en-suite, toilets and bathrooms were at the end of the corridors on each of the three floors. Luke's room was on the second floor but Morton had to trudge up to the third to find his. There was a sickly smell of bleach or carpet-cleaner on the stairs and the narrow corridors. His room was small, described online by Hotels.com as 'compact'. It was stuffy; the single window, double-glazed by means of a thick perspex panel screwed across the single-pane window frame, could not be opened. The obscured view through the perspex was of ventilation ducting and brick wall of the neighbouring premises. The noise of the city centre; traffic, trains, sirens, a hundred discordant sounds. Morton tested the bed. It looked okay. The sheets seemed clean, if shiny. The TV with its attached coin-box looked old-fashioned. The ancient plumbed-in radio on the bedside table didn't work. There was no bulb in the bedside light. He sighed and rummaged in his rucksack for his mobile and phoned Emily. She answered almost at once. He told her he had been missing her and was annoyed to be stuck in Glasgow instead of being with her. He could picture her on the sofa, sipping a glass of Malbec.

'You're not completely wrong. It's vodka and coke!'

'Aw. And here I am, in this stinky hotel.'

'Is it stinky?'

'A little greasy. Cheap though. The alternative was inviting him to stay at my place. I couldn't have that. I've already had that pair of spooks sniffing around there. Blenkinsop and that Dunan fellow. I didn't like them and I don't want them coming back. I know we probably shouldn't talk about this on an open line,' he said, 'but things have degenerated into farce here.'

'Oh. What did Brodagh say?'

'She's going to try and come up with something for our friend, but it doesn't look too hopeful. Do you know, there was not a flicker of recognition when she saw him? She had never met him, didn't know him. Oh, he tried to pass it off. "She's so busy" he said, "must have forgotten" but when they shook hands she said: "we finally meet". They had never met before, so the idea that she was going to help him, well… And then there was the ludicrousness of the so-called Cerberus link. Either he's made it all up to make himself look important or the person who is Cerberus – assuming it isn't Luke himself – is no longer there, or has been compromised in some way. Luke asked him for help and there was no response. Frankly, I just want to get out of the whole thing and get on with my own work.' He chuckled dryly, 'not that I have very much on the go at the moment.'

'We've got that holiday trip to arrange,' Emily said. 'We missed the boat with the spring vac but must get something sorted for the end of May.'

As the Montrose provided accommodation on a room-only basis, he had arranged to meet Luke in the foyer at 9 a.m. He awoke hours too early and lay on his back trying to identify the numerous sounds, as the room became stiflingly hot. It was like being underwater. He got no sense of daylight behind the grey, faintly illuminated perspex. Radiators clanked, cars tooted, heavy Lorries rattled, buses, sirens, even trains at Queen Street station. There was a big hospital nearby, several multi-storey carparks and Junction 15 of the M8; restless, invasive noise pollution. At 8.30 he went downstairs and was surprised to see that it was a bright and sunny day outside. He sat on a black couch in the foyer and read yesterday's *Herald* but couldn't concentrate. The editor, Bill Devane, was an old friend and rival of his. Finally, Luke appeared, as dishevelled as ever, rucksack on one shoulder. His hair was wet from a shower, even more straggly than usual.

'Come on, let's get something to eat.'

'Brodagh's texted, no?' Luke asked as they walked along the pavement, blinking in the sunshine.

'Not yet.' The city centre had a yeasty smell, as of last night's spilt beer intermixed with a stewing milk. Morton's stomach was craving a coffee. He tried to work out how many hours had passed since he'd had one. Over fourteen, he decided. They ambled from sunshine through dappled light into the gloom of Queen Street station and made for the cafe. Commuters were streaming off the platforms although it was twenty minutes after nine. There was a small queue for the take-away coffee stall but plenty of red plastic seats in the cafe. Morton looked around and selected a table against the back wall from where he could observe the comings and goings. The clientele were few. A shabby man in two raincoats with orange corduroy trousers halfway up his shins, shoes without laces. A couple of businessmen at separate tables reading the pink business newspaper. A tousle-haired student, eyes glued to the screen of his tablet, thumbs in a blur of activity. A pair of middle-aged ladies freed from the drudgery of the office-cleaning nightshift. No spooks, he smiled grimly.

When the waitress came, a weary Glaswegian grandmother, they ordered fry-up breakfasts, toast and coffee, the full works.

'That was a ghastly place,' Morton commented. 'I couldn't sleep, and when the heating came on…'

'I slept okay.'

Morton looked critically at him, once again wondering at his self-containment, his lack of any obvious anxiety. He sniffed. 'At least it was cheap.' He checked his mobile and saw there was a text from Brodagh. He was about to say something, when he read: *can I phone you. Privately?*

Luke looked over. 'Anything?'

'Na, nothing.'

'I hope she bloody remembers.'

'She will. Be patient. Right, I'm off to the Gents before the food comes.'

He went into the corridor, straight past the Gents onto the concourse and sat on an unoccupied bench out of sight from the cafe. He phoned Brodagh's mobile. It was answered on the third ring.

'Willie? Where are you?' He told her. 'On your own?'

'Yes.'

'Listen, I don't want to alarm you but I'm not convinced that the young man is who he says he is. There's something not right about him.'

159

'I've been having that kind of feeling myself, off and on.'

'Quite. Look, not entirely because of that, but partly, I'm afraid, I can't help you – him – if you see what I mean. Might sound paranoid but I've reason to believe there's some kind of attempt to compromise me, incriminate me or something. I've no evidence of course, just that a few things don't add up. But don't tell him any of this.'

Morton frowned deeply. 'Of course not.'

'Delete the text I sent you and I'll send another you can show him if necessary. I'm sure it will give you an opportunity to extricate yourself.'

'Okay. I'm not sure what's going on, but for now, thank you.'

'Bye.'

Morton deleted the text and went back into the corridor to the Gents where he washed his hands. As he returned to the cafe and saw that the waitress had delivered their breakfast, he felt his mobile buzz.

'So what now?' Luke asked him, dipping his toast in fried egg.

Morton glanced at him. 'I'll check.' He looked at the phone. 'Oh, here she is. Ach, she can't help,' he said, reading her text. 'Busy all day filming an interview. Couldn't come up with any ideas… sorry… ah well, there it is.'

'Bloody hell. She's useless.'

Morton looked at him with distaste but said nothing. They ate in silence for a while. The tannoy announcements began again from a speaker mounted in the ceiling. He couldn't make them out. He was keen to go. He finished his coffee. 'What did you expect? She's a busy woman. Anyway, best thing now is to go back to Edinburgh. I've got things to do. That's what I'm going to do anyway.'

'What about me?'

Morton gave him an incredulous look. 'That's up to you. Haven't you got any pals here, maybe from your Uni days? No-one? What about family?'

'They're in Newcastle. What's left of them.'

'Well, maybe you should head down there? Anyway, I'm keen to get home.' He stood up and hefted his rucksack. 'I told Emily I'd find you, check you were okay and I've done that but I can't really spend much more time…' The words he meant to say but didn't, went unsaid: 'on social care.' That's what it was beginning to feel like. Morton had always hated a clinger, someone who didn't know when to push off. But Luke followed him out. Morton noted on the timetable display suspended above his head that the next train to Edinburgh would depart in ten minutes.

'I'm going to get that train.' He moved to the ticket machine and began to key in his journey. Luke was still with him. Morton tapped his Visa card on the payment screen. 'What are *you* going to do?' Luke was right at his shoulder.

'I'll get one too.'

'You got money?' Morton asked. He'd already had to pay for the hotel and for their breakfast.

'Some.'

He frowned. 'Want me to pay for yours?'

But as he half-turned, he saw surprise register on Luke's face. He was being grabbed from behind by a tall man in a dark coat. Short curly hair, squint nose: Dunan! On his other side, Morton intuited the presence of the other man, the chunky one: Blenkinsop. He idly wondered what they were doing in Glasgow even as a strong arm grabbed him. He evaded the hand and twisted backwards, grabbing his rucksack off the floor.

'What the fuck!'

'Morton – careful! You don't want to be assaulting me, now, do you?'

Luke was trying to wriggle out of Dunan's grasp, kicking and bucking against him.

'Got the pair of you, now!' Dunan exulted.

Morton backed to the ticket machine. 'Get your hands off me! I've done nothing.' Customers fell away from them and there was an audible gasp of alarm. Excitement spreading on the concourse: an altercation. The two men looked like policemen. That was the trouble. Capturing two illegal immigrants, or vagrants or drug-dealers. Morton imagined how it would look. Blenkinsop had a detaining grasp of his forearm. Morton shrugged it off. Luke was resisting Dunan – the stronger man – Morton wondered.

For a couple of seconds there was a stand-off, like a *tableaux vivant* then with a sudden explosion of energy, Luke kicked, Dunan slipped and fell and Luke was running and clear. And Morton, with blind instinct was running too, chasing Luke out of the concourse into the daylight of North Hanover Street, past the taxi queues and straight up the hill. What was he doing? Why was he running? Later he would be unable to explain it to himself. In his right hand, his rucksack and in his left he clutched his Visa card and the ticket to Edinburgh.

CHAPTER SEVENTEEN

They managed to get over the M8 on the footbridge and up the hill into Sighthill. They stopped, out of breath near a primary school and took off their rucksacks.

'I think we've lost them.'

'What the hell do we do now?' Morton gasped, searching in his rucksack for sunglasses. The light was hurting his eyes. 'This is all your fault!'

'My fault? How do you make that out?'

Morton looked at him with disgust. 'If you hadn't run, I wouldn't be in this mess. I haven't done anything!'

'Well, neither have I!'

Morton put on the sunglasses. He bent over, inhaling deeply, trying to catch his breath. He heard a train nearby and wondered if it was the one he should have been on. He could imagine the joy of sitting looking out the window, dozing in the heat, heading back to his flat in Edinburgh. Instead, he was stuck with Luke, making it look like he had something to hide, by running away. He wondered if he should phone Archie, get his advice? Or Emily? She would know what to do. Mostly, he wanted to be back in Edinburgh. He felt like a fish out of water in Glasgow. It was a city he didn't know well.

He straightened up. 'You must have done something illegal – or they must think you have – for them to be pursuing you.

Now, of course, they can do you for resisting arrest, possible assault too, and you've got me implicated. Frankly, I've no time for this. I'm heading back to the station. I'll take my chances. I don't know what you're going to do. But it's time we went our separate ways.'

'Very supportive,' Luke sneered. 'And you think they won't arrest you and detain you in custody, harass you, make you say all kinds of things, charge you with all sorts?'

'I don't think so. I'd get my solicitor on it.'

'Don't be naive,' Sangster said, sitting on the low wall that bordered the play-area. 'These are not the regular police. These are British spooks. They have no interest in helping little old ladies across the road. What they are interested in is stopping subversives like us; taking us off the streets. Teaching us the errors of our ways. Don't you get it? This is what they do. Harass, intimidate, disperse and divert people doing perfectly legal things on the grounds that later we *might* do something affecting the security of the state. It's not about chasing criminals. It's about dissuading political activity.'

'I think you're overstating it,' Morton said, breathing deeply. 'And don't forget I've already been a target of these spooks. I have a damn good idea what they're capable of, but I think you're exaggerating. The Scottish Government is in charge of policing and they play a big part in curbing the excesses of…'

Sangster snorted in disgust. 'There are some very naive people about!' He spat on the pavement. Morton was surprised at his vehemence which seemed out of character and sat down beside him on the low wall, looking at the church up the street. A crocodile of hand-holding primary kids in high-vis tabards went past, shepherded by school staff. The teachers looked absurdly young, Morton thought and one of them caught his eye. Nice looking, thick dark hair, nice legs. She probably wondered at the two men with rucksacks sitting on the wall in the middle of the day. She looked so cheerful and optimistic. Morton wondered if she was. Teaching kids that age must be a dawdle.

Sangster was still sounding off. 'The kind of people who think there'll be another referendum and everything will just fall into line. A Scottish state will be formed and everyone will give three hearty cheers. These people have no idea – no idea – what the British establishment is capable of, no knowledge of the brutality, the deception, the decades of hostility, the assassinations, the misinformation, the 'disappearances,' the torture, yes – torture – that was perpetrated in even the least of their former territories. Not to mention the dirty war in Ireland. And these were just the remote acquisitions of empire, the furthest-flung dots on the map. The kind of place which, apart from the profit and the pride of conquering, of being the overlords there, offered them little emotional significance. But Scotland – almost a member of the family… can you have any idea how such treachery will be regarded in Whitehall? After three hundred years of so-called 'partnership,' Scotland is just going to walk away? And they are going to stand by and shake hands and… what? Agree that the whole project was a big mistake? That these three centuries were wrong-headed? Perhaps open themselves up to criminal prosecution for it? Think on, as they say in Yorkshire. Listen – the Union will not be dissolved. There is no chance of it. Democracy will not be allowed to prevail, vote or no vote. If it comes to it, they will shoot people, people will disappear, the radio stations, TV, newspapers will be closed, social media will be suppressed, Holyrood disbanded, or neutered. Public opinion will be diverted, divided upon itself. The movement will be destroyed and the causes of it will be trashed, its key people neutralised, with the full force of the law. It will *not* happen.'

Morton clicked his tongue in exasperation. 'What a rant! Sometimes I wonder whose side you're really on.'

'They won't hesitate to scoop you up and trash your life. What do you mean, whose side am I on?'

Morton ignored him. 'There's no point in arguing here. What are you going to do? Because I am going back down to Queen Street and getting on a train.'

'Don't do that. I can drive us back to Edinburgh.'

'What? Since when do you have a car?'

Luke grinned. Morton was surprised again at his sudden change of mood. 'Haven't you heard of car-sharing schemes? Helping to protect the environment.'

Morton frowned. 'What are you blathering on about now?

Sangster stood up. 'Wait here and guard my rucksack. Back in a minute.'

Morton assumed that Luke was going around the corner to have a surreptitious pee. He contemplated walking away, just going without any explanation, but sat recovering his breath, breathing deeply in and out. Only a couple of minutes later, a red car coming down Pinkston Road tooted at him. It was a Ford Escort. Luke was the driver. He stopped opposite Morton and rolled the window down.

'Get in, Willie!'

'What the hell!' Morton snarled. 'Whose car is this?'

'Told you,' he grinned. 'Car sharing scheme. Ride with a friend. Share petrol, blah blah.'

'You've *stolen* it! You think I'm going to get in a stolen car?'

'We're only borrowing it to get to Edinburgh.'

'Not me. I'm getting the train. This is the last straw.' He stood up and shouldered his rucksack and began to walk off.

Luke drove the car slowly alongside him. 'They'll be there. Waiting for you. Get in, you silly tosser!'

'Not with you!'

'An hour and you'll be home. Easy, come on!'

And just like at the station, when Luke had said run and he, having no good reason to run, ran, now he got into the stolen car. Why? He had no idea. Or he had no better idea. He simply wanted to get home.

Luke started up and rolled down the hill towards the M8. 'Observe,' he said, holding up his hands, which were muffled in the extended sleeves of his grey hoodie. 'No fingerprints. We'll be in Edinburgh before the car is missed, so there's zero danger. Happens every day.' He began to whistle.

Morton clicked his tongue in exasperation. 'Well, drive carefully then,' was all he could find to say. 'That means slow down. This is a 30 mph zone. Don't draw attention to yourself.' He just had to hope the car didn't belong to that nice young teacher. Now he was a criminal too.

Emily was in the Boardroom on the fourth floor of David Hume Tower, waiting for the meeting of the University Court to get under way, in her role as one of four Senatus Assessors. She could see blue sky out of the window, fluffy clouds rolling by. Other members of the Court were helping themselves to tea and coffee from the side table. She noted a few were still to arrive. The Principal and the Chancellor's Assessor were deep in conversation at the head of the table, beneath the oil portraits of former Principals. She nodded at colleagues, smiled at Amy Okinawa, President of the Student's Union, who was a member of the SNP, and took out her mobile. She noticed a new WhatsApp message from Marco Vanetti. Sent an hour ago. She'd missed it. *LS sighted in Leith. Definite, seen by Alasdair. Will check out today and try to make contact.* She frowned and switched the phone to silent. What? He was in Leith?

Ainsley Fairbairn, the Principal, did a series of throat-clearing coughs that made everyone turn and look. Emily saw that there was no text from Willie. Nothing since the previous evening. Hopefully he'd be at his place and she'd see him later. She wondered if Brodagh had been able to help. Still, good news about Luke. She pocketed her phone and waited for the meeting to start.

Donald Watt, the Chancellor's Assessor, tapped his fountain pen on the table-top and made the series of placatory mumbling sounds recognised as the start of the meeting. Emily was fascinated by his nose, a large, lobular object that looked like it was moulded out of red Plasticine. Hairs sprouted from it. She tried not looking, or thinking about it, and picked up her Agenda. She had scanned the reports and other business related to revenue and property, staff salaries, foreign students fees, anxieties over changes to the funding of the Erasmus Scheme and the forthcoming Higher Education Governance (Scotland) Bill. It was going to be a long meeting. Two hours at least, then, home and hopefully a glass of wine and hearing what Willie had been up to.

Dunan clicked on the key fob to unlock the Ford Mondeo parked in third floor gloom of the Mitchell Street multi-storey car park. They sat in the car digesting updates on their phones.

'Well, that went well,' Dunan said. 'Worked out perfectly, I'd say.'

'We'll have to be careful what goes in the report,' Blenkin-sop mused. 'It's a contact that never happened. Armoury's movements are increasingly erratic and difficult to explain otherwise. Wait a minute, have you got this from Desmond?' He showed his screen to Dunan. 'He's secured the onward transportation.'

'That's good.'

'And – DIGINT suggests the likelihood of Sangster being in Edinburgh.' He read out the rest of the text: 'Based on lack of any FR scan activity it is concluded the target is not moving therefore is most likely to be in his home area, somewhere he knows he can avoid CCTV.'

Dunan scrolled through his messages. 'I have it. That makes sense. Okay, well, we'd better get over there, boss. What do you think?'

Blenkinsop agreed. 'I'll tag us as heading there. We can use the Edinburgh office, maybe stay over. Change of scene will do us good.'

'Aye, boss, away from McLennan.' Dunan drove round and out of the tight bends and narrow ramps of the car park, headed under the Heilanman's Umbrella and west through the congestion of Argyle Street, heading for Junction 19 of the M8.

As they sped east, they discussed the Claymore operation and rehearsed how their initiative could be explained within it. Their original remit had been to shut down the hacking operation of Sangster. As a backer of the current UK Government, the interests of energy giant Viroil and its billionaire owner Brian Treanor were regarded as synonymous with theirs. Although there were plenty of relevant laws such as the Communications Act 2003 and the Computer Misuse Act 1990 to allow Police Scotland to step in and make an arrest, the operation was handled by the British Security Service. To prevent a turf-war on the question of who had overall authority, MI5 had naturally assumed control as the senior authority throughout the UK, including in the devolved nations. They had tried to locate Sangster and the sinister figure called Cerberus in charge of the hackers' group. Pressure on the journalist Morton, codename Armoury, would lead them to Sangster and possibly to Cerberus. They infiltrated a support agent into position, having previously established that other members of the group did not have the information. Secondary targets were the writer McLanders and the broadcaster Brodagh Murdoch but they proved more wary of 'volunteers' or strangers popping-up with helpful suggestions. Meanwhile, in the background, another team worked to disperse the members of the Claymore group and reduce the group's effectiveness over time. They had someone on the inside there too and it was this operation that was being shared with Special Branch. This looked good. Full inter-departmental co-operation and the liaison working well. But it was a smokescreen. Because behind it, MI5 were running their own op. Desmond Thorpe's terms for these ops was 'external' and 'internal.' MI5 had learned from experience that an op tended to break down and fail because of the stretched links and compromises of sharing with other agencies, so 'internal' MI5-only operations were never revealed outside MI5. To all intents and purposes MI5 was happily collaborating with Special Branch. And in Scotland, where the politicians were nervous about security intelligence matters, they were grateful to defer to the UK Government's civil service, naively trusting that they were being given full unobstructed oversight on all operations: which was far from the truth.

'So, if our intervention works,' Dunan concluded, driving fast under the pedestrian footbridge to Harthill Motorway Services, 'and Armoury reveals the information, we pick up Sangster and this Cerberus geezer and Armoury will be of no further use to us.'

'Correct. But nor will he be in a position to embarrass us. No need to harass him further. He can go back to writing stuff for his paper. No problem.'

'We don't care,' Dunan grinned. 'He could do what he bloody well wants. Wouldn't bother us.'

'Just as long as we get Sangster off the streets and safely tucked away… and Armoury never gets to share notes with him, then all is well. And best of all, McLennan will never find out what we've been up to.'

'You've got to wonder though,' Blenkinsop mused. 'Why, when he had this Condor fella right there with Armoury, he pulled him back. That's a puzzle. We don't know what Condor's cover story was but undeniably Armoury seems to have trusted him. Then the tweedy tosser throws away his advantage and calls Condor off. Odd?'

Dunan glanced over. 'With that fella, you never know what he's thinking. He's capable of all sorts.'

Blenkinsop had a sudden misgiving. 'You don't think he's already got the information, do you? Holding out on us?'

'No, boss. No way. He's not that good.'

3: OGESTRÜM

CHAPTER EIGHTEEN

Morton looked sceptically at the *Jesper Larsen* riding high against the harbour wall at West Granton Harbour. The reassuringly-modern marine satellite and radio masts on the wheelhouse, rust-streaked hull, heavy lifting gear for rolling out the nets at the stern, the boom crane from moving stuff on its deck. It was about a hundred feet long but he knew that a boat that looked big in harbour could look insignificantly tiny on the swells of the open sea. The boat was modern but it wasn't a ferry. He had little trouble on ferries. They were stable. However it was practically summer and the seas would be calm. He glanced at the ranks of little yachts on their trailers behind chain link fencing at the nearby Athenian Yacht Club, heard the melodic tinkling of the halyard ropes rattling against the masts. Apart from the *Jesper Larsen* there were two other boats at the Middle Pier. A rusting derelict hulk that might once have been a container ship, and a sleek modern catamaran, shiny white, whose tinted glass was reflecting the ever-changing light of the declining sun. He watched the colour rising in the clouds pondering whether there would be a spectacular sunset over the Forth Bridge.

Luke pulled his arm. 'Come away before we're seen. We're too early. Let's go for a pint.'

They walked along the dock in silence, into the wind, to Lochinver Drive and out to Lower Granton Road. There had been a surprising turn of events on the way back from Glasgow. They'd stopped at Harthill Services. Luke had gone to the toilet, Morton to get a coffee and when he returned to the car, Luke was excited. 'Brodagh's come to the rescue,' he said, holding out his mobile as Morton put his coffee on the dashboard and got into the car. 'Look what I've got!'

Morton did a double-take. 'What? Brodagh texted *you*?'

Luke grinned. 'Yeah. Pretty cool, uh?'

'How did she get your number? Why didn't she text me, like before?'

Luke laughed derisively. 'Maybe she likes me more than you?'

Morton turned sharply. 'What's going on? She didn't even have your number. Let me see that!'

'I'll read it to you…'

'No, I want to see it. Give!'

'Okay.'

Morton scrolled through the message. *2nd thoughts, u 2 b safer in EU. Meet Sgurd, Old Pier Inn, W Granton 7 tonite. Go 2 Uppsala. Contact will ph u in 2 days dont use mobs till then B x*

'Bloody hell!' Morton exclaimed. 'That's a long text message. Uppsala? That's in Sweden! This is ridiculous.'

Luke took back his mobile. 'Well that's what she's arranged.'

'Long bloody way to go. I don't see why I have to go.'

'You don't have to, but she does suggest it. Maybe she knows something we don't?'

'Right.' Morton thought about it. He opened the door. 'Now I need the toilet.'

'Didn't you go already?'

Morton glared at him. 'Well, if I had I wouldn't be needing now, would I?' As he walked to the toilet, he felt a mounting anger. Uppsala? Sweden? Fuck that for a game of soldiers! It occurred to him to call Brodagh to check the text was kosher. Her number was engaged. He typed a text: *Uppsala? Really necessary? Long way? Me as well?* He stood at the odorous men's urinal, in the light from thick whorled glass bricks, staring at the green fungus on the pipes and the dripping cistern. He heard a text alert. He zipped up and read it: *My best advice. Bon voyage B x* He rested his forehead on the cold metal of the hand towel dispenser while he dried his hands. It was too much. He wanted to go to his flat, not halfway across Europe. He balled up the paper towels and tossed them into the bin and walked back outside.

'You were a while,' Luke said suspiciously.

'You'll get old,' Morton told him.

He was silent on the rest of the way to Edinburgh. When they got to the outskirts of the city at the Newbridge round-about, Luke began heading north on a spur of the M9 to the Kirkliston roundabout and then onto the M90 to Dalmeny. Morton knew then that he was heading for Granton.

Luke glanced round. 'We'll abandon the car in the Pilton estate,' he said.

Morton grunted and looked out of the window. A part of him felt like it would be fun, exciting, although also scary. He tried not to think about the voyage, the depth of the sea, the waves.

They came down off the Cramond Road onto Ferry Road and from there into the Pilton estate. Morton knew the area from previous stories he had worked on. Luke navigated narrow streets made narrower by cars parked on both sides of the street.

'We'll get as close as we can,' he said. 'Somewhere around here will do fine.'

'Wardieburn,' Morton said. 'Not Pilton.'

Luke frowned. 'So what? Listen, we'd better put our phones out of action now, in case they are tracking us. Which they probably are.'

Morton sighed wearily. 'I suppose you're right. First thing they will do. We should have done that earlier.' He remembered being tracked by his mobile phone when he was investigating GB13. He took out his phone and switched it off.

Luke glanced over. 'Take out the battery too. I'll do the same with mine. We'll put them in our rucksacks. Right, no-one about. Let's leave the car. First you'll need to wipe the car door where you've touched it. Use a Kleenex from that box on the backseat.'

'Okay, done. Let's go.' Morton was quite glad to be out of the stolen car and walking in the fresh Edinburgh air, away from the scene of the crime.

They walked out onto Granton Road, away from the windows of the terraced houses, out towards an industrial estate and large superstore carparks. 'We could have left the car there,' Morton said, pointing. 'Among the hundreds parked there.'

'They have security cameras,' Luke said. 'Don't be such an amateur.' He laughed.

'Okay, what now?'

'Look, Willie, best idea is to get to the Old Pier Inn, it's just along here.'

'A rendezvous with Sgurd. What kind of name is that?'

'I don't know. Maybe he's from Uppsala? Brodagh's arranged it. She must know him. We'll find out.'

The Old Pier Inn on Lower Granton Road is a ramshackle two-storey grey stone building, favoured by the evening sun, facing out to the rocks of the Eastern Breakwater. Inside, the well-used bar is patronised by sailors, rascals of various types and folk musicians. A pool table is squeezed into a smaller lounge, and there are four guest bedrooms upstairs. Morton and Sangster pushed through the narrow swing doors into the bar and found it warm, bright, noisy and crowded.

Standing at the bar, Morton looked around. There were no women. That was the first thing he noted. But they served real ale and had several guest ales on tap.

They took their drinks to an unoccupied table in the corner near the unlit fireplace.

'I don't see anyone that might be Sgurd,' Sangster said. 'Must be around though.'

Morton was hoping they had already gone. He had a growing anxiety about a trip abroad. He was not convinced it was necessary. However, the trip was bound to cost money anyway and that might give him a good excuse to back out. Or he could pull out on the grounds that he didn't have his passport. They observed the activities of tipsy patrons in the bar, half-listening to maudlin conversations, repartee, familiar jokey insults. Morton wondered if he could slip out and leave. It wasn't a long walk to Emily's place, about three miles, maybe three and a half. And Sangster didn't know where she lived, he was fairly sure. What did Emily see in him? She'd called him brilliant, talented. He couldn't see it. He finished his pint and was thinking carefully about his next move. Mostly, he found it hard to comprehend Brodagh's sudden change of mind and was incensed that she had contacted Luke instead of him.

'I think we've had it,' Morton said, flipping a beermat. Outside the evening was growing darker. Streetlights were coming on all along Lower Granton Road. He wondered how long it would take him to walk to Restalrig.

'Another pint,' Luke suggested. 'They're bound to turn up

soon.' He leaned forward and in a lower voice said. 'High tide in less than an hour.'

'Not for me,' Morton said. He glanced at his watch. 'I'll give them five more minutes then I'm off.'

'Oh, that must be them!' Luke said, standing up. 'One of those guys is bound to be Sgurd.'

A group of foreign men who could by their appearance, and heavy bags, be fishermen, were clumping down the wooden stairs. Morton was surprised to see how young they were except for one man, who turned, gazing around the bar and saw them.

Sangster stood up and pushed over to him. The man looked to be in his fifties, tall and well-built with short white hair and a goatee beard. Morton saw him glance round. He wore a thick sweater, dungarees and a heavy outer jacket. Morton heard him say: 'We go now.' Sangster was beckoning him. He stood up reluctantly, wondering if he could find a way to slip off. Decision time.

'These are our guys,' Luke told him excitedly. 'Let's go. It's the high tide.'

Outside, after the heat of the bar, the wind was raw, colder now that the sun had gone down. The others sprawled across the road onto the rough ground, heading for Lochinver Drive and the pier. Morton could see the cluster of lights of Burnt-island and Aberdour, six miles away across the dark water of the firth. He let the distance grow between himself and the men and was about to turn and slip away when Sangster appeared behind him: 'Come on, let's get aboard before they change their minds.'

'Eh?' Morton said. He'd been convinced Sangster was up ahead with the crew. 'What's the deal?'

'All sorted. They'll take us to Denmark. Sgurd's got to sign the paperwork up at the harbourmaster, and as long as no-one sees us, we're all set.'

'I don't have my passport,' Morton demurred. 'Crazy for me to go to Denmark without it.'

'You can't use it anyway. They'd arrest you.'

The boat gnawed on the high tide and as Morton looked down, he saw the dark gleaming water. The men were aboard and had laid down a narrow gangplank.

Sgurd stood on the dock wall and held out his hand. 'Step over now, please.' Morton had no option. He had to go. They were all aboard. 'I go now to harbourmaster, then we go,' Sgurd said, relinquishing Morton's hand.

A young blond Dane, the one with the nose ring, showed them to the living quarters. They had to climb down a metal ladder. The boat was bigger than it seemed, Morton thought, three decks. Was it an adventure? Maybe, but did he want an adventure of this kind?

The ladder ended in a cramped space facing four bulkhead doors. The young Dane, Matsen, opened the second door. 'You stay,' he pointed, grinning. 'I bring coffee soon, yes?'

It was a small cabin familiar to Morton from cross-channel ferries. There were four bunks with high sides. That was ominous, he felt. Did the seas get so rough people might fall out? He told himself there was no risk. The boat was modern, safe and used to all kinds of rough weather. 'I'll have this one.' He put his rucksack on a bottom bunk, reckoning it might be less prone to motion. He sat heavy-hearted, his thoughts in turmoil. Could he simply go out, get up on deck and climb back onto the dock?

Sangster sat facing him on the other low bunk. The cabin was about eight feet by eight feet, functional, painted yellow with an over-bright lamp making it like a prison cell. The floor was steel with a kind of red rubber matting on it. 'Well, here we are,' he said. 'Those spooks won't get us now!'

They heard and felt through the floor the tremulous vibrations of the engine starting, the hammering of the propellors. It was too late now. The bulkhead door opened. Matsen looked in and handed them enamel mugs of coffee. Both, Morton discovered had milk and sugar in. He sighed.

'Okay?' Matsen gave them the thumbs up. 'We go now. I bring food soon.'

Morton was imagining the activity on deck, waiting for the sensation of the boat casting off and moving out into the incoming tide of the cold, dark, Firth of Forth. Ten minutes went by as he sat miserably aware that he could easily have walked away in the pub, and be, even now, walking to Emily's. He could imagine her warm welcome as he turned up on the doorstep. Instead he was in a fishing boat moving away, heading into the North Sea with a man he didn't trust and a gang of Danish fishermen he didn't know at all. And why? On Brodagh's advice. A woman he didn't know either. Well, he pondered, she was a woman to trust. At least she was on their side, looking out for them.

CHAPTER NINETEEN

And others were looking out for them. Standing on deck in the swirling sea-mist, an hour after lunch, Morton was fascinated by the four giant white stone figures looking out seaward as they approached Esbjerg. It was an unusual, even unnerving sight. As the boat moved closer to the Danish shoreline through an archipelago of small, uninhabited islands, it was indeed as if these giants were searching for them. But Sgurd appeared at the wheelhouse window and reprimanded him with violent hand signals to get back down the ladder into the living quarters. He had spent more than an hour there, holding onto the rail looking out at the undulating sea, the gradually-thickening line that was the Danish coast. It had been a calm crossing and he had slept through most of it which puzzled him and yet made him feel much better. The boat had gained nearly an hour and expected to be docking around 4 p.m., Central European Time. Down in the cabin, Luke was reading a comic book, or looking at the pictures, because it was in Danish.

'We're coming in,' Morton told him. 'I still don't see how we're going to get past customs.'

Luke shrugged. 'These boys know all the ways to do that,' he said. 'Sit down and relax. We've got a long drive ahead of us today.'

They heard the engines change tone, reducing speed and

felt the boat's momentum reducing, as they lay on the bunks in silence. The boat was going through the process of docking. Sgurd came halfway down the ladder and put one finger to his lips. 'Stay there. I come for you when is ready to go.'

Half an hour went by as the boat slowed, reversed, manoeuvred and came to rest. Then the machinery on deck started up as boom and crane began to unload the catch of frozen shellfish from the hold. They could hear the men's shouts, loud industrial noises of engines and equipment. Morton was convinced Customs officers would come on board. It couldn't be as easy as this to get into another country. Then all went quiet. Morton anticipated the sound of the skipper's boots clumping down the ladder. Ten, fifteen, twenty minutes passed.

'They've all gone to the pub,' Sangster joked.

'Sounds like it.'

Then at last the clatter of boots on deck. Sgurd came halfway down the ladder and wordlessly beckoned them.

They climbed after him and stood amidships behind an open bulkhead door with a clear view of the deck and the harbour beyond.

'Now we be careful,' Sgurd said. 'I go. You wait. I tell you when to come, okay?'

Morton looked at Luke. Denmark. Almost. Sgurd was out and over onto the harbour wall. They could see him standing, looking both ways. They waited for the sign. Sgurd casually lit a cigarette and smoked it. They heard a vehicle moving nearer. It stopped, its doors opened. Another of the crew appeared and lifted a box of gear into the car. Sgurd tossed the cigarette butt into the dock and urgently signalled them. Luke went first, across the wet, fish-smelling steel deck to the ladder and up and over the harbour wall. Morton hurried behind. They were ushered into the boot of the estate car, fishing gear piled on top of them so that they lay in darkness. Morton smelled fish and petrol. The doors closed, the car began to slowly move along the dock. He heard the two men in front laughing and joking. The car began to accelerate. Five minutes later the car was stopping. He heard the handbrake. The tarpaulin was pulled off and the boot door opened. Morton saw daylight. He swung his legs out of the car boot. Sgurd stood grinning above them. 'Welcome to Denmark,' he said.

Morton and Luke picked up their rucksacks and watched the car speed off. It was a fine, sunny evening with the embers of a magnificent sunset high above them. He saw that they were in a car park behind the massive seated figures he had seen from the sea. To his left was the dock, ferries and ships and the *Jesper Larsen*. Tourists were walking around the base of the white stone giants, which, reflecting the sky, looked ice blue. Their sightless eyes stared outwards at a distant horizon. He read on an information board that they were nine metres high and they reminded him of pictures of the figures from Easter Island.

'Creepy,' Luke commented. 'Come on, let's get into town and get on our way.'

'I think they're splendid.'

It took them fifteen minutes to walk into town. Luke quickly identified a car rental agency.

Morton was baffled. 'But you can't get a hire car without a passport.'

Luke nodded. 'Well, but I have mine.'

Morton was astonished. 'Bloody hell! You kept that quiet.'

'Yes, well, don't worry. Look, in case they ask for yours, I'll say I'm a solo driver. In fact, I'll do all the business. You go to that shop over there and get us some sandwiches and a bottle of water. Here's some Danish notes.'

'Right,' Morton replied. He wondered where Luke had got the cash from. Maybe from Sgurd? He turned back to check that Luke had actually gone into the agency. He didn't want to be driving across Denmark in a stolen car. And he was thinking: *All this time and he had his bloody passport and said nothing!* Morton waited in the street for Luke to reappear. There were spaces for him to park on the street.

Finally, he saw him driving along in a bright blue four-door Ford Fiesta. Luke parked and leaned over to open the passenger door. It was a left-hand drive. Morton tossed his rucksack into the back seat and got in. Luke told him he had booked it one-way to Stockholm, which was not far from Uppsala. The interior smelled fresh and new and there was plenty of legroom. Luke set off, following signs for the E20.

'Stockholm. How far is that?' Morton inquired.

Luke rubbed the stubble on his chin and checked the Satnav. 'Depends on the route, but around about a thousand kilometres.'

'Jesus! I'll do my share of driving,' Morton volunteered. 'That's a long way.'

'Well, you can later, if you want. It's mostly motorway. Says here it's about eleven hours driving time. We'll do it in two days easy.'

'If you say so. At least this car's legal. I didn't know you had your passport with you. That's a stroke of luck. I don't have mine, of course.' Morton was perplexed. If the plan was to evade surveillance by going to Europe, wasn't it crazy to hire a car using a passport? 'But won't they track your passport to the car rental place?'

Luke glanced at him and smiled. 'No. The chances of the spooks getting that bit of information from Interpol is unlikely. Their surveillance at boat and plane exits in the UK is so good, they will believe that we must still be in the UK. They won't expect us to be have been able to get abroad illegally.'

Morton sniffed. 'You mean, the UK spooks' electronic surveillance doesn't run in Europe?'

Luke nodded. 'Interpol wouldn't pass on the information unless specifically asked to. Which they may do later of course.'

'So I could have brought my passport and used it in Europe, once I was out of the UK?'

Luke looked at him as he slowed for the junction. 'Don't worry about it. This is the EU. You shouldn't need it.' Morton wondered what he meant, but lay back and let Luke drive.

They turned off the junction on the E20, heading to Aarhus. Luke made good progress, the roads were dry, the sky clear as they headed due east to the more populous island of Fyn, which Morton learned from the English-language guidebook, helpfully provided with the car, was pronounced Foonan. The pattern of the declining sun on the side-window and the reflections from the windscreen and the warmth in the car pushed Morton gradually into a doze, and when he woke up he found they were approaching the big city of Odense.

'Crikey, we're on Fyn already? That's good going.'

'Nothing to it. Good roads.'

They stopped at a roadside Kondotori stall for coffee and sat at a wooden table looking at a glassy blue lake and thick black forest on either side of it. For some reason, Morton found himself thinking back to the roadside cafe on Loch Linnhe just two days earlier. And now he was in Denmark. He wondered where Ross Mackie was; probably at his cottage near Friockheim, doing DIY. Mackie must be okay. If he was some sort of spook, he'd have pushed harder to find out what was going on, wouldn't have been so happy to drop them off and skedaddle. He looked sideways at Sangster. He had seemed to have no money in Glasgow, now he was paying for everything. The car rental. That must have cost a packet. He wondered about the Uppsala connection too. They had no information at all about that. Just the word of Brodagh that someone would call them. It was a bit dodgy. What if no-one phoned? It seemed a long way to go. Surely there was a safe house somewhere nearer? A thousand kilometres? He was still not quite reconciled to the idea of this trip as an adventure. Also, he had decided he was going to phone Emily as soon as he could and to hell with Luke! He would have to ask her to send him his passport out, so he could get a flight back. And he just wanted to hear her voice and know that she wasn't going crazy wondering where he was. He smiled, thinking how nice it was to have someone care for him, to be in a real relationship after so long on his own.

'Something amusing?' Luke muttered.

'Just thinking,' he smiled. 'Remembering that cheesey snack bar near Fort William. We were there with Ross.'

'I remember. He was a funny guy. Just appeared, out of the blue. That's a bit suspicious. I mean, what do you really know about him?'

'Well... maybe. He was a volunteer and I remember someone wise telling me never to trust a volunteer.'

'Damn right. It was someone in our group who grassed me up. Or that's what I believe anyway. But I can't work out who it was. Emily ever mention to you any suspicions of an informer?'

'Don't think so.'

'You only went to one meeting, right? Anybody there strike you as suspicious?'

'I never really knew any of them. Apart from Liam, Emily and Marco – but he wasn't at the meeting I was at.'

'It's not Marco. He's no grass.'

'I wouldn't have thought so. Or Alasdair. Sound as a pound.'

'But someone grassed me up. I've been thinking about the group, trying to work out which one…'

'There was an older woman called Alison.'

Luke sniffed. 'Don't remember her. What's her last name?'

'No idea. And a woman with blue hair and a lip ring. Cecelia. Who didn't seem to like you.'

'Cecilia?'

'You must remember her.'

'Oh yes. She never liked me,' he said, scowling at the dashboard. 'Look, the Satnav's predicting lots of traffic delay after Nyborg, all the way over the bridge to Trelleborg. That's the run up to the big bridge, the…'

'The Storebaelt.' Morton felt the onset of dread. He'd heard of this long, high, super-bridge. He wasn't good on bridges.

'So I think we'll head south to Svendborg. There's a short ferry trip then over to an island and then up to Copenhagen. It's a little longer but not much.'

'I have absolutely no problem about missing the Storebaelt Bridge,' said Morton with feeling. 'I've seen pictures of it. Gives me the creeps.'

'We'll try to make it to Copenhagen if we can tonight. Then we could stop and crash out for a few hours in the car.'

'The seats recline?'

'Yeah, it'll be a bit cramped but we'll manage.'

CHAPTER TWENTY

Morton had become aware that their route would inevitably take them across the Oresund Bridge. It was twenty kilometres long; sixteen kilometres across open sea between Copenhagen and Sweden a mighty feat of engineering no doubt, but for Morton a test of his nerves. If necessary he might have to make his seat lie flat so he could lie with eyes shut to try to calm his ridiculous fears.

Luke shrugged. 'A road is just a road, even when it's a bridge.'

Morton grimaced. 'The Oresund is different. It's the longest in the world. Except for the Storebaelt which we managed to avoid by going by Svedenborg and that ferry to Lolland.'

Luke grinned. 'Ah, you'll be alright. It'll only take fifteen minutes.'

They had reached the outskirts of the city the day before and slept in the car on a dusty piece of waste ground off the road under some trees. Sleep proved elusive even with the windows open; too hot and stuffy. As dawn broke, they drove to a city centre parking area and got out to stretch their legs and have breakfast.

'Best to take a break for a couple of hours,' Luke suggested. 'Do the tourist thing.' It felt odd to think of themselves as tourists, Morton thought. Fugitives from justice more like, although he had done nothing. But then neither had Luke and they were off on this crazy adventure. If it *was* an adventure. They spent a couple of hours walking in the city centre, looking at the colourful houses at Nyhavn, the seventeenth century waterfront, passing buskers playing jazz on the quayside and admiring the modernistic Opera House across the water, a huge glass structure with an oversized flat roof. They clocked the bronze statue of Hans Christian Andersen in a square. Through the gates of the nearby Tivoli Gardens they could see walkways festooned with red Chinese lanterns.

'Sort of funfair,' Luke said. 'Overpriced. You been here before?'

'Me? No,' Morton replied.

'I've been once. Apparently it gave Walt Disney the idea for his theme parks.'

The weather was dull. Squalls of drizzle had left the cobbles wet with puddles forming in places. Morton couldn't relax because of the thought of what he was going to have to face later. Also, he could not phone Emily, or anyone, as Luke never left him alone even for a few minutes. Their mobile phones were in the car boot, batteries out, disconnected. The safest way, Luke had said. We don't want them to track us. Yet it felt like they were in a different world, with no feeling that they were being watched. They could conceivably be tourists, on holiday. There seemed to be few CCTV cameras. Or maybe – he wondered – I'm just not seeing them?

Finally, in mid-morning they got back to the car and set off into the Copenhagen ring road system heading for Sweden. The E20 was busy and filled with drivers racing to and fro. Soon, they were passing the airport and going down into a long brightly-lit tunnel. Traffic raced by in four lanes. Why couldn't they have built a tunnel all the way, Morton wondered? Then they were queuing at the toll gates. Morton could see no sign of water. The vehicles, including theirs, were left-hand drives. That would mean he would be sitting near the outer edge of the bridge. He tried to stay calm, felt he was nurturing the onset of a headache. Luke stopped at the toll gates. Morton was surprised to see him hand over banknotes. Where had he got the cash from? But he was too pre-occupied with other things to think about it anymore as Luke drove onto the bridge structure. There was no sign of land. They were in the middle of the ocean. He shrank back in his seat, wound it halfway down and tried closing his eyes. That was worse, less control.

'Yes, where *is* Sweden?' Luke joked. 'Must be around here somewhere.'

Morton lay rigid with anxiety, right hand on the door handle and all he could think about was the eighteen inches or so between his door and the bridge parapet, which looked so flimsy that it wouldn't stop a toddler falling off. He vividly imagined spinning wheels, tarmac, concrete and the *void*. He stared fixedly ahead, counting the seconds, but already, in the distance, saw the towering climb of the main bridge structure snaking in a loose bend over the ocean, away up in the air, miles ahead, tiny dots of vehicles visible on it. Sweat was all over his body, racking up stress, the headache obscuring his vision. His knuckles, gripping the door handle, were sore. The high bridge section reared ahead, sixty metres above the sea, and they were already curving round onto it. Minutes passed, the wheels spun, Luke was impassive and still no sign of land in the distance. Where the hell was Sweden?

'This is fucking scary!' he burst out, his voice sounding like someone else.

'I can see you're not enjoying it,' Luke said, 'don't worry, it's perfectly safe. Nothing to worry about. It's only sixteen kilometres. Not as bad as the Storebaelt. That's twenty-four kilometres. To take your mind off it, I'm going to tell you something I've never told anyone else.'

'Uh?' Morton said through gritted teeth. He didn't want to lose concentration on the task in hand; battening down his terrible fears. It was taking all his effort.

'I wasn't sure if I was going to tell you, but now might be a good time.'

'Right, get on with it! Don't take your hand off the wheel for fucksake!'

All he could think about was the height… the depth of the sea beneath them, the vast, open space. What *was* this disease he had? He had looked it up in medical tomes. Was it gephryophobia (fear of bridges), thalassophobia (fear of deep water) or acrophophobia (fear of high spaces)? Or all fucking three?

'When I was a student at Durham Uni…'

'What?' Morton forced himself to close his eyes. They must be more than half over now. Must be!

'I met this girl in the student Union. Brooke – very glamorous. Not at all my sort socially. A posho and one of the best-looking girls around. Way above my aspirations if you know what I mean, me being a greasy nerd.'

Morton was barely aware of what Luke was saying. They were approaching the highest bend, the crux of his fears, almost floating in the clouds.

'… she approached me and said she'd been speaking to… someone I knew. I was flattered and in awe. I suspected she was just a *yah* if you know what that means?'

'Oh yah!' Morton said grimly staring straight ahead.

'Anyway we had a date. Except it wasn't.'

'What?' Morton wished he would shut up.

'She met me in the coffee bar but then a guy came in and she introduced me and then buggered off!'

'Uh. Why?'

'Well this other man was like her, another yah. I ignored him. I felt I'd been had. But I soon realised there was something going on. He seemed to know stuff about me. Asked me about IT interests, my hacking. It was like he was *interviewing* me. You know, for a job like.'

'A job?' Morton repeated. He had suddenly become aware of land in the distance. Sweden. 'Look – is that land over there?'

'Yes. Not long now. Wow, look at this, coming up on the right. It's a huge shipwreck!'

'Don't look at it!' Morton instructed. 'Please keep your eyes on the road,'

An enormous ship had foundered close to the bridge and lay on its side, rusting, rotting, a fascinating sight – the sheer scale of it – but the road was now sloping downwards, descending towards dry land. They had nearly made it.

'That's Malmo over there,' Luke said. We're in Sweden.'

And the sunshine came out as they rolled onto terra firma. Morton's fear dissolved, and his stress and headache. He felt a hot flush of relief. They swept into a tunnel and emerged at the Swedish tolls.

'What do we do now?'

'That's okay. I paid at the other side. I got Euros at the car hire place. You can pay in Euros or Kronor.'

'Right. I wondered.' He was marvelling at the ripe corn fields and dazzling yellow of oilseed rape.

'Sunny Sweden,' Luke said. 'Feel better now?'

Morton closed his eyes and deeply inhaled. He exhaled. 'I don't know why I have these fears. I never used to have them. What was it you were trying to tell me, back there?'

'You're just a mass of neuroses really.'

Morton scowled at him. It was an unfair comment, overly critical. Or maybe he was too sensitive. But there was a bitterness, an edge to the remark. Morton did not like to feel diminished by his phobias. 'It's not my fault you know,' he said finally. 'When I was your age, I did all kind of scary things. Never bothered me then. Anyway, *was* it a job?'

'A job? Oh yes. You'll never guess…'

Morton scoffed. 'Really, I've no idea.'

'MI5. Can you believe? Five!'

Morton was astonished and speechless. He stared at Luke. Then he recovered himself. 'What the hell? MI5?'

Luke laughed as if it was all a big joke and worked the indicators, turning onto the main road north. On either sides, arable fields, with no dykes or fences at the road edges. Trees and stone cottages. 'Could you believe it?'

'So?' Morton demanded.

'Went for the interview. Hotel on the South Bank. Had to stay overnight. It was a pretty intensive two days. They made me do all kinds of tests and participate in various scenarios. There were about a dozen others there, men and women, most about my age. I didn't like many of them and the instructors were nasty. But… I guess they knew my heart wasn't in it.'

'You didn't get the job?'

Luke laughed incredulously. 'Of course bloody not! What do you think? They said they'd be in touch but they never were. That was my one big chance of getting my licence to kill.'

Morton was thinking about the story and wondering why Luke had told him. Was there a hidden meaning to it? 'That was MI6 – licence to kill, not…' he murmured absent-mindedly.

'They're all the fucking same. Trust me.'

So… do you think this is maybe why… they are after you now?'

Luke half-turned. 'A definite maybe, I think. Don't you?'

'Bloody hell!'

The scenery was familiar from Nordic-noir dramas. Morton stared at it blankly. Huge open fields, the vast blue sky, stone dykes, low houses. There was a bleakness to it, peripheral. It looked like Fife. 'So you are known to the security services? Why didn't you tell me before now?'

Luke grunted. 'It's just something that happened. I'm sure they interview loads of people. Anyway, they interviewed me under my real name.' He grinned. 'Luke Sangster is my new name.'

'For fucksake, Luke! Morton burst out. Then he found he had nothing else to say. He sat in silence, ruminating on what he had just been told as he was driven through the flat, unfenced landscape. Was there more to it? If they'd never contacted him, and that seemed unlikely, why had he changed his name?

'We'll give Malmo a body swerve,' Luke said. 'Heavy traffic, according to the Satnav. We'll head directly north via Lund, cut across to the E4.'

'Whatever you say. I don't mind driving a bit.'

'Maybe later. No problem.'

Morton drowsed a lot of the time. The endless forests, the bleak similarity of it. He was being taken farther away from where he wanted to be. What was the point of it all? He had done nothing. He wanted to be on a plane back to Edinburgh. He wanted to be able to speak to Emily but Luke had insisted they remove the batteries from their phones and that they couldn't use them. Morton didn't believe they were fugitives. There was little evidence of it. Dunan and Blenkinsop had no authority to arrest them. Unless Luke hadn't been completely honest with him? He felt Luke was dragging him into something, that it was only Luke's problem. And why on earth had he changed his name? It seemed that the more he found out about Luke, the less he knew him. Who the hell was he really?

Luke drove hard all that day stopping once for petrol, twice for toilet stops, when they had peed into the trees at the side of the quiet, shaded road. Then they hit the E4 dual carriageway. As it began to grow dark, the headlights illuminated a large sign and Morton saw they were approaching a town called Värnamo.

'Yeah, I'm knackered. We'll stop here for the night,' Luke said. 'If we can find a guesthouse or something.'

'I'm hungry.'

'Me too. Tomorrow we'll be on real motorway. Still a long way to go.'

'Well, I'm not necessarily going all the way. The nearest airport will do me.'

Luke just laughed. 'Keep an eye out for guesthouses.'

After hours on the road, the dulling repetition of the endless miles, Morton found his spirits and his sense of adventure slipping away. He couldn't sustain a steady line of thought. He craved the cool, still, quietude of a bedroom, motionless and peaceful.

He woke fuzzily in the night, panicking about being on the high bridge. But they were across. He was safe. He felt the nagging need to urinate, stumbled out of bed, eyes half-closed and went out into the corridor, heading to the toilet. From there, he fumbled his way in the dark to the communal kitchen and drew a glass of cold water from the tap. It wasn't cold; he'd not let the tap run long enough. He put down the glass and, passing in front of the window, looked out. He felt like he was very far away from home. There was an almost full moon. He saw a figure at the guesthouse gate, standing motionless in shadow. He had almost missed it. He rubbed his eyes. It was Luke, leaning against the street wall and his left hand was… he was using a mobile phone! Morton blinked the crust of sleep from his eyes. It *was* Luke. He fumbled his way to the hall and felt Luke's door with his fingertips. Open. The room was empty. He went back to the kitchen window. The figure was not there. Morton fled to his own room and listened behind the door. He heard furtive sounds and knew the truth. But who was Luke phoning? He got back into bed and let his breathing slow to normal. Should he confront him in the morning, he wondered? Or bide his time? He couldn't see where this was leading. What was the point of it? But Luke had lied – that was a new fact. That was definite. That was something he now knew. And if there was one lie…? He went back to bed and fell fast asleep. He was on autopilot, confused enough to sleep dreamlessly.

Next day, Morton lay in bed and couldn't decide what to do. He went downstairs and breakfasted, made small-talk. Luke seemed unusually keen to get on the road. Morton couldn't see how to get away without revealing what he knew about Luke's phone call. They set off at 8.45 a.m. They were heading for the city of Jonkoping, or that was the plan, according to Luke, who again insisted on driving. Despite his full night's sleep, Morton could barely keep awake. He woke up to find they were stopped in a layby.

Luke was looking sceptically at him. 'You're awake?'

'Want me to drive?' Morton yawned. 'I'd better do my bit.'

'No, you're alright. Have a cup of coffee. That'll wake you up.' He waggled a thermos flask.

'Right.' Morton sat up and accepted the plastic cup. 'Don't know why I'm still so sleepy.'

'Here you are.'

'Where *are* we?'

'Oh, we're getting there,' Luke said with a wide grin. 'Don't you worry.'

'Good.'

The next thing Morton knew it was evening, the sky getting dark. He saw from his low vantage point that they were in a thick deep forest. He couldn't see the sky so he couldn't absolutely certain that it *was* evening. They weren't moving. So much for Luke saying they were getting there. They were getting nowhere. He felt warmly amused. He tried to focus his eyes on Luke but couldn't see him. He felt the first stirrings of alarm, but there he was, out of the vehicle, looking down at him.

'You must be needing a piss by now. All that coffee. Come on. I'll help you out.'

Morton drowsily wondered why he was so unsteady on his feet. And why Luke had to help him. He saw that they were in a small clearing in the forest but couldn't see the road. It was silent, no other cars. 'Where... we?' he tried to ask.

'Come on, Morton. We haven't got all day, Jesus Christ! Now you go over there and have a pee...'

Morton swayed unsteadily, tried to remember what he was doing, struggled to unzip his trousers, began to urinate. Then pain and oblivion....

CHAPTER TWENTY-ONE

It wasn't Marco who had spotted Luke, it was Alasdair Robertson. He and Celia had been driving back from Haddington. She had had an opinion survey to complete, Alasdair had tagged along and they'd made a day of it. He had been tagging along with Celia for several months now. She enjoyed having an assistant, a confidante and companion and the repartee and the constant banter sparkled. Their days were brighter together. Alasdair worked as a heating engineer but conspired to get days off so that they could do things together. They came off the A1 into Musselburgh and along the coast road through the centre of Leith. As Celia drove sedately along Commercial Street, and he idly glanced out of the window, he spotted Luke on the pavement. Although he was wearing his hoodie up and had a scarf at his neck, there was no difficulty in recognising him.

'There's a fella I know,' he said. Celia was too intent on the slowly-moving traffic to comment. 'Thought he was missing, but there he is.'

'Missing?' Celia was bemused. She had her specs on for driving and peered forward as the lights changed and the lines of traffic slowed. 'What do you mean?'

So Alasdair told Celia about Luke's flight. 'I'd better let Marco know. Funny thing. I thought he was up in Assynt.'

When they got back to Celia's baronial mansion, Pilton

Mains, in the trees above parkland in Muirhouse facing the estuary, Alasdair phoned Marco on his landline. He knew he should have send him a WhatsApp message for security reasons, but couldn't be bothered. Alasdair disliked mobile phones and used his so rarely that it was often found to be battery-dead. He had a different phone for his work, which belonged to the company but couldn't use it for personal calls.

'Hello?

'Alasdair here. Guess who I've just seen strolling about? Our old chum.'

'What? You *saw* him? Where?

'Dock Street, in Leith. We were just passing, didn't get a chance to speak but no question, it was him. Wearing his hoodie and a thick scarf around his neck. He had a Co-op plastic bag so I guess he was just going out to the shops and lives nearby. Thought he was up in Assynt?'

'Last known sighting was Glasgow. Right. I'll check it out. Leave it with me. Better ring off now.'

Marco put out a WhatsApp message to key figures in the group and went off to his U3A evening class as normal.

The next day, he phoned the University and took the day off. He got the bus down to Leith and walked along Commercial Street. It would be like looking for a needle in a haystack but he had worked out a simple circular route, using Google Maps, connecting all the possible places Luke might go if he was living in the area. The corner shops, Library, post-office and of course Dock Street. And all had to be on routes that didn't have CCTV cameras because he knew Luke would avoid those. That would narrow it down. He walked around the wider loop noting CCTV cameras and was then able to reduce the loop, centring it in the North Leith area and found he could complete the circuit in twenty-five minutes.

He turned and retraced his steps. On the fourth pass, just outside the Lifestyle Express convenience store in Portland Place, he saw him. He followed him round the corner into Portland Street, got closer, stepped off the pavement and passed him, stopped and turned sharply around.

'Aha! It *is* you.'

'Marco!'

'I dinnae believe it! You were so easy to find. Come on, keep moving.'

'How *did* you find me?' Luke asked, sounding a little resentful. 'I've been really careful.'

'You were spotted yesterday by Alasdair. We presumed you were living in the area because you were carrying a Co-op plastic bag.'

Luke looked around him then seemed to relax. 'Yeah, well… I'm in a friend's flat. They're away. Good to see you, man. I've been going stir crazy. Was thinking about getting over to Holland.'

'We need to get aff the street. Is your place far?'

'Just up here. Come on.'

A few minutes later, they were in Jed's flat on the sixth floor and he gave Marco the guided tour.

'At least this one has a proper door,' Marco commented. He squinted out of the skylight. 'And a sea view.'

'Yes. They kicked in the door of the last place, although I was on the roof by that time. Had planned my escape route in advance. Had to leave a lot of gear there though. I suppose there's no chance of getting that back?'

'What dae you think? Naw! Listen, where is Willie Morton? He came up to see you at Assynt, yes, and then…'

Luke turned. 'Eh? Assynt? I've never been to Assynt.'

'You phoned me to say…'

'Not me, Marco. I never phoned you. Assynt?'

'It wasnae you that phoned me? Well, who the hell did?'

'Tell me from the beginning. What did this person say, exactly?'

Marco slumped onto a kitchen chair. 'I've been conned,' he said. 'Somebody's been playing silly buggers.'

'I haven't seen Willie since we took him to the portacabin at Bo'ness. That was months ago.'

Marco left Luke in the flat and leaped down five flights of stairs onto Portland Street. The sun had moved around and now shone directly on the roofs of the giant Ocean Terminal building and the Western Harbour. Marco made rapid progress and as he passed Leith Job Centre, saw a taxi cab sitting outside. There were red tasselled Islamic symbols hanging from the mirror and a small text from the Koran on the dashboard. He gestured to the driver who lowered his window.

'You on hire?'

'Aye. Nae problem.'

'University. Buccleuch Place.' He got into the back seat.

The driver, an elderly Asian looked at him in the mirror. 'By tower building, is it? Near tae the mosque.'

'That's it.'

'Nae problem, my friend.'

The driver turned up the hill and headed to the Old Town. Marco tried to analyse what was going on. The tip-off he had relied upon had been fake. He remembered that it had been brief, difficult to hear, but the person on the other end was not Luke. As a result, he had sent Willie on a wild-goose chase up to Assynt. And now Willie was missing. He had put Willie into danger. Who would cause him to do such a thing? It was a malevolent act. It wasn't a prank. There was danger in it.

As Marco sat musing, ordinary people passed him, going about their everyday activities. Crowds of people, a sea of faces on the pavements, going into and out of shops, pubs and newsagents, waiting to cross roads. Workers, hurrying students, jeering schoolkids, businessmen, painters and decorators, greengrocers unloading trays of lettuces. The life of the nation continued in its normal frenetic, disconnected, dysfunctional way. Murders, courtroom dramas, accidents, rapes, rising sales figures, political arguments, cancer victims' brave defiance, penalty shoot-outs; the day's headlines.

When he stepped onto the pebbledash concrete plaza walking towards the dark bulk of David Hume Tower, he glanced over to Salisbury Craigs and could make out tiny dots walking along beneath it. He wasn't looking forward to the meeting. Would Emily blame him for putting Morton in danger?

The road developed into a motorway, snaking through forests and large lakes towards the coast, the airport and the city of Gothenburg. He had stopped for fuel at Bollebygd and, heading straight for a deepening sunset, put on sunglasses as he reached the outskirts of the city. He intended to go straight home and return the Ford Fiesta to the rental office the next day. It had been a tiring day and he had his report to complete. He navigated the ring roads and turned down towards the university and the quiet, tree-lined streets of Annedal in the southern suburbs of the city. Parking the car in the underground garage, he removed the two rucksacks and sleeping bags from the back seat, checking there was nothing left in the boot. He momentarily remembered his passenger as he stuffed the blue sleeping bag into Morton's rucksack, but it was over, finished, all in a day's work. He had never had a problem switching off after an op. The sixth-floor apartment was owned under a different name. The main room had a view of the Gota as it joined the Kattegat. The sun was now barely an orange smudge on the horizon but the purple, red and burgundy stain it threw up was darkening the entire sky, like a scab closing on a wound, as the night coalesced. He turned the dimmer switch, bringing the room lights to a warm glow. Across the river, streetlights and house lights of the western suburbs of Lundby and Lindholmen were an attractive patchwork with the regular pattern of red and white of vehicle taillights and headlamps moving on the high Alvsborg Bridge.

Hamner upended Morton's rucksack on the carpet and knelt down to sift through the contents. He found the mobile phone and replaced the battery. It was flat. He inserted the charger and plugged it in. He'd have to wait till it was charged before he could look into the texts, emails and other personal stuff. He'd do the other parts of his report in the meantime. He made himself a pot of coffee on the stove and looked into the fridge. Nothing – of course, he'd been away more than a week. He went into the bedroom and stripped, showered, washing out the hair dye and the stink of a week of living rough. Washing off all trace of Luke Sangster. As he towelled dry and dusted himself with talc he began to feel more like himself. The first thing he would do tomorrow was get a haircut. Check his account at Nordea Bank to see his bonus had been paid in. Dump the clothes and Morton's rucksack in waste disposal. Then return the car, as arranged. Have a nice slow lunch at Hamnkrogen with a beer. He had a week's vacation due and it might be a while before they found him a new assignment. He would sleep well. Driving long distances had that effect on him and he hadn't slept well for quite a few days. He sat down at the computer near the wide window and wrote up his report, itemising the information he had gathered and the actions he had taken, under the file name Armoury. By the time he had finished, he noticed that it was fully dark, only a shining blade of river could be seen and a full moon was rising over the switchboard of lights across the great northern city.

Professor McKechnie's office on the south western corner, third floor, of the David Hume Tower had had several previous uses in its forty years. A store-room, a staff common room, departmental conference room, and for the previous ten years, the room of the Secretary to the Department of Political and Constitutional Studies. Professor Kikollo-Gombally, the previous Head of Department, had used a smaller room on the first floor near the lift, because of his disability. When Emily replaced him she had swapped rooms with the Departmental Secretary. It had a window that looked out over the Meadows and Melville Drive from where it was possible to see Brunstfield Links and the far side of Warrender Park. The room got the afternoon sun. There had been a bit of a struggle but Emily had emerged victorious.

When Marco arrived, Emily and Liam McLanders were standing at the window looking out at a view, backlit by the sunshine that was only partially impeded by the bulk of the University Library on the corner of George Square.

'Marco, good,' Emily said, turning. 'What's going on?'

'It's a mystery,' Marco told her nervously. 'Honestly, it's a total mystery.'

'Let's all sit down,' McLanders said, taking his hands out of the pockets of his tweed jacket. Ushering Marco to a seat around the large table, surrounded on two sides by the high shelving unit, his long fingers smoothed wavy silver hair.

'I'm worried about Willie,' Emily said. 'Where is he? Have you heard anything from him?'

'Let's keep calm,' McLanders said. 'Look at this logically.'

'You're right. I'm sorry.'

'No problem. Okay, Marco, fill us in about Luke.'

Marco told them about his meeting with Luke; about his never having been to Assynt and that the tip off had been a fake.

'Remind me,' McLanders said. 'What did the caller say exactly?'

'We've been through this,' Marco complained. 'I messaged you at the time. It was brief and I couldn't hear it well. It could have been Luke. It only lasted twenty seconds or so. And that fitted, because he was on the run, didn't want to stay on the line.'

'But why Clachtoll? What's there?' Emily wanted to know.

Marco shrugged. 'It sounded like Clack-toll, the way he pronounced it, but Willie seemed to know it.'

'Yes, he's been there. But then they came back to Glasgow, Willie, the man pretending to be Luke and the other man.'

'Ross Mackie. I met him,' Marco told them.

'And what was *his* role?' McLanders asked. 'Where did he pop-up from?'

'He was advising Willie about off-grid living. I met him at Willie's place. He seemed genuine and it was kind of him to offer to drive Willie north.' He rummaged in his curly hair and grinned. 'Although Willie didnae trust him entirely. He was not pleased when I mentioned Luke's name. See, it didn't occur to me that he had not already told Mackie the name. Anyway, Mackie took them north and then back to Glasgow, dropped them off and disappeared. Or, at least he went off.'

'So, he's not involved anymore?' McLanders said. 'Willie and this other man then met up with Brodagh?'

'Yes. But Brodagh couldn't help them,' Emily said. 'That was the last communication I had from Willie. He phoned me from his hotel. That was Monday night. It's now Friday. He's not answered any of my texts or calls. It's like his mobile is dead. I phoned Brodagh yesterday. She confirmed that she had texted him on Tuesday. You know, she told him she didn't trust the man calling himself Luke Sangster. Maybe this man, whoever he was, got wind of that and didn't like it?'

'There's no proof he's in danger,' Marco said. 'We have tae try and work out who this man is, and what he wants?'

'Is it possible this man has some connection to Viroil?' Emily suggested. 'I mean that was Luke's target and who his hacking affected.'

'But why impersonate the person you're trying to trace? Makes no sense.'

'Unless they think Morton knew something, like maybe where Luke is?'

'But that's preposterous! If Willie knew where Luke was, he'd know this other man was a fake!'

'Good point.'

'But maybe this man is a diversion?' Marco suggested. 'Willie met Luke briefly and might not recognise him again so easily.'

'Meaning,' McLanders continued, 'that he might mis-recognise or more easily accept a fake?'

Marco nodded. 'Whereas Emily or me would spot a fake right away. Was that why he wanted Willie to come up and not me, or Emily?'

McLanders sighed. 'I think we're getting somewhere. That must be it. Willie would validate the fake and establish his credentials for the meeting with Brodagh. Maybe this man was hoping to entrap her in some scheme?'

'And meanwhile, the spooks hunt for the real Luke and…'

'*And* doesn't bear thinking about!' Emily said with a shudder. 'Who are these people? And is Willie still with them?'

'We don't know,' Marco said. 'I've told Luke to stay put. He's reasonably safe for a day or two more.'

'It's time we brought in the professionals, I think,' McLanders said. 'Whether these people who have Willie are spooks or not, we need to bring this to the attention of the authorities. We should contact the Justice Secretary, or go direct to Nicola?'

Emily stood up abruptly. 'Sean Kermally, the SpAd would advise us,' she said. 'Let's ring him right now. Liam, can you make some coffee, while I phone. It's probably best if we try to get him to come here if he can, rather than go barging in to Holyrood.'

CHAPTER TWENTY-TWO

When Morton began to recover consciousness, he found that he was lying on moss, bark or perhaps earth. It was dark and silent as a grave. No bird sounds, no sounds at all, near or distant. He had a headache and felt cold and numb. A long time after his eyes opened, he was unable to move, even to twitch. Gradually feeling returned to his legs and arms and he could move his head. He lifted his face off the soil and saw he was in deep shade. Black and impenetrable, cool and pine-smelling; a forest. Then he remembered the clearing, the car... Luke. He was in Sweden somewhere. Panic began to flood his bloodstream with urgent messages. He forced himself to move and lifted his arm up to the back of his head to explore the pain. His fingers came away wet but it was several minutes before he put together the idea that he had been hit from behind. Luke – the man who called himself Luke – where was he? Morton pulled himself up into a kneeling position, realised he had blood on his fingers and smelt urine... remembered. So had Luke lured him here and hit him? And was this Brodagh's plan all along? He started to get angry, forced himself forward on all fours, feeling the weight on his knuckles and hands. Slowly he got to his feet. He leaned against a pine tree, smelling the strong sap, and began to imagine what Emily might say, her wry remarks. It warmed him. Emily. He wanted to be with her again, warm and slightly tipsy on her couch at Lochend

Grove. He stood unsteadily upright. Staggered twenty feet into the small clearing where the car had been. It wasn't there now. The fragment of sky he could see between the tops of the tall trees all around was the dark blue of evening. A cold shiver of fear ran in his veins and nerves. He was cold too; he was in his shirtsleeves. No jacket. He peered closely at his wristwatch: The green luminous digits showed it was 7.05 p.m. He could barely discern the narrow track they had come down. It was slightly less black than the trees. But why had they come off the road? There was no other explanation. He had been abandoned in the middle of nowhere. It was deliberate. But he was alive and he realised that couldn't be part of Luke's plan. If it was Luke's plan and not someone else's – like Brodagh – but he couldn't believe it of her. No. She couldn't be involved. An intoxicating sense of anger and outrage swept over him. He probed at the wet place on the back of his head. He was sure it was blood. He brought his fingers to his nose. But that didn't help. Did blood smell? He rolled down his shirtsleeves and buttoned them with difficulty at the wrists. He wished he had his jacket. He felt in his trouser pockets; no wallet, but he had his Visa Debit card and a folded Kleenex tissue. He took out the tissue and dabbed at the back of his head. Blood? Yup. But not much. He stood in the middle of the clearing, less than twenty feet wide maybe and looked up. How far from Edinburgh? The thought made him shiver. There was a moon in the sky above the great mass of trees though he couldn't see it. The longer he looked around, the more he saw, began to differentiate black from almost-black and the many shades of grey. He remembered that the previous night, in Värnamo, there had been a full moon. He stretched his neck to loosen the tension and began to swing his arms. Had Luke meant to kill him? If so, he had failed. He did some cautious leg stretches, knee bends. He didn't feel too bad, cold, hungry... Anyway, no time for reflection. There was the track, barely visible, but as it was the only one, the one they had come down, it was the way he had to go. Not dead yet! Not by a long way. He began to make his way down the twin ruts in the forest. It was soft underfoot, sandy, dry, with pine needles deadening his footsteps. It was a narrow path and he estimated the distance between the trees on either side couldn't have been more than seven or eight feet. The forest was featureless, dark, pine-smelling and silent. And very still. He listened. There were no distant sounds, no sounds at all. Morton had heard of the vast forests of Sweden, inhabited by wild boar, wolves. He wasn't sure if there were still wolves. But he heard nothing. Not like most UK forests, where you soon heard traffic in the distance. Apart from the track there were no signs of human habitation, no lights, no man-made objects, no gates or fences. At one point, the dim moonlight illuminated a long silver line of water in one of the ruts of the track and he realised then the forest had gone away on his right. Almost at the same moment, the full moon became visible to him. On his right was a vast open sea or moor, but he quickly established it wasn't water. It was too black, too resistant to the moonlight to be water. It was dull, matt, sinister. He carefully stepped off the track and explored but soon found his feet squelching in unforgiving marsh, sucking him down. He quickly got back onto the track. If he went that way, he would be lost forever! He continued, the forest on his left and on his right, this vast empty marsh, the beautiful moon above; his personal torch. He wondered if there would be a mist, or dew. Walking was helping, swinging his arms, keeping blood pumping through his veins was driving away the fogginess in his brain. Luke had drugged him. The coffee in the flask. Bastard. And he had even told him he'd been recruited by MI5! Pretended he had turned down the offer. As if! Morton now suspected that he had been telling him the truth in plain sight. Couldn't resist showing off how clever he was, how completely he had enmeshed Morton in his deception. The texts from Brodagh must have been fake somehow. Why had he been so easily deceived? But *was* the man Luke? If so, Luke had been a spy in the group all along. Or if he was someone impersonating Luke, where was the *real* Luke? If they – whoever *they* were who employed the fake Luke – were intending from the beginning to leave him for dead in Sweden, what would they do, or *have already done* to poor Luke? And did that mean that all members of the group were at risk? Liam McLanders, even... Emily. And how did Brodagh fit in to all this? Was she too some kind of spy? And a bitter irony struck him. Hadn't he, just three months before, impersonated Philip Gallimont to get inside GB13? Now history was repeating itself with a vengeance. As he worked his way along the interminable track, the moon rose higher in the sky and cast more light on the narrow rutted track. He saw millions of stars twinkling and remembered the night at Clachtoll and the thought made him feel acutely lonely. He looked at his watch and was astonished to find that it was 11.15 p.m. Had he misread it earlier?

At some point, he stumbled, fell, and rested for a few moments on the dry forest floor. He couldn't get his thoughts properly in order. The blood on his scalp had dried into a thick scab and that was a good sign, so maybe it was hunger and the effort of stumbling miles in the dark? Maybe he was going in the wrong direction? This thought constantly returned. Maybe he was going round in circles? Or maybe there was no way out? He knew that was silly. There *was* a track. The car had come along the track, from a road. There was a road somewhere, a way in to the forest from the outer world. He had to sit down and rest. It was 1.13 a.m. But he came to and realised he had made a mistake. It was 2.47 a.m. He remembered he had seen daylight when Luke had 'helped' him into the trees to pee. How long had he been here? He found that he couldn't add up the numbers. Maybe some of his brain was shutting down? Maybe the blow on his head had... He got painfully to his feet and began again, lurching forward.

And then he saw the gate. It was difficult to differentiate forest dark from ground, trees from sky but this structure jumped out at him because... it was *man-made*! He felt it with both hands. It was dressed wood, smooth and mossy in places and it lifted and moved. He realised that the man who had taken him here had had to open it and had shut it after him. The man... wait a minute! Durham University. He'd said he met the girl and then the man, MI5 recruiters... at *Durham* University. But Luke had gone to Edinburgh University! So it wasn't Luke. Not the real Luke. He wasn't losing it. He was working it all out. He got to his knees beneath the gate and felt for the tyre tracks. He believed he could feel the extra indentations of the tyres as he had braked. Wishful thinking or not, it was definitely the right track. He was getting out of the forest. Yes, he bloody well was!

Fridays at the Scottish Parliament were relatively quiet as apart from some committees, Parliament did not sit. Most MSPs were holding surgeries in their constituencies. The First Minister was on a day of visits in Glasgow and Liz Farrell was accompanying her. So Sean Kermally was able to take a leisurely lunch, eating a filled baguette which he had brought from home, in the Garden Lobby. He was considering taking a stroll across the road into Holyrood Park. It was good to get out of the Parliamentary bubble, away from his fourth floor desk in the Ministerial tower and inhale some fresh air. He always had both his mobiles with him; his personal one and the Scottish Government media one. A SpAd was never 'off' always in standby mode. As he sat, legs stretched out in front of him, drowsing in the sun, in the background, the murmur of schoolchildren on a visit, being mustered by teachers and parliamentary tour-guides, his personal mobile chirruped. With a sigh, he retrieved it. Emily McKechnie.

'How's my favourite Prof?'

Emily concisely summarised the situation. Morton in trouble. Again. He'd never heard of Luke Sangster. Yes. He could manage this afternoon. He glanced at his watch. The walk over to the Uni would do him good. He could be there by 2 p.m. He moved inside and got into the lift. On the fourth floor, there were few people about. Alasdair McDougall, another of the SpAd team, nodded in his direction, Krystal Mazotos and Fiona MacInnes, heads bent over their computer consoles. Seonaid Nicoll was out at lunch, according to the yellow Post-it in the centre of her screen. He pinged a message round the team, grabbed his jacket, thrust a note pad in his pocket and entered the lift. He headed for the front entrance. It would be quicker walking by Holyrood Road and the Pleasance than via the Queensferry Gate and up Canongate.

Liam McLanders had left before Sean arrived. Emily introduced Marco Vanetti. They shook hands.

'Nice to meet you. You work with Nicola?'

'I'm part of the media team, Marco.'

'Sean's being modest. You'll remember the GB13 footage on YouTube? That was down to Sean.'

Sean expostulated. 'No – Willie did that. He put himself at huge risk. But you know all that.'

'Of course, but without you organising him getting in and equipping him and editing the footage he got, it wouldn't have made any stir at all.'

'So… where is Willie now?' Sean asked. 'Is that why I'm here?'

'We don't know. It's a complicated story. We're very worried.'

CHAPTER TWENTY-THREE

Shortly after finding the gate, Morton stood in the bright glow of the moon. The light was so dazzling that he had to shade his eyes. His feet were on the tarmac surface of – undeniably – a road. It was a tiny road, barely ten paces wide, and the forest closed around it ahead and behind. As his eyes grew accustomed to the moonlight, he began to feel that he would make it; get back home, survive. In his trouser pocket he fingered the edges of the small plastic rectangle that was his Visa Debit card. Surely another oversight by the man who had dumped him? He had no wallet or other ID but that Debit card might be the key to his survival. He swung his arms and thumped his sides to warm himself up. There was dampness on his shirt. Was that sweat or dew? He looked left and right and chose left. The road seemed to be heading downhill. He had no idea of its real direction. There must be houses, a village or a town. In the moonlight walking was easier, less stumbling around. He found that he was looking for litter, signs of human existence. He felt the cravings of human companionship, food and hot coffee, talk, relaxation, warmth, of course. Even just thinking of these things warmed him. How long had he been walking? How long since he had eaten? He couldn't bear to look at his watch. He saw a shiny object in the verge and went over to it. A squashed plastic water bottle! He almost felt the need to pick it up, but it was partly covered in moss. It exhilarated him. The road was heading downhill and he was hearing distant sounds. He wondered if the road would lead him to a city. But the sounds were nearer. Right behind him. He turned. Twin lights coming at him!

He froze for several seconds, slowly understanding that the lights were from a car. It must stop. He must make it stop. He stood in the middle of the road and held up his hands in surrender.

Maybe it was the man who had dumped him, coming back to make sure he was dead? He was too tired to care. The car stopped short and sat there, blinding him with its headlights. If he stepped to the side, it would drive off and leave him. It must pick him up.

After a few moments, he stepped forward, holding up his hands. Squinting in the powerful beams he saw that the driver was a woman. She looked scared. Then after a few seconds, he realised she was indicating the passenger seat and gratefully, slowly, he went forward beyond the headlights into the darkness and grasped the door handle. Gratefully, he got into the seat and closed the door behind him.

'Thank you,' he said and felt tears well up in his eyes.

The elderly woman spoke soothingly to him. He couldn't understand what she was saying. The only Swedish word he knew was for thank you.

'Tag, tag,' he said, 'Help me.'

The car started moving and as they moved down the narrow road between the dense forests, Morton fell instantly asleep.

When he awoke he was confused and his body ached. He was being awoken. It was dark but there were lights and he was in a car. He didn't understand what they were saying to him. But he could see there was a house and the old lady who had picked him up was standing at the front door. The man doing the shaking must be her husband, a man with profuse walrus-like moustaches and white facial stubble.

'Tag,' Morton kept repeating, a magic talisman, and tried to lift his wobbly legs out of the car. The woman came forward and they both helped to lift him out of the seat and to stand unsteadily and hobble towards the bright light at the front door. He heard the word *Polis* and found it funny that it was the same as in Scots. They brought him inside and he knew they were looking at the back of his head and talking. But he swayed and fell asleep standing up.

When Sean Kermally got back to his desk at Holyrood, he quickly set the wheels in motion. Contacted the Diary Secretary in the Justice Secretary's Department. Established the fact that Martin Masterson MSP was available to take a call: dialled the internal number.

'Martin? Sean Kermally here. I've got a situation you need to know about and I'm hoping you can get a briefing from your police liaison, possibly get Special Branch onto it. It may be something illegal, might be nothing at all, at this point I can't be sure, but…'

'I've got a few minutes if you want to pop along now, Sean.'

'Okay, on my way.'

The offices of the Justice Secretary were on the third floor, one below the rest of the team. It took Sean barely a minute to jump into the lift and walk through the open glass doors of the outer office where the PS and PPS and admin staff sat at three separate desks. There were two doors, one which Kermally knew led to a small storeroom cum pantry. In the modern Parliament there were no visible filing systems, not much evidence of paper files, just a few computer screens here and there. Up on a corner bracket above the doors, Holyrood

TV was showing proceedings in a committee meeting. The sound was off. Kermally saw a junior minister giving evidence and read the subtitles beneath.

Kermally caught the eye of the young blonde intern who was acting as Diary Secretary and continued to the door at the far end, seeing a panorama of the afternoon sun moving over the rock faces of Salisbury Craigs in the glass panes. He knew the intern was from Salt Lake City although you couldn't tell that from her accent of course. He pushed open the honey-coloured wood of the other door and entered the surprisingly small private office of the Justice Secretary. Masterson emerged in his shirtsleeves from the door of an adjacent conference room, a slight smile on his usually worried-looking pale face, patting self-consciously at the rapidly-thinning hair on the back of his head.

'Now, Sean what's all this about?' Illegal… Special Branch? How can I help?'

Kermally filled Masterson in on the details concisely and efficiently as Masterson sat and swivelled his chair to and fro.

'And that's it in a nutshell. So you can see why I suggest a police briefing.'

Masterson sighed. 'So poor old Willie Morton is with… this man… who he believes to be a hacker called Luke… in Europe because he thinks he is in danger in the UK?'

'Correct?'

'He thinks *he* is in danger or this other man is in danger?'

'That we don't know. But I can't imagine Willie has done anything illegal.'

'And this man is impersonating the hacker Luke in order to discover some information about this group… this Cerberus? Which seems to me,' he sniffed and searched the pockets of his grey waistcoat for a tissue, found one, dabbed at his nostrils…

'a very dangerous strategy. Surely if or when the real Luke turns up, this man will be exposed as a fraud?'

Kermally thought about it. There was only one possible conclusion and it scared him. He hadn't wanted to say anything to Emily because it would have upset her. 'Minister, in my opinion they didn't expect the real Luke to turn up. In fact, they probably intended to locate him and kill him.'

'Who are these people? Who are *they*?'

'I can't say for sure. But I can't believe Police Scotland are involved.'

'Hmn. Well, whoever they are, they seem to have failed.'

'Yes. We know that. But do they?'

'And where is Luke now?'

'He's safe. That's all I am allowed to say.'

'I get your point.'

'So Morton is in the company of a man whose existence, as an impersonator, is an embarrassment to those... whoever they are, who sent him,' Kermally said. 'On the other hand, Morton may come to know that this man is a fake and therefore that someone organised this whole charade on the strong belief the real Luke will not turn up. Do you see?'

'I do,' Masterson concurred. 'Of course, you can only produce a fake when you know the real thing is not going to be around. So, if the real Luke is bumped off, Morton will be the only person who knows the truth of their deception – and why.'

'That's what scares me,' Kermally said. 'Who *are* these people?'

Emily had been to Willie's place in Keir Street on Wednesday, using her key to get in. She had found nothing untoward. Now, with Marco, she walked across George Square and alongside the boarded-up site of the old Royal Infirmary. They entered Willie's second floor flat.

'What are we looking for?' Marco asked.

'Anything out of place. Has someone been here? I want to check if his passport is still here.'

'Where would that be, do you think?'

'In his desk?'

It took them twenty minutes to find the passport, which was underneath the small bedside table. 'Well, it's in a hiding place,' Emily said. 'And it's still there. What does that tell us, Marco?'

'That Willie is still in Scotland?'

'Yes. But where? He spoke to Brodagh from Queen Street Station around 10.40 a.m., suggesting he was getting a train back to Edinburgh. The person calling himself Luke was there too. What happened then? Where did they go?'

'Try not to get upset,' Marco said. 'I'm sure he's alright.'

'I wish I'd never got him into this. It's all my fault. I practically forced him to get involved in the search for Luke.'

Emily's mobile rang and made her jump. But it was Sean. She gestured to Marco and switched the phone to loudspeaker. 'Emily, I've had a word with Martin and he's asked for a meeting with someone senior in Special Branch to see what they know. He's happy for you – and Marco – to sit in on that. It'll be in Glasgow this evening at 6 p.m. Can you get to Glasgow City Centre Police Station, in Stewart Street? It's just five minutes' walk from Queen Street, on Cowcaddens Road.'

Emily and Marco looked at each other and nodded. 'Yes,' Emily said, 'we can do that.'

Morton awoke to birdsong and through half-closed eyes

felt bright sunlight and warmth on his skin. He saw that he was lying face down on a single bed. It took him a while to remember what had happened to him. He felt relaxed and safe, calm. He knew now he would get back to Edinburgh and Emily. They would go off on holiday together; everything would be alright. He tried to move and rediscovered pain. His muscles ached, but he had to get up and persisted despite the stiffness, swung his legs over the edge of the bed and sat up. He was in a small dormer bedroom, naked except for his briefs. He saw that his trousers, socks and shirt were folded neatly on a wooden chair with the watch and his Visa Debit card on top of the pile. He tried to stand up and found himself a little dizzy but grasped the window ledge and looked out between the screens. The fresh air helped. He looked down on flowering fruit trees in which little birds sang. He saw a wall, a driveway, the black Citroen 205 that he had been in last night, a metal table and chairs, lawn. It was idyllic but across the road was the forest and that made him remember the ordeal he had been through. What he thought about most of all was the dispassionate way the man had drugged him and driven him into deep forest and hit him over the head, despite the four days' companionship they had shared. It was hard to believe there were people like that around. He turned from the window and found his clothes. The room was small and bare, a box room, his mother would have called it, the wallpaper an apple green shade.

He went out into a pine-floored corridor and creaked down the wooden stair, shoes making a lot of noise on the treads. He wondered if his hearing had been affected by hours of absolute silence in the forest. The large kitchen was a sunny, warm space. The old lady stood at a cooker while her husband ate at the wooden table.

She smiled and beckoned him in. Her husband, a stout fellow with large walrus-like moustaches and braces, looked up and studied him. Morton went over and sat at the table, wincing at the pain in his joints. He felt profoundly grateful to them for rescuing him but had no idea how he could tell them that.

The woman pointed to her floral apron and said: 'Gretl och Jorge,' pointing to the man, who nodded sagely.

'Willie,' he said.

She repeated his name. The man laughed. Morton smiled. There was a relaxation of the tension in the room. The woman placed a plate of scrambled eggs, slices of gammon and cheese in front of him and then a large mug of coffee. She brought milk, but Morton shook his head.

'Tag. Tag,' he said, trying to signal his gratitude with his eyes and his hands.

As Morton began to eat, savouring the unusually wonderful tastes of the food and the coffee, Gretl produced a cordless phone and rang a number and began to talk volubly into it, while looking at Morton. He hoped it wasn't the police. The coffee was wonderful and he inhaled its flavour as he took long gulps of it. The cheese was gorgeous, the gammon and the scrambled eggs were perfect. He continued to eat as the woman talked on the phone and her husband, Jorge, stared rather mournfully into the distance.

He looked up to see the phone being offered to him. 'Polis?' he asked.

She shook her head.

Morton put the phone to his ear. The woman was speaking to him in English. It was their daughter, Maja.

'My mother has told me how she found you on the old forest road. You gave her a bad fright. She thought you were a ghost. It is a long road out of the way, a back road. She did not expect to see anyone there. How did you get there without a car?'

Morton thought carefully. He did not want to get the police involved because his attacker might have police help or support. The ease with which he had been able to obtain a passage across the North Sea, hire a car and cross frontiers suggested to Morton that he was not working alone. Leaving him in the forest was not a random act. It was part of a conspiracy. And now here he was, alive against the odds, in a foreign country with no passport. He had to be careful who he trusted. 'I came there in a car, with a person I thought to be a friend,' he told her. 'But we had a quarrel and he left me there.'

'And my mother says you have blood on your head. He hit you, this man?'

'Yes. But I don't see the point in going to the police. This was just a quarrel.'

'What will you do?'

'I'll go back home.'

'To England?'

'Scotland. Do you know if there is a train from here? Where am I?'

'You are in Svenabo. The nearest train station is Gnosjö. It is about thirty kilometres away. I'm sure my parents would take you there and from there you could get the train to Gothenburg. It is about two hours.'

'I see. How far is Svenabo from Värnamo?'

'Is that the way you came? That is about eighty kilometres away. My mother picked you up in the woods at Ogestrüm. That is a dangerous place. Very remote. No-one lives there. She was coming back from my aunt's house at Dalstarp. Usually my father goes with her. You were lucky she went that way. She saw no-one else on that road.'

'Yes. I was very lucky. I am so grateful to your parents and to you for your help. I wish I could tell her that.'

'I will tell. I will speak to my mother now.'

4: AFTERLIFE

CHAPTER TWENTY-FOUR

The train raced through the Swedish sunshine, diving into the gloom of forests, over bridges and along the shores of great lakes that flickered in the sun and hurt his eyes. Sweden was a land of forests, isolated white wooden houses with red roofs, silent lakes with boardwalks and handrails leading down into them and signs he had seen warning swimmers of Brännmanet; stinging jellyfish. It was a land of the outdoors; remote cabins and hidden trails, the possibility of seeing families of moose browsing peacefully on fruit bushes at road verges. Morton felt relief that he was back in the normal everyday world, heading for the safety and anonymity of a big city where he could re-organise himself and take stock. Already he had got beyond his experience of fear in the forest of Ogestrüm, downplaying it in his mind. Had it happened as he remembered? Had he really been in danger? Had the man meant only to scare him? At the town of Gnosjö, Gretl and Jorge had taken him to a public health clinic where a maternal nurse fussed over the cut in his scalp, binding the wound with plastic sutures. The nurse had been clear that he had received a blow to the head with a blunt instrument, probably a piece of wood. That couldn't been denied. So it was assault with intent to murder. Morton gingerly touched the back of his head, felt the ridged hard skin of the scab and the plastic stitches. It didn't hurt much and he had been lucky not to have suffered concussion or worse.

Morton's plan on arrival in the city was to purchase a pay as you go mobile, charge it up and phone Emily. She would be going out of her mind with worry. It had been five days since he had spoken to her on the phone from Glasgow. He had a pretty good idea, from memory, of most of the thirteen digits of her mobile number. He was sure of the international dialling code and the first eight numbers. It would be trial and error after that for the final two digits. The scrolling message on the screen in the carriage indicated they would arrive in Gothenburg in ten minutes. He stretched his legs and reached up to the overhead locker to retrieve the jacket they had given him, which had belonged to their son, Hassi. It was a zip-up denim jacket, faded dark-blue and somewhat out of date, but not a bad fit. He liked the texture of the fabric and that it had two inside pockets. It was kind of them to donate it to him. Apparently Hassi hadn't worn it for years and wouldn't miss it. Morton had been lucky in his rescuers. By sheer chance Gretl had driven through the forest at that time on a route she never used. And by a further lucky chance she had been delayed two hours at her sister's otherwise she might have driven past while he was still blundering about in the forest.

Morton saw the approaching signs of Gothenburg, end of the line. He put on the jacket and in his trouser pocket fingered the edges of the all-important Visa Debit card. He had things to do.

The meeting on the first floor office at Pacific Quay went ahead without a representative from Special Branch; an internal MI5-only meeting, called at short notice. Even though it had mostly been a dull day with rain showers, the warmth of the infrequent sunlight, through the metal window blinds, allied to the central heating, had made the room too warm. Most of the participants had removed their jackets and hung them on the backs of their chairs.

Desmond Thorpe was chairing and got things underway with little preamble. 'This extra meeting has been called at short notice to update you all on Armoury,' he told them, adjusting the positioning of his tortoiseshell specs on the bridge of his nose with thumb and forefinger. 'Colleagues from Special Branch are not attending. They were not, in fact, notified. There will be no notes taken, no record. Okay? Speak freely.'

Blenkinsop held up his forearm, finger pointing like a pistol. 'Boss, to give you a swift rundown… we infiltrated a contractor into Claymore, or EH4I if you prefer, and he convinced Armoury of the need to leave the country.' He coughed several times, then cleared his throat. 'Actually that was accomplished by the use of a hacked mobile phone account of… a third party, to provide additional bona-fides.' He paused. 'It worked. Then transport was facilitated to Denmark and thence to Sweden. This was accomplished without passports or appropriate legal procedures. Initially, it was intended that this would buy time for us to locate Sangster.'

'Excuse me,' Joe Miller queried, 'I must have it wrong, but…' he grinned self-consciously '…wasn't the original intention to create a tie in between the group's illegal activity and other outside agents such as Brodagh Murdoch?' Miller's tanned good looks were shown to advantage by white tee-shirts that showed off his upper body musculature. He looked around for support. 'That's what I understood, anyway.'

'Well, yes, that's correct Joe,' Blenkinsop told him, 'but it was thwarted when Murdoch refused to play ball, so a secondary aim was to divert Armoury while we located Sangster.' He laughed. 'Actually, in a very economical way, we were able to get her to help us. Not willingly of course.'

Blenkinsop and Dunan shared a knowing smile.

'How?' Miller asked.

'Glad you asked that Joe, man,' Dunan smirked. 'Digint hacked her mobile, see, and two text messages were sent that helped our man to persuade Armoury what he ought to do. Very clever.'

'Yes. And…' Thorpe interrupted.

'The contractor we have used before, is Sweden-based, very reliable,' Blenkinsop continued. 'But regrettably he may have overstepped the mark a bit this time.'

Thorpe looked up from his papers. 'Better explain that point.'

'We have been aware for some time…' Blenkinsop looked to Dunan for confirmation, who nodded, '… that our *local* colleagues may have been attempting to subvert the operation. We established that they had put their own support agent into contact with Armoury, though they did, belatedly, admit this. We've also suspected for a while that our inability to locate Sangster was due to their, shall we say, interference. In the light of this…'

Thorpe nodded. 'He overstepped the mark. Yes, but what exactly has he done?'

'He saw an opportunity to remove Armoury altogether from the scene. I mean permanently.'

Thorpe took off his specs and placed them on the table. 'Good grief! I hope you're not saying…?'

There was an awkward silence as Blenkinsop's explanation was digested.

'Christ!' Freddy Blake groaned. 'A fuck-up!'

Blenkinsop tried to spin it. 'He was given specific

instructions simply to remove him from the scene for a week and let him find his own way back to Scotland, unharmed, but instead…'

'So Armoury is in Sweden?' Miller concluded.

'Yes, Joe. Regrettably, he is. He has no ID, passport, money or mobile phone, in a location where I am informed, he will never be found.'

'Bloody hell! I get the picture,' Thorpe said, wiping the lenses of his spectacles with a little cloth and sighing heavily. 'This is definitely a serious fucking over-stepping of the fucking mark.'

'You're telling me,' Freddy Blake said. 'We'd better cut and run. Get shot of the contractor, sever all links.'

Thorpe nodded. 'Freddy is right. Is it deniable? Is it fucking deniable?'

Blenkinsop nodded. 'Oh yes. Absolutely, agent Hatchet operates only on that basis.'

'And Hatchet's not on the books? There's no record of transit? What about CCTV in Denmark and Sweden? Transaction traces?'

'No transaction traces. Car rental, toll charges and accommodation were all under Hatchet's real name. CCTV will exist in places. It will be patchy and Armoury will be more or less undetectable in that. Anyway as his passport is still at his home, there will be no call to look for him abroad.'

'Time to drag the rivers and search waste ground?' Dunan grinned. 'And perhaps we can find a quack who can testify to his psychiatric issues?'

Thorpe cut in: 'No need for that kind of remark! There will have to be an investigation into how this was set up. Who said what to whom, the precise paper trail, or digital trail more like, of instructions given to Hatchet. And since you mention our colleagues in Special Branch, how involved is *their* man in this operation? Is he in a position to be aware of Hatchet, for example?'

'No,' Blenkinsop reassured him. 'His involvement seems to have ceased in Glasgow before Armoury was spirited back to Edinburgh and from there to the EU.'

Dunan said: 'We think he made a serious error there, boss. He had his man right there, with the target but he pulled him back. Crazy!'

'That is odd,' Thorpe concluded. 'He builds up confidence and the bona-fides of his agent then removes him and lets the target walk? But this operation of theirs was not mentioned in this room, was it? They never confided in *us*?'

'No – not until recently, so we simply returned the favour.'

Thorpe cleared his throat then sat back. 'Right. And where in all *is* Sangster? We know he must be in Edinburgh. Are they hiding him, do you think?'

'I can't see that,' Blenkinsop muttered. 'That would be going too far and our liaison officer, McLennan would have had to disclose it.'

'We don't trust him at all but we think he trusts us a little!' Dunan grinned. 'Tweedy tosser!'

'Colleagues, that's no way to speak of our sister organisation!' Thorpe rebuked him with a lop-sided smile. 'Perhaps now is the time to pre-empt this by directly asking them if they *have* made contact with Sangster? Maybe even drop a hint that we suspect Sangster has had special help from them?'

'Nice one. Keep them on the back foot.'

'But as to Armoury. There will be repercussions. This could turn into a steaming crock of shit. We need to work out how to proceed. Also how to finesse our contact with Special Branch. We need to list all those who might start to jump up and down when it is disclosed that Armoury has disappeared and produce a list of actions we have taken to try to find him. Richard and Saul, you'd better continue on that task. Joe and Maureen establish last points and times of contact. We still need to locate Sangster, but perhaps that will have to wait for a while, till the dust settles on this.'

Police Scotland's A Divisional headquarters in Stewart Street, Glasgow, is a Cubist's dream, introverted, defensive. Its three-storeyed facade is striped in dark blue, pale blue, dark blue dotted with distinctive small, square white-framed windows. A Cubist's dream, it looks introverted, defensive. The taxi had taken them through city centre streets of umbrellas and traffic lights and rush hour buses. Crossing Cowcaddens Road into McPhater Street, it traversed the base of a tower block and lines of cars parked in Maitland Street and delivered Emily and Marco to the front door ramp under the large silver-on-blue logo of Police Scotland.

Emily got out and saw, at the end of the street, six concrete tiers of walkways leading into Council flats.

Inside the foyer, Martin Masterson MSP, the youthfully slim but balding Justice Secretary was waiting for them by the lifts, a serious expression on his sharp-featured pale face.

He came forward. 'Professor McKechnie, good to see you again. This is Adrian Thompson my PPS and Shirley Edwards is my Admin Secretary. You must be Marco?'

'Aye, that's me. Cheers.'

'Right, now we're all here, we'd better go up,' Masterson said.

The room on the top floor was functional – no frills. Its small square windows looked out onto a spaghetti junction of wet roads, including two elevated sections of the M8. As they entered, one of the two men sitting there, a short bulky man at the far side of the table stood up and came forward. Nearly bald, he had thick grey mutton-chop sideburns. He wore a grey suit in a way that indicated he didn't normally wear suits; the collar of his checked shirt stuck up awkwardly, an old-fashioned war-torn tie that might have been green or grey. 'I'm Chief Inspector Colin McLennan,' he muttered and shook hands with the Justice Secretary and no-one else, Emily noticed. 'This is Detective Sergeant Rankine.' The DS was a bulky youth whose cheery face and small pink mouth contrasted with an ugly scar above his right eye running though his eyebrow.

'Hello.' Introductions made, they sat down around a table that was clearly too small for six. By some intuitive notion of inverse importance, DS Rankine and Shirley Edwards pulled over two aluminium chairs and sat alongside. Shirley Edwards pulled out a Dictaphone and a notebook. Seeing the Dictaphone, the Justice Secretary said: 'Ah, yes, just to inform you, this meeting will be recorded, if that's alright, Chief Inspector? For note-taking purposes, once the transcript is made and approved by you, the recording will be destroyed.'

'Aye, of course.' McLennan sat back and loosened his constricting wool tie. 'Now I was told you wanted a discussion about a missing journalist?'

Masterson opened the file in front of him. 'Perhaps I should outline our concerns and then we can summarise the questions we need answered. The journalist, William Morton – who is a friend of Professor McKechnie and Mr Vanetti here – went missing while in the company of one Luke Sangster after they met up in Clachtoll in Assynt. Then they had a meeting in Glasgow and then both completely disappeared. That was,' he paused, checking his notes, 'five days ago.'

Marco coughed into his hand. 'Excuse me. Willie went to Assynt because I got a phone call.' He told the meeting about the brief call he had received and their subsequent reservations about it. 'We now know that the call was fake.'

Masterson frowned. 'How…?'

'Because the real Luke Sangster has been in Edinburgh all along. Never went to Assynt or Glasgow. Never made a phone call to me.'

'I see,' Masterson sat back. 'Good grief. Do you mean someone…?'

'Someone with malevolent intent has lured Willie up to Assynt,' Emily told him. 'And then back to Glasgow and now, goodness knows where he is!'

'Can you shed any light on this, Chief Inspector?'

McLennan sighed deeply and hunched forward at the desk. 'Aye, I can. I know a little about it. This is what I know. I was aware of Morton's journey to Assynt to meet Sangster. And the subsequent meeting in Glasgow with Brodagh Murdoch but that's all I know. What happened next is not known to me, or my colleagues, however, as you are aware, we are not the only organisation monitoring these kinds of groups and individuals.' He sighed deeply and hesitated. 'I am rather constrained here, Minister, as you know I cannot discuss operational details or even remits. Although if you were to request specific information, I would be able to…'

'Other organisations?' Emily queried. 'You mean British spooks?'

McLennan looked at her for a long moment, then at the Justice Secretary, who nodded. 'Well,' McLennan continued, 'we have a close liaison with MI5's Scotland Station, here in Glasgow. They have also been monitoring Luke Sangster. Of course, that's all they are entitled to do. Monitoring. He came to their notice because of his hacking activities, but MI5 have no powers of arrest in Scotland, as you know, Minister.'

'Correct. That is why the liaison process is so important.'

'Yes, we do have regular liaison of operations like this, where our operatives are active alongside theirs. Both our organisations had been apparently unable to locate Sangster. But for a while, I have had my suspicions that they are not fully sharing all of their knowledge with us. For example, if it *was* Luke Sangster that Morton went to Assynt to meet, why did they not tell me? They didn't, even although I found out from our own operatives. I waited to see if they would tell me, but they never did. According to them, Morton's trip north was for some unspecified reason and they kept that up, even though I got to know that that wasn't true. We were already aware of the circumstances of the meeting with Brodagh Murdoch and what the intention behind it was…'

'What do you mean, Chief Inspector?' Masterson asked. 'The *intention*? Brodagh is a friend of mine.'

'This is little more than speculation, but it looks like they wanted to enmesh her in the activities of this hacker and the group. Get her involved, for whatever reason.'

'Entrap Brodagh?' Emily said. 'That's outrageous!'

'I didn't use that word,' McLennan reproved. 'But you may be right. My colleagues in MI5 are a little bit more…'

Masterson intervened. 'A little bit more what?'

'Gung-ho, I suppose. They don't like mysteries, want to link everybody up into one big conspiracy. Get them all in the same bag.' McLennan's smile caught them off-guard. 'You know what I mean, they think everybody up here is a rabid Nat.'

Emily and Marco exchanged glances. Masterson frowned. 'I'm going to have to take action with my UK counterpart if this is true,' he said. 'Are you indicating to me, Chief

Inspector, that the liaison between Special Branch and MI5 is not working properly?'

McLennan frowned, thought for a moment, shrugged. 'I have my suspicions and I don't mind admitting it. As far as I am concerned, we are the senior investigating force in Scotland and should be able to report to you, as the Justice Secretary, that we are fully aware of everything that is going on in Scotland, but I can't. They' – he gestured peremptorily – 'have never really accepted devolution or the fact that Police Scotland, the Scottish Police Authority and ultimately you, as Justice Secretary, are in charge of all policing and security matters in Scotland. They believe they are the senior force, and should answer to no-one except the Chief of the Joint Intelligence Committee and the Prime Minister, ultimately.'

'That's a grave criticism you are making,' Masterson said. 'And I'll be sure to raise these matters with the Cabinet and the First Minister, though I'm not convinced there is anything we can do about it. Security and Intelligence matters are reserved and there is undoubtedly a grey area in terms of authority. As I know only too well.' He smiled grimly. 'Yes, I've been put in my place more than once.'

Emily sighed. 'Yes, that's well-known, or perhaps not so well-known to the public, although it's a grey area that no-one wants to talk about. The Scottish Government in its sixteen years of existence has soft-pedalled on the issue and let the UK Government take precedence. When MI5 opened their Scotland Station in Glasgow and the smaller office in Edinburgh, it was partly to improve liaison. And partly to show an acceptance of devolution, albeit belatedly.'

'Yes, that's right,' McLennan agreed. 'That was the plan. And I wouldn't say there *hasn't* been some effective liaison. I hope I'm not giving that impression? Just that it breaks down from time to time. Some of their operatives are, well, *arrogant* is the word I would use. Others are better. Don't get me wrong. There has to be operational liaison, but in this case, on this investigation, in this operation, I suspect there's been a lot less than complete openness and transparency. This is highly sensitive, but I believe that the person Morton believes to be Luke Sangster, the *fake* as you referred to him, the person he met in Assynt, could be an operative of MI5.'

'Surely not! That would be going too far!' The comment came from Adrian Thompson, the young floppy-haired PPS to the Justice Secretary. 'I apologise,' he added, conscious that he should be listening and not contributing. No-one registered the remark anyway as if everyone present thought that they had made it themselves.

'I'm sorry but that's the conclusion I've come to,' McLennan told them, gesturing with his hand. 'We initially suspected that Sangster had been removed from the scene with MI5 help. It was difficult to believe that he could have evaded our search so effectively without assistance but there were no traces at all. And that's unusual. We suspected he was dead.' He saw the alarmed looks on the faces of Emily and Marco and coughed discreetly. 'What I mean is, at that time, we suspected it, as a possibility. Now of course we are told he is at large, and alive. But the point is, he then turns up unexpectedly in Assynt, an out-of-the-way place. Very unusual. Then there was the apparent need this person had to contact Brodagh. It looked odd to us, like a fishing expedition. And there was something not right about this person purporting to be Luke – the fake – as we now know. Hence my suspicions.'

'And how do you know all this? I mean, the insights about the *fake*?

McLennan smiled wryly. 'We had our own source very close to the operation, who was in direct contact with Morton and this other… the fake.'

'I see,' Masterson said, raising his eyebrows, 'or rather, I don't see, but what does your source say about Morton's whereabouts now? Is he – or she – still in contact with him?'

'I can't really go into operational details but no, my source is not now in contact with him. The last-known piece of information we have is that Morton bought a ticket to Edinburgh from Glasgow Queen Street railway station. That was on Tuesday morning at 11.02 a.m. Five days ago. He has not left the country.'

'Yes, we know that. We have his passport which was in his flat,' Emily said. 'What needs to happen now is… put pressure on MI5 to reveal what more they know. If their agent is involved, god knows where Willie is.'

Masterson agreed. 'Yes. We will do that. We need to get to the bottom of what they've been up to, as a matter of urgency. I will brief the Chief Constable tonight and get him to request an urgent review with his counterpart at the Joint Intelligence Committee. From the very top.'

'And I thought you were the very top,' Marco muttered.

Sitting beside him, Emily's mobile phone buzzed and she stiffened. She took it out from under the table and saw it was from 'unknown number'.

'Good grief!' she exclaimed and jumped up, knocking the table. Everyone looked at her.

CHAPTER TWENTY-FIVE

'Hello… hello…' Emily stood up, mobile clamped to her ear, everyone watching her in anticipation. She listened for what seemed to them like ages, possibly a full minute, then with a great exhalation of breath said: 'Ah, thank god you're safe!

'It's *him*?' Marco mouthed, but Emily was too engrossed, straining to hear. It seemed so happy a coincidence that everyone in the room wanted to believe, not to be disappointed, but no-one yet knew for certain. Then Emily smiled and gestured '– Willie.' And everyone exhaled in relief. 'Where are you? *Sweden*? What on earth? How…? Right. I see. I will. Text me that. Of course. I'm in a meeting in Glasgow with the Justice Secretary, Special Branch, Marco, we're all here. So glad. Right, you do that. I will, okay. Speak soon love, bye.'

Emily sat down, closed her eyes and sat still for a minute. No-one said anything. Finally, she cleared her throat and said, in an emotional voice. 'That was Willie. He's in Sweden. The man persuaded him to go in a fishing boat to Denmark. Apparently it was advice from Brodagh Murdoch.'

Matheson started. 'What? *Brodagh?* Why?'

Emily looked from him to Marco. 'I've no idea why she would suggest such a thing. Then he – this man – drove him to a remote forest, hit him over the head and left him. But he was rescued and now he is safe, in Gothenburg. He's asked me to post him his passport so he can get home.'

The tension dissipated and everyone began to talk at once. Marco and Emily awkwardly embraced while sitting down. 'So pleased fur ye,' he said. 'Poor old Willie.'

'Right,' Masterson said. 'Well, that's amazing. Astonishing. But this fake has a lot to answer for. That's attempted murder, no question. Who is he?'

'But why would Willie go there with him? Would Brodagh really give them such advice? That doesnae make any sense,' Marco said.

'What doesn't make sense is why you didn't know anything about it, Chief Inspector,' Masterson said. 'It's all happened behind your back.'

'Yes,' McLennan agreed, bitterly. 'But it's pretty clear who's behind it. I've never come across this before. This is way beyond their remit. Five have no business operating outside the UK. The man must be a support agent, a freelance or contractor maybe. Arrogant doesn't even begin to cover it. But we need to be cautious. We must keep this to ourselves.'

Everyone turned to look at the Chief Inspector.

'What do you mean?' Masterson asked slowly.

'If the man took him there, and left him, that's attempted murder right enough,' McLennan stated. 'And for sure he isn't working alone. If, as we believe, he was ordered to do it, then they, whoever they are – and we mustn't assume we do know who they are – might try again. Their agent is probably still in the area. If they get to hear Morton has *survived*… well, they might try again, stop him telling what he knows.'

'Of course!' Masterson said, frowning.

Emily turned pale and fainted, dropping her mobile phone on the table.

'Glass of water please,' McLennan said, 'DS Rankine can you…?'

Shirley Edwards, the Admin Officer, filled a paper cup from the watercooler in the corner of the room, took it over to Emily who had already come out of her faint. Someone took her specs off and held them while she sipped water.

'Thank you, so sorry for disrupting the meeting. I'm alright, honestly. It was just the shock of...'

'Yes. Getting the call,' Masterson said. 'You must have been under a lot of strain.'

'No, it wasn't that. It was hearing that he might still be in danger.'

'It *is* possible,' McLennan said. 'But I intend to take steps to ensure that he isn't. We'll take immediate action to liaise with the Swedish authorities. I'll send a good man out there, to work with them and bring Morton safely home. He's in Gothenburg? Right, I'll need the number of his mobile phone. Presumably it's not his own phone, I mean, it'll be a new one? We'll keep contact at a minimum in case of hostile surveillance.'

'Right, Chief Inspector,' Masterson said, rubbing his hands, 'that sounds good. We're relying on you. And we will keep this matter private until we know he's safe. In the meantime, my briefing to the Chief Constable and the nature of it, will alter to reflect what we now know or suspect.'

'And you're sending someone out?' Emily asked. 'When I speak to Willie can I tell him that?'

McLennan sighed. 'Yes, you could. Keep the calls short but reassure him we're working hard to get him safely home. Tell him it's someone he already knows. Someone he can trust. That's all I can say for now.'

Willie ended the call in the huge Nordstan shopping centre two streets across from the railway station, practically outside the shop where he had bought the phone. He felt a sense of being reborn. He had escaped and was enjoying little things like the evening sunlight on his face, the newness of an historic old city like Gothenburg, the pleasure of having time to stroll the wide streets and boulevards. Emily would send his passport out and until then he needed a place to sleep. It might take several days for the passport to arrive. He thought it might be difficult to check in to big hotels because he had no passport or ID but if he could find a smaller place, perhaps a guesthouse, where they spoke English, he might be able to convince them that it had been stolen and that a replacement was on its way. There'd been no problem in the small guesthouse at Värnamo. No-one there had asked for passports or ID. He didn't want any police involvement. Once his passport arrived, he'd buy a ticket and fly home. It was an hour and a half to Edinburgh. He crossed a canal, enjoying the waning sunshine, wandered around the edge of a tree-lined park into the heart of the city; a wide boulevard busy with cafes, bistros and music hang-outs. Following a sign that had a ship on it, he found himself in a curious district of trendy flats, chic design studios and shops selling art materials. There were a few antique shops. He was intrigued by the sight of marzipan-makers in white chef's hats and overalls pummelling almonds on marble worktops in a basement bakery. The streets became narrower, cobbled. Most of the houses here were stone at the ground level with two wooden storeys above. There were B&Bs here too with a variety of Swedish names. He felt anonymous and safe away from the busy centre. A hundred yards along he spotted a sign angled out from a pink harled wall: Buck House B&B. It made him smile. He crossed the cobbled street to look more closely. The windows were whorled glass, like an old English cottage. It was small, probably only a few rooms, and quirky.

The owner must be English or have a UK connection. This might be a good place to try. He went up three steps beside the potted geraniums and rang the bell.

A face appeared in the whorled glass pane of the doorway. A young old man in denims and black running vest opened the door. He was bald but exuded a youthful vigour. White body hair at the neck of the vest that stretched over a six-pack appeared on his muscular arms and shoulders. Bare feet in flip-flops, he looked like an athlete or an artist. He smiled down at Morton. 'Can I help you?'

'You speak English? I am looking for a room for a few days but I have a problem.'

The man's face widened into a joyful smile. 'Ah! You have no money?'

Morton frowned. 'No. I have money but no passport or ID. It is being sent on to me.'

The man made an elaborate gesture of welcome towards Morton and stepped back a pace. 'Then you have no problem my friend. I am Johan. Welcome to Buck House. Come.'

Morton followed him into a varnished wood-lined hallway festooned with mirrors in ornate carved frames and miniature oil paintings.

'Come into the kitchen. We have a cup of English tea.'

Morton chuckled. 'A cup of tea in Buck House!'

Johan turned and searched his face. 'You like the name? I used to watch on the TV Spitting Image. And being an old queen myself…'

'Ha!' Morton chuckled.

'So now I need to look out my Tupperware!'

Morton got the joke. 'Best china will do.'

'Of course. Nothing but the best for my guests. You will be happy here. Home from home as you say. But you are not

English, I think? And how does it happen that you are here but your passport is not?'

Morton told Johan a complicated story of airports and baggage and implied that he had got through the EU Nothing to Declare line at the airport without even noticing he didn't have it.

'Earl Grey tea is your preference? With a slice of lemon?'

'Fine.'

'Then I will introduce you to Cleopatra, the house cat. She reigns here, this is her kingdom.'

The Justice Secretary offered Emily and Marco a lift to the station after the meeting as it was raining heavily. Three of them squeezed in the back of the Government Mondeo. Adrian Thompson sat up front next to the driver.

'I don't mind telling you I'm furious at the turn of events,' Masterson said as the car swept onto Cowcaddens Drive. 'It's outrageous that this is happening in Scotland on our watch. We're supposed to be the Government with full authority over policing matters and they treat us like this.'

'Yes, well,' Emily said. 'We know the history. Scottish Governments have always been afraid to rock the boat on such matters, always deferring. And you know why.'

The windscreen wipers did four sweeps of the screen, clearing the pattern of red and green drops of water as they waited at traffic lights. Masterson nodded sadly. 'Aye. Politicians up here are nervous of an area they don't have much experience of. Security and intelligence. In the referendum it was a subject we tried to avoid and we were hammered for it. I was aware of that although we are developing experience and competence now alongside Police Scotland as that beds in. And it's not been easy so far.'

'You can say that again!' Emily agreed. 'Little short of catastrophic. A lot of bad luck too. Internal squabbles. Bad blood left over from re-organisation. Hopefully it will bed down soon.'

'But we're damned if we do and damned if we don't, Emily. Of course, our ultimate aim must be a separate Scottish Intelligence Service. Huh – we could call it SIS!' He made a mournful attempt at a smile. 'Or perhaps not. Like the Irish whose DJ2 and NSIS services were commended by the UK Joint Intelligence Committee as a model of co-operative effort in the Five Eyes alliance. We would be the very same. We could be the Sixth Eye. Or the Seventh, because Ireland is really the Sixth. They've a separate service but just get lumped in as 'Britain & Ireland' when it suits Whitehall. Well, we could be in the same category. Madness to suggest otherwise, in fact. But in the meantime, if we complain of being ignored or mistreated, or if we cause any problems at all, they threaten to make it look like we are trying to weaken the UK's defensive shield against potential terrorist threats. They accuse us of inexperience, being incompetent, unfit to handle security matters. Or worse, as potential traitors. They would stir a tabloid storm against us.'

'Not easy,' Emily conceded. 'But we can work inside the liaison partnership. Than man McLennan looks like he takes things personally.'

'Yes, first time I've met him. I usually deal higher up the food chain – Chief Constable level – it was refreshing to meet someone at the sharp end. Oh and by the way, Emily, I intend to give Brodagh a call this evening to get to the bottom of that advice she gave them to flee the UK illegally. Doesn't ring true to me. Not the Brodagh I know. But we'll see.'

'That's good,' Emily agreed. 'Let us know what she says.

Yes, the Chief Inspector was very frank about them not giving full disclosure. We can work on that, make them respond and open up. I wouldn't like to get on the wrong side of Colin McLennan!'

Marco agreed. 'Aye, that man looks the part alright. I'm glad he's on our side and that's the first time I've ever said that of Special Branch! I must be cracking up.'

Marco and Emily caught the next train to Edinburgh and as it was nearly 8 p.m. their carriage was almost empty. They discussed the meeting, going over what Masterson had said, what McLennan had said. They had just stopped at Falkirk when Emily's phone rang. 'Willie,' she exclaimed. After a few minutes of conversation, she fumbled with her right hand in her handbag looking for a pen. Marco handed her his notebook and pen.

'Say again, Willie.' Emily wrote down his temporary address in Gothenburg. 'Okay, you take care. Keep your head down until it arrives. There might be a problem with the man who… they might still be looking for you… to hurt you… please take care. Can you get WhatsApp? So we can keep in contact more safely? They might be listening in to me.'

As the train passed Linlithgow, Emily sat back, numerous worries flitting across her mind's eye. 'Marco, I wish I hadn't made him read his address over an open line. That was stupid. What do you think?'

'Don't worry, Emily. They're not going to try anything now that the Special Branch are onto them.'

'But they don't know that yet, do they?'

'Well, no, but they think Willie is lying dead in a forest somewhere.'

'Oh God, just think. Poor Willie.' Emily had a sudden

thought. 'Why post the passport? Why don't I fly over there and take it to him? It'd be a lot quicker.'

Marco sighed. 'I don't think you should do that. Tempting as it sounds. They might have us under surveillance. You might end up leading them to him. Much better to post it tomorrow – special courier – that'll get to him in twenty-four hours without alerting anyone.'

'You're right. Unless they can intercept mail to Sweden?'

'How could they do that? No. That's a bit far-fetched isn't it?'

'Well, it is tempting. I'd love to see his face if I turned up with it.'

'We've got to stick to the plan, Emily. It's the safest way. You know something funny?'

'What?'

'At the meeting, no-one actually mentioned Luke, the real one! Did you notice? That's what all this was supposed to be about!'

'You're right. That's weird. Apart from mentioning that he was in Edinburgh alive and well, no-one asked us anything more about him.'

'Once Willie's safely home, we'll get the Justice Secretary to look into that too.'

'I'm not sure I'll be able to sleep tonight. I feel jittery.'

'Try to relax. Willie's in a safe place. Good people are doing their best to get him safely home.'

CHAPTER TWENTY-SIX

Morton found the first floor room in Buck House B&B in Husagarten perfect for his needs; comfortable and anonymous, the window looked across the street above dwarf tulips growing in a window sill planter. He sat on the bed and breathed in the lavender scent of the pillows. There was a residual tiredness at the back of his eye sockets. It did not seem that twenty-four hours had passed since he had been lost in the forest of Ogeström. It had been a close call, he had been lucky! But he had come through it. He would make it home to Emily. He was reminded about WhatsApp and immediately downloaded the app, using the free broadband, watching the clock graphic complete the installation. He opened it and added Emily's mobile number. Immediately it located his two calls and he added Emily's name in his empty contacts list. Once again, he began musing about why he had let himself be persuaded… the image of the man came into his mind's eye. A spasm of incoherent anger passed quickly. Now he was safe he wanted to track him down. Not revenge, just a need to find out the truth about him. Who was he? Who did he work for? Who had issued the orders to drive him to that forest and leave him for dead? He glanced at his watch. It was 9.15 p.m. An hour ahead of Edinburgh, there was still light in the sky. He decided to take a stroll and get something to eat.

He tucked the mobile into the top pocket of Hammi's

jacket and went out, pausing to stroke the languorous Persian cat at the bottom of the stairs.

It was mild in the street, even warm and there were a lot of people about. He took the street that looked the busiest, Haga Nygata. It was a pedestrians-only zone. Soon he came to a square with statues and large trees, trams gliding past, signs to the Stena Line ferry terminal, and in the distance the high bridge. There was a Burger King, a coffee shop, a couple of snack joints nearby. Further on a vegetarian restaurant and then he saw a neon sign, Feske Nils.

It was a low-roofed glass-fronted place, smart and comfortable. He went in. Although there were few diners, he waited until a slim blonde waitress came over and ushered him to a table near the door.

'I'd prefer to sit in the window, if you don't mind?'

'Ah, yes, you are English?' She beamed her wide smile.

'Something like that.'

'Perhaps over here?' She led him to a cloth-draped table for two that had a view out over the square where the streetlights were casting light and shadows on the pavement under the lines of trees. He studied the menu which was in English and Swedish and ordered a steak, chips, salad and beer. When his beer came he studied it for a moment or two, the condensation on the glass, the frothy head. He took a sip, savoured it, the hoppy flavour like being reacquainted with an old friend. It tasted great and all the better as he reflected philosophically on his lucky escape. He was back in the land of the living.

Saul Dunan and Richard Blenkinsop were in the Mondeo on their way to the Baird Street Police Station to meet Colin McLennan. He had left them a message asking to meet on 'an urgent matter'. A call from Desmond Thorpe came over the car radio.

'Two things you need to know, guys. Surveillance has discovered the location of Sangster. We're sending a team to the address to apprehend him.'

Blenkinsop was in the passenger seat. 'Okay. That's our shout, surely? We're happy to do that.' He winked at Dunan who was driving. 'Too bad about the liaison meeting.'

Thorpe's voice, with a brittle edge of command, cut across as if he was in the car. 'No, not you two! Attend the liaison as requested. Find out what this 'urgent matter' is. Give nothing away, about either Armoury or Sangster, and try to see where they are at. Have they got wind of anything? Keep it low-key. And, Saul, try to avoid antagonising him. You know who I mean?'

'As if, boss!'

'Okay,' Blenkinsop replied. 'Anything else we should know?'

'Sangster's in Leith,' Thorpe told them. No idea how he eluded us for so long. I'll get the other team to pick him up in the early hours. And meanwhile, Hatchet will fade into the ether.'

'Right. That's clear.'

'One other thing that might be relevant. Armoury's girl-friend – Professor McKechnie – got a call from an unidentified number in Scandinavia an hour ago. Digint are liaising with GCHQ on narrowing down the call location details through telecoms providers and local masts. It's odd though, isn't it? You need to check this with Hatchet. Has there been some slip-up?"

There was silence in the Mondeo as Dunan parked in the Staff section of the carpark behind a line of trees across from the main entrance.

'Unidentified number in Scandinavia?' Blenkinsop said. 'That's sounds decidedly fishy. We'd better call Hatchet after the meeting.'

'Sounds like a cock-up right enough. Look, nothing to lose, Richard, let's try and rile the tweedy tosser now and see what comes out. I mean, let's accuse him straight out of assisting Sangster's escape. See what he says. See if he's aware Sangster's been found – or if the fucker knew all along where he was.'

'Attack being the best form of defence you mean? Good idea.'

'Yeah, and let them know we're aware of their little meeting. McKechnie was there so it must have been about Armoury, though they've not given us a sniff. I think they must be co-ordinating a search. Bringing in the heavy artillery.'

Blenkinsop scoffed. 'Heavy artillery? Masterson? He's a lightweight. More like a water-pistol than a howitzer. Out of his depth. Anyway, we'll soon know what it was about.'

Dunan frowned as they walked across the car park. 'How do you mean?'

'Well, he's going to tell us, isn't he? One way or another.'

Dunan squinted at him. 'I shouldn't have thought so, boss.'

'Watch and learn. Watch and learn.'

There is no doubt that there are lovelier places to dine in Glasgow than the staff canteen of the Police Scotland station in Baird Street where shifts of uniforms and plain-clothes boys from various Divisions mingled to eat. It was in serious need of repainting and the plasterwork needed repairs. The yellow walls gleamed with condensation. The windows, located above head height, let in a dim, poor light attenuated at all times of the day and night by electric strip lighting. They were entirely opaque due a layer of grime that could not be cleaned because of iron grilles protecting them. The place was functional, the food basic though hot and plentiful, cooked and served by a team of stout, no-nonsense Glasgow ladies of a certain age. No matter how busy the canteen was, you could find a table even at peak times. It was like the dining room of a modern Dotheboys Hall. Except that you could always get more. Another dollop of whatever. The place was still half full, Saul Dunan saw, even though it was gone 9.30 p.m. McLennan was already there, at a table against the far wall and he had a colleague with him, a tall young man in a grey suit, with sandy hair.

'He's at eleven o'clock, boss,' Dunan muttered. 'Looks like he has his bagman with him.'

'I see him. Let me do the talking, okay.'

'You're welcome.'

'Chief Inspector.' Blenkinsop approached the table. McLennan looked up. He was eating a piece of millionaire shortbread and drinking a yellow mug of tea.

'Sit down, ye're blocking ma light. This here is DS Rankine, one of my team. Ken – this is Blenkinsop and Dunan, Five's version of Laurel and Hardy.'

'Very funny!' Blenkinsop muttered, sitting on the wooden bench opposite the two Special Branch men. 'Right, what's so bloody urgent we have to come all the way here on a Saturday night?'

McLennan grinned sourly and half-turned to DS Rankine. 'See that's what we need in our team: manners and sheer enthusiasm!'

Rankine's cheery face lit up in a smirk and his pal eyebrows lifted the trace of a scar. He was young, Dunan thought, early twenties, straight out of uniform probably or more likely months out from graduation. He shuffled along the bench clutching his folder in front of him, wondering if he was tougher than he looked, or just a flabby boy.

'Okay,' McLennan said, scowling. 'Now we've just came from a meeting with the Justice Secretary no less. Where we were hauled over the bloody coals about this missing journalist, Morton – Armoury your cryptonym – and practically accused of doing away with him.'

'Oh, my heart bleeds for you,' Blenkinsop smirked.

McLennan gave him the stare. The look famous in the city of Glasgow that invented it. The Saturday night stare, preparatory to 'putting the heid on' as described in a hundred city tourist guides.

Blenkinsop coughed and looked away from the serious stare that searched his soul and found him trembling. 'What I mean is,' he said apologetically, is there any truth to it?'

'What the *fuck*?' McLennan exploded as his fist hit the table top. 'Truth?' Is that the word they're learning you now, boy? The disappearance of Armoury is nothing to do with us, as you damn well know, but you – you know all about it!'

'*What*?' Blenkinsop challenged but it was unconvincing from the off. 'We had come to the conclusion that Armoury was…' He hesitated at the vital moment, searching for a less confrontational way of putting it. '… getting some kind of assistance from local police or Special Branch.'

'Oh you *did*? See that, Rankine. Lesson one: when faced with an accusation, accuse the accuser. Well, let's look at the facts? I put my cards on the table. This is what we know. My man Condor was with Armoury when by some mysterious tip-off, the missing hacker Sangster is revealed to be in Assynt, hours up the bloody road. He goes there to meet him and by all accounts this supposed missing hacker is a strange bloody kettle of fish altogether. But, nevertheless, Armoury is convinced by him, or convinced enough to go with him to Glasgow to try to meet up with Brodagh Murdoch. So we have this farce of a journey up to the north and back again, like the Grand Old Duke of York. But Murdoch, wise old owl, spots him a mile off and declines to help him. Then, well, then, they disappear. Armoury buys a ticket for Edinburgh but never gets on the bloody train. No FR scans, no sightings, no financial transactions, no CCTV. This is what we know for certain, yes?'

Blenkinsop nodded. 'We've been over this already.'

'So the last known location is Queen Street Station at...' he glanced at DS Rankine, who quickly scanned the document in the folder.

Rankine cleared his throat. 'Um, ticket purchased at 11.02 a.m.'

'What's your point?' Dunan said. 'We know this.'

McLennan was staring them out, both fists on the table. For a long few seconds no-one spoke. Then McLennan inhaled deeply. 'The point is... what happened at Queen Street Station at 11.03?

'We don't know that, do we?' Dunan protested.

'You bloody well *do*!' McLennan snarled. 'Did you not think we would get video footage from the station concourse? Took us a while to find it, but we got there in the end. Didn't we, DS Rankine? And what did it show?'

'An altercation sir, on the concourse,' Rankine replied.

'An altercation, yes.' He grinned bitterly. 'Want to tell me about it *now*?'

Blenkinsop and Dunan glanced at each other. This was unexpected. The CCTV footage was supposed to have been deleted by the techies of A Branch. How could he have retrieved it? But they couldn't be sure. Was he bluffing? They'd have to try and find out.

Blenkinsop sat back and tried to plot ahead a few moves. He had to be ambiguous, give nothing away but seem to co-operate. There really couldn't be footage with them on it. The tech boys didn't make that kind of mistake. On the other hand, this was Scotland, they did things differently here. Maybe Police Scotland had deeper access? 'I'm not sure what game you're trying to play here, Chief Inspector,' he said. 'It's a fact that Queen Street station is the last known sighting and I'm sure you tried to obtain CCTV footage there – as we did – but there is none. By the time we looked, it had been taped-over, if it was ever recorded at all.'

'Not so, sonny. There's good clear video, perfect quality. Could show it on *Reporting Scotland*. And you know what's on it, or *who's* on it?'

'Why don't you tell us?' Dunan intervened, smirking. He was enjoying the confrontational nature of the encounter.

'I don't need to, do I? You already know.'

'You're bluffing of course,' Blenkinsop said quietly. 'But I just don't know why or what you expect to gain. There is no footage as you well know. First thing we looked for. So come on, what's your point? Why are we here?'

McLennan calmly stroked his sideburn, left elbow on the table, the fingers of his right tapping the table top. 'Okay, here it is, the lowdown, the point, the shit hitting the fan… you're correct. Yes. There is no CCTV footage any more. Oh yes, there *was*. There should have been, but some bloody spooks came in and destroyed it. Oh that was you. We know it was you. No point in trying to deny it.'

Blenkinsop sat back and smirked. 'Well you can say that…'

Dunan shook his head. 'You had us all going then. What a story! Almost had us believing you.'

McLennan had a weird smile on his face as he suddenly winked at DS Rankine and that friendly gesture threw Blenkinsop and Dunan into a panic more than his blaspheming or violent moods might have done.

'But what you overlooked,' he said forcefully, pointing at them with two fingers extended like a pistol. 'Is there is *other* coverage of the station from 11.03 to 11.06 a.m. that clearly shows what happened, the… altercation. Oh yes. We have footage. See, we did a social media sweep of the location at the time in question and we have several minutes of footage. And what it shows…'

Blenkinsop and Dunan exchanged quick glances. It might still be a bluff but this was not playing out as they had expected.

'… and what it shows is clear. Armoury and Sangster attacked by two men who bear a very, very close resemblance to you two. You grab Armoury and Sangster, there's a struggle, they get away and run out of the station.' He sat back and folded his arms.

'Okay, it's a fair cop,' Dunan said provocatively. 'So what? We were doing our jobs but they got away. So. Big crime – didn't mention it in our report.'

'No, you didn't, did you? But you see that's what happens when you fight in a public place. Some people call the police, some people actually join in. Isn't that right, DS Rankine?'

The DS nodded, serious-faced. 'Aye, that's right sir.'

'Yes, that happens here in Glasgow,' McLennan grinned. 'A lot. But also people whip out their mobiles and film it. Everybody has a mobile and everybody is looking for a good punch-up to put on Facebook or Instagram. So you didn't mention the incident and you didn't mention that you got your people to remove the CCTV footage too. And the reason why you went to all that trouble is in the last few seconds of the footage. It's absolutely clear.' He pointed his finger-gun at each of them in turn. 'You start to run after them, then you stop, let them get away although you could easily have caught them – given they were hampered by rucksacks – instead, you stop in the entrance to the station and give each other a high-five! How the *fuck* do you explain that?'

CHAPTER TWENTY-SEVEN

Sunday morning in Edinburgh. Litter lifted by a hesitant wind shuffled back and forth along sticky pavements of the Cowgate beside over-stuffed litterbins. Early double-decker buses with few passengers made headway over South Bridge. Too early for tourists, the Royal Mile deserted, even the kilt emporia and the vendors of Jimmy wigs were closed. Waverley had yet to disgorge the first of its day's horde of visitors. Grey on grey masonry, iron railings, the smell of last-night's beer, seagulls swoop on remains of takeaways; curry stains on polystyrene. At the Kiosk on Bank Street, newspapers are displayed in perspex sections at the door. The spry, grey bearded newsagent, Ahmed Asif, was rather too full of the joys and the lights were too bright in this time zone between the streetlights going off and the natural light of dawn.

And for Sunday readers, the usual tabloid guff; half-truths at best, at worst, downright mendacity, prurient finger-pointing, secret sins exposed (again), new instalments of royal arse-licking by prominent toadies, rabid Nat-baiting *ad nauseam*. The formerly austere broadsheets lapsing too into this lexicon, albeit with longer words, although they too had shrunk to fit the new mentality, the diminished attention span.

Out of this swamp of information/misinformation, diversion and dalliance, the discerning reader would perhaps select the *Scottish Standard on Sunday*, and head homeward to cereal and toast, marmalade, coffee. Prop the paper up against the milk jug, peruse, eat, defecate, urinate, repeat. Drink, read, peruse and inwardly digest.

At the top of page four, the head and shoulders photograph was of a man in his forties described as a long-term contributor to the *Standard*, but the strapline in sixty-four point Myriad Pro bold was: 'Mystery over Abduction of Journalist' by Staff Writer. The reader, scanning the article, might have felt the lack of detail and substance; there was little evidence of the 'abduction' angle. Perhaps Morton was simply missing, out on a spree, had forgotten to phone home, or over-slept for five days? Or was lying dead somewhere, or had fallen foul of criminals… Or? It seemed a little self-indulgent or premature though the writer had thoughtfully appended details of Mr Morton's previous 'disappearances' and his run-ins with secret police agencies. But this was not the Middle East or South America the reader might smugly conclude. Our Mr Morton will reappear, tail – no doubt – firmly between his legs, safe and sound. The apocryphal reader then turned to the Sports pages and died of a surfeit of fitba guff.

Eighty five miles away, Ross Mackie was up and about in his cottage near Friockheim. He was a natural early riser and the fact that his abode had no central heating helped. It had no roof, or, at least, part of it had no roof. The main roof was, as yet a framework of rafters, beams and joists and held up a creaking blue tarpaulin. He'd had to nail that down to prevent the wind removing it. But the kitchen and bathroom end of the cottage had a roof, albeit the original corrugated iron one. He was awaiting a delivery of rolls of Roofshield breathable membrane. The previous material had had to be sent back; not approved by the planning gestapo at Angus Council. Mackie took these hassles in his stride. *Illegitimi non carborundum*: Don't let the bastards grind you down. He could make coffee though. The gas supply was not yet re-connected, but he had rigged-up a Calor gas cylinder to a two-ring cooker and soon was boiling up coffee grounds, standing in long johns and wellie boots in the concrete space where his kitchen floor would be. A light rain pattered on the tarpaulin. In the corner of the room, on the fold up bed, his sleeping bag and pile of blankets and beside it a cardboard box of jumbled clothing. He must get his van back from the garage. It was a lot more comfortable than this bombsite! The coffee was almost right. He reached for the mug and the milk carton. He didn't need a fridge; the place *was* a fridge. Showering was out of the question. He glanced at his watch. He was going to have to drink up and get out. He had to be at Leuchars by 10 a.m.

Marco Vanetti was still in bed, half-asleep under the duvet when his mobile buzzed. He rolled onto his side and peered at it in the light from the skylight window where rain was sliding down and across in wavy lines. Emily. He pulled himself up against the headrest.

'Hi, Marco, sorry if I woke you. You're not still in bed?'

'What time is it?'

'It's nearly nine. You won't have seen the paper then?'

'No. What paper?'

'*Standard*. There's a piece about Willie: Mystery over abduction…'

'Where did they get that from?'

'Exactly. Well, what worries me – is this going to put Willie at risk? It doesn't have much detail. Says he was last seen in Glasgow. But just to check, I'm going to speak to Willie's editor today, if I can.'

'Aye, that's a good idea. As long as you don't give him anything he can use as another story. Try to find out where he got the information.'

Emily sighed. 'I didn't get much sleep last night. I've got the passport all ready to post off tomorrow. I had a WhatsApp message from him, just to test, so that was good. But I hate all the waiting around. I need to be doing something. I might ring Martin later today to see if there's been any progress and I thought maybe tomorrow first thing we could speak to Sean – Nicola's SpAd – he'll have seen the story too. Put him in the picture.'

'I could come with you, if you like,' Marco offered. 'But hopefully, Willie will be on his way home by then.'

'Hope so. Okay, Marco, speak soon.'

Marco got out of bed, stretched and put on his bathrobe. He looked out of the window at the roofs and trees vague and fuzzy with rain. Padding in bare feet into the carpeted corridor, he listened outside the guest bedroom door, tapped on it. No answer. Tapped again.

'Uh? Come in.'

He went in. 'Luke… time to get up.'

The tousled head lifted from the duvet. 'Uh… any chance of a coffee in this joint? Or even a joint in this joint?'

'Huh, you'll be lucky, nae dope here. But a coffee I can do.'

Mackie's motorbike trip to Leuchars military base took him down the coast to Arbroath, to Dundee, over the narrow Tay Bridge, then the St Andrews Road. The rain was a problem though it was a road he knew intimately and on a Sunday it was relatively quiet; few Lorries and commercial traffic. The rain cleared as he was bypassing Monifieth on the A92. It was sunny and clear at Leuchars. He pulled in beside the sentry box and pushed up his goggles. The two sentries, one with rifle at the ready, stood waiting for him to show ID. Mackie fumbled in the chest pocket of his leather suit and handed it over. As he waited, he noted how the soft landscaping had been redesigned so that no visible sign of the base was obvious from the road. The buildings, the runways, the barracks all hidden behind muddy fields and low drystone dykes.

The sentry in the box checked his manifest and nodded. The other sentry lowered his rifle. 'Okay, mate, you're good to go. Have a nice one.'

Mackie turned the throttle, let in the gear and waited till the boom gate fully opened before releasing the clutch and lifting his boot off the ground. He rolled in to the base. He'd done it in forty minutes. He didn't want to be late for his first solo posting.

He knew the layout vaguely having been here some years before when it had been an RAF base and he supposed it hadn't changed much since the handover to the Royal Engineers and REME just a month ago. It was still largely unoccupied, though he had learned from mates that the Royal Scots Dragoon Guards were soon to relocate there from Germany. He was looking for Block 4. He stopped to study the camp layout board but it had not been updated. Idling out along the narrow tarmac road he was approaching the forest and the estuary of the Eden river that marked the farthest boundary of the base. He could see marram grass and dunes and the mud banks of low tide. On a clear day, St Andrews would be visible from here and the famous East Sands, but there was no chance of it today.

Block 4 was on the periphery of the base, quite a distance from the canteen block and he had been told that his present unit shared it with another group. He didn't yet know the details, but suspected that the arrangement was to do with providing cover for their presence here. There were, he knew, several 'lodger' units at the base whose precise deployment was kept vague. It was a large base and it would take just one person to drop an incautious word into an interested ear and… As he brought the bike to rest alongside a military jeep in the four parking spaces in front of the two storey brick building, he wondered if he had time to get a coffee and maybe a bacon roll before meeting Chief Inspector McLennan. But in the deserted front entrance of the block he soon realised services of that kind were unlikely. In fact, it looked derelict, unused. Bare wooden floors with patches of what looked like rotting linoleum. Dust on window ledges. What a shithole! Through the dim window he could see gorse bushes advancing, already encroaching on the block. He heard boots moving about on the bare floor above. Boots coming down the wooden stair.

'Sergeant Mackie?'

He recognised the voice. McLennan had got here before him. He unzipped the front of his leather suit and took off his goggles.

McLennan appeared in the hallway. He looked like a middle-aged Glasgow keelie, Mackie thought. Tough bugger.

'At ease, Mackie. You're not in the army now,' McLennan told him. 'And you don't need to salute.' Then he clocked the leather suit. 'Fucksake, is that what you're wearing?'

'Came by bike, sir.'

'I heard,' said McLennan drily. 'Well, you're on the plane in twenty minutes, as soon as the pilot is ready. You're cleared through to Gothenburg.'

'Gothenburg?' Mackie repeated. 'Sweden?'

'Yes, it still is in Sweden! First, I have to fill you in on what you're being sent to do. Christ, man!' he said exasperatedly, 'you're dripping water all over my files! I had expected you in civvies… normal urban wear.' He looked up at Mackie. 'Did you no get the message?'

'Ah, no sir. Problem with broadband at my place at the moment.'

'Well, we'll see if we can rustle up some kit in the meantime, but you're tall… what height? Six two?'

'Six four.'

'Christ. Let's go over this first and then you can try the Camp stores.'

It was sheer coincidence Hugh Leadbetter was in the *Standard* office on South Bridge when Professor McKechnie turned up at the front desk. He did one in four Sundays, a half-shift, starting at a sedate 10 a.m. and finishing at 3 p.m. when he would be expected to take Daniel, his four-year old and Tammy his two-year old, somewhere so that his wife could go boozing with friends. Fewer staff worked the Sunday shifts.

His phone rang as he studied staff rosters for the week ahead. 'Uh?' he grunted. 'Oh, aye, the Prof. Whit, *here*? Awright, tell her to come on in. It's a wee bit…' he paused. Untidy didn't quite cover it. Untidy was almost acceptable. His office was a health hazard, a unique example of how one busy human being can make such a mess despite the efforts of others.

Emily appeared in the glass portion of the door.

'Come in.'

'Jesus!' Emily exclaimed as the door opened grudgingly.

Leadbetter grinned. 'Naw – despite the beard!' He sniffed, seeing the direction of her glance. 'Aye, I'll grant you it's a bit out of hand. I let the cleaner go to Blackpool for a week and now look at it. All her fault, you see.'

'Of course,' Emily said, sarcastically adding: 'You're lucky you can find a woman to blame. Anyway, it's about the piece in today's.'

'Willie Morton? That man is a genius but he's even better at getting himself intae tight spots. And you and he are...' he grimaced, searching for the socially appropriate word... 'winchin?'

Emily laughed and adjusted her black specs on her nose. 'Good grief, I've not heard that expression since... I suppose we are.' She looked around and perched on the corner of the table. 'I wonder if that's a nautical term? Must look it up. *Winching*. My, you fair take your life in your hands here!'

Leadbetter rubbed his beard. 'Ah've apologised. Now whit can I do...?'

'Well, I want to know how the piece came to be. Who tipped you off?'

Leadbetter grunted as if baffled. 'What, is he *not* missing?'

'No.'

The editor clicked his teeth in exasperation and leaned back so that the chair creaked loudly. 'Bloody hell! Well, I'm glad to hear it, of course. But how did that happen? I was assured it was kosher.'

'It came from a tip off?'

'Aye,' Leadbetter nodded, 'from a trustworthy source. Not usually wrong.'

'What puzzles me is the 'abduction' bit. Yes, Willie went missing for a few days working on a story but... abduction? That's a very specific claim.'

'So he's not missing now?'

'No. I know where he is.'

'Where is he?'

'I can't tell you that.'

'What? Is it a secret?' The editor scoffed. 'Jings. He's hiding, is he?'

Emily ignored the jibe. 'I can't tell you for very good reasons. But I can give you some information privately on condition you do *not* use it. Willie's safety depends on it.'

'Cripes!' Leadbetter catapulted forward on his seat. 'You've got my attention now, Prof. You know I wouldn't ever do anything to endanger the man.' He grinned wolfishly. 'Even for a good story! That was a joke.'

'Ho ho,' Emily smiled sourly.

'Come on – Willie's one of my top guys. He trusts me. I've been there for him in his last couple of run-ins. He's always getting in bother. That's why we like him, I suppose. I assumed you came to me because you know you *can* trust me. And there's no many newspaper people you can say that about, eh? Aw, you *know* you can, come on, love. Shove that crap off the seat. I'll get coffee brung in.' He stood up and jerked the door open, put his head around it and bellowed out into the press room. 'Coffee needed here, someone. Pronto!' He edged around the desk and heaved a pile of books, newspapers, letters and other detritus from the leather chair onto the floor in the corner, on top of other stuff, raising a mighty cloud of dust.

Emily coughed. The editor moved around to the window and heaved it open. 'Sorry about that, I must get something done about this place.' Fresh air blew in coldly, relieving some of the fug.

A young man in his shirt sleeves came head and shoulders into the room around the door frame. 'Wanted something boss? Oh – hello – you've got company?'

'Coffee for two, Des,' Leadbetter muttered. 'Black for me and…?'

'Milky or latte if you have it.'

'Naw. There's milk but. Sugar?'

'No,' they chorused.

While they waited for the coffee, Emily filled in Leadbetter on the circumstances of Willie's disappearance but refused to say where he was now.

'We think the people who attempted to murder him may try again if they hear he's alive.'

The editor jerked upright. 'Jings! So now you want to know who gave us the "abduction" theory?'

'That would be helpful. We're meeting senior people at Nicola's office first thing tomorrow to discuss issues arising from this.'

'Aw, the First Minister's going to be involved?' Leadbetter scratched noisily in the depths of his beard. 'Sounds like an even better story is building up?'

'But it's one only Willie can give you. In a day or two, I'm sure. Assuming you want the full story, the truth.'

'Of course. Right. Well, the story came tae us intact and complete. In other words, all from the same source. Someone I've known for decades, from my earliest days as a reporter in Glasgow. A polis, senior now. That's all I can tell you, really.'

'Senior in Police Scotland?'

Leadbetter hesitated. 'On the operational side, yes. He disnae wear a uniform and that's a bit of a hint. He's not a desk-jockey, he's at the sharp end, shall we say. Now do you see what I mean by a "trustworthy source"?'

'Not really, but what I want to know is when this tip-off came in?'

'That's easy. Saturday night. During *Match of the Day*.'

'What time is that?'

Leadbetter's eyebrows twitched. 'Don't watch the beautiful game? Around 10.30 p.m. It had just started.'

'So it came to you, directly?'

'Yes, well he's my source. Well-placed. Usually, I'd pass something like that over tae one of the reporters, but this source is something special. I've used him for years.'

'And does he get paid?'

'Oh, no, nothing like that.'

'So what's in it for him?'

Leadbetter scratched in the wiry depths of his beard. 'Thought about that over the years. We've never met face to face. Always just a phone call. The essential bones of the story each time, no small talk. I have the sense that he uses it as an opportunity to right wrongs as he sees it. Mostly the stories are about what you could call the failings of the secret state, if you know what I mean? It's his way of exposing injustices, things that might never come to light without a tip-off of this kind. What's now known in media parlance as a whistle-blower or deep throat.' I mean, I think this guy is in a position to do a lot of good and that's why when he gives me something, I use it.'

The young reporter elbowed his way into the room with two paper mugs of coffee and third paper mug with milk in it. 'I'll leave yous to put your ain milk in, awright?'

Emily was aware that the reporter's thumbs had been inside both the paper mugs. She tried to keep the distaste out of her voice. 'Thanks.'

'Thanks, Des. Nae biccys?'

'Naw, nae biscuits, boss. Some fucking cunt's had the lot. 'Scuse my Greek.'

'So, you won't do anything more on this until Willie comes back?' Emily asked, finding a nook where she could dump the paper cup between a stack of boxes where it might never be found.

'Of course not, if there's danger to the man.'

'I'm not overstating it. There is.'

'And maybe you won't mention what I've told you? I like to protect my sources.'

'Not unless I have to. Unless I'm directly asked by the Justice Secretary or Nicola herself. I mean… if it comes to that, I'd just say the source is from within Police Scotland. That's about twenty thousand people.'

'Well, only if you have to,' Leadbetter grumbled. 'So Willie's not in any *immediate* danger?'

'We hope not. I'm hoping to see him within twenty-four hours. And then he'll have quite a tale to tell.'

'Good. Tell him I'm asking after him and looking forward to hearing the tale.'

CHAPTER TWENTY-EIGHT

Morton had slept well, fresh air fluttering the window blinds and raising lavender scent from the pillows. He lay listening to the peaceful sounds of the street below, Church bells striking the hour. He wondered if it was the bells of the historic Hagakyrkan which he had passed, in its wreath of trees, on the edge of the park. He counted the peals: Nine. Other church bells too, in the distance and nearer, the sibilance of street conversations merged with distant traffic noise, laughter, car doors, even bicycle bells. He got out of bed and looked up at the sky. It was blue with small clouds drifting quickly across it. He showered and dressed in the same underwear, the same shirt and jeans. He looked at his face in the mirror. Nearly three days of stubble. He should have bought a disposable razor. He had no toiletries or luggage whatsoever. Worst of all, no toothpaste. It occurred to him he might ask Johan but it would be better to buy some stuff after breakfast. He might have to stay another day, or even two. Emily wouldn't be able to post his passport till tomorrow. It might arrive on Wednesday but it could be a day or days later. He'd just have to be patient.

Downstairs in the front parlour, Johan was serving a young couple whom Morton had seen on the stairs. They exchanged greetings.

'Morning,' he said to Johan, 'mind if I…?'

Johan fussed over him, ushering him to a table at the window where bright sunlight was illuminating the glassware, glinting on steel cutlery. Fresh flowers in a vase stood on the windowsill.

Morton tucked in heartily to a selection of cold meats and cheeses, freshly baked crusty bread and fruit, orange juice and two cups of strong black coffee.

He left Buck House around 10 a.m. feeling relaxed and rested. Sending Emily a brief WhatsApp message, he strolled along Haga Nygata past the church glimpsed through trees. He continued into the park, crossed the canal and drifted through wide streets. Crossing another, wider, canal – he saw the Stadsmuseum and went in, mingling with crowds of mostly young people. Under 25s got in free, he wryly noticed. In the stagey low lighting of the vast rooms he admired the remains of Sweden's only original Viking vessel, the Äskekärrkeppet and weapons, silver and jewellery from the same period. For a while he watched an artist sketching the boat with a charcoal stick. She was very good but when she caught his eye, he moved on, drifted out into the little courtyard garden and sat on the bench beneath the trees. Finally, suitably impressed, he strolled onto the street. Morton continued towards the river, the giant casino, Cosmopol, and the floating ship museum which, he read on the notice, had more than twenty historical vessels, including a submarine, the Nordkaparen, which you could go inside. He was tempted but the sun shone and he wanted to get close to the spectacular glass frontage of the opera house that looked to the main docks and harbour. He ate a snack lunch in a sunlit coffee bar, and decided to walk up the river as far as he could, stretch his legs. He wanted to look at the red and white striped building he could see. He took off his jacket and swung it over his shoulder, wishing again that he had his sunglasses. He wondered where his rucksack was, what had become of it. There had been little of value in it, except his sunglasses, phone and a notebook he'd barely used.

The odd building known as 'the lipstick' because of its colour and shape, had a white tower section emerging from its slanting sides. He read on a plaque that it had been built by a Scottish architect, who had also designed the Sydney Opera House. There was a cafe on the top floor but he wasn't one for heights. He started to walk under the bridge until it turned into a big building site so he turned back and passed some impressive conference centres by the river.

Emily was in the garden at Lochend Grove around midday hanging out washing when a car stopped outside the front gate. She ignored it and continued to peg up clothes on the line. A man got out. She glanced over and recognised Chief Inspector McLennan. A sudden dread descended upon her. She dropped the pegs into the basket and met him on the path outside the front door.

'What is it? What's happened?'

McLennan moved his hands to reassure her. 'Nothing has happened. Our man is en-route to Gothenburg. He'll be there within the hour. Can we have a chat please?'

'Come inside,' Emily said.

McLennan hesitated, hands in his leather jacket pockets. 'No, better not. You never know if those devils have it bugged. The shed – is there seats in it?'

Emily looked around, bewildered. 'The shed? Oh, well… there's a packing case we could sit on. It's a mess though.'

'That's okay. Nice and private. They're not likely to have bugged it.'

'You really think my house is bugged?' Emily whispered.

'No, I can't definitely say that but I don't want to take any chances. Even now they may be watching us.'

Emily could not resist looking out at the quiet street.

'Don't look round,' McLennan said, peering into the shed. 'It is a bit cluttered. Oh, you've a bench. This'll do. Come and sit down.'

They sat together on the bench against the house wall. 'It's not bad news... definitely?' Emily asked nervously.

'I told you. Nothing has changed since last evening. Our man is well on his way there to extricate Morton safely and he'll not need his passport. We've liaised with our Swedish counterparts and established customs clearance for him. All being well he should be back here by this evening.'

'Oh great. So I won't need to send the passport?'

'No, that's what I came to tell you. The only thing that's worrying me and it's not *really* worrying me is whether that other lot whose-name-we're-not-going-to-mention have been tracking Morton in Sweden.'

'But they think he's... he's dead, don't they?'

'Let's hope so. But we've been tracking his financial trans-actions since he arrived in Gothenburg and maybe they have been doing that too.'

Emily was aghast. 'But you said... you said...'

'Don't worry. We can get there a lot quicker. Our man is...' he pulled back the brown leather sleeve and glanced at his steel watch. '... over Danish airspace now, landing in forty minutes. He'll be getting co-operation from the NI there, our Swedish equivalent. They'll be waiting for him at the airport and then it's just a matter of locating Morton and whisking him safely to Edinburgh.'

'You make it sound so easy.'

McLennan pulled at his sideburns with thumb and

forefinger. 'It's not easy, Professor. Just organised. So, anyway, if they have been tracking his Visa card, they'll know where he's staying. And that's just me being careful. I don't have any grounds for thinking they're aware he's... around. Anyway, I want you to send him a WhatsApp message to meet our man at a specific place, to help avoid any issues.'

Emily gulped. 'Issues?'

McLennan smiled, although it was a tense kind of smile, Emily thought. She was feeling the tension and wasn't sure if the Chief Inspector was telling her everything. What was he not telling her?'

'You saw the story in the paper?' Emily said. 'The *Standard on Sunday*?'

'Oh, yes.'

Emily had a sudden thought. 'Did you tip them off?'

'No comment.'

'I see,' Emily said, frowning. 'Well, I've got my mobile right here. What do you want me to say?'

'Ah, we need him to go to a place away from his lodgings, somewhere easy to find, because he doesn't know the city. Have you been in contact with him in the last hour?'

'No. We exchanged WhatsApp messages around 10 a.m.'

'Okay. Our man doesn't know the city either but should have a police escort, well, someone in plain clothes from the NI, the Nationella Insatsstyrkan.' He grinned briefly. 'And try saying that with your teeth out!'

'I see.'

He cleared his throat. 'Hmn. So it has to be the ferry terminal but there are several. I want Morton to go to the Stena Line Denmark Ferry terminal and wait in the passengers' waiting room there.' He pulled up his sleeve and looked again at his watch. 'Now, I'd estimate our man is about an hour away from there, counting landing time, meeting his contact and getting there by car. So let's send the message.'

'Okay,' Emily said, fishing her mobile out from the zip-up pocket of her fleecy. She found that her fingers were surprisingly nervy as she typed out the message that McLennan dictated.

Ross Mackie had flown in numerous military and civilian aircraft of all sizes and shapes over his career and was used to basic interiors and lack of frills but the Beechcraft King Air 200 twin turbo-prop that awaited him on the runway at Leuchars was probably the smallest plane he'd been on, not counting helicopters. It was on loan from a private contractor and had at one time been an air ambulance for the NHS in Scotland.

'How old is she?' he inquired sceptically of the pilot and co-pilot as they walked across to it from the jeep, only yards from the Eden estuary and the woods.

'Well, she's not new,' the pilot, Flight-Lieutenant Menzies conceded, 'but reliable. Comfortable inside. And there's good insulation to cut down the noise. You'll be surprised.'

And he had been. Yes, the cabin was small, only sixteen feet by five feet high and five feet wide; he had to crawl in on his hands and knees, but the well-padded seats were like something out of Emirates Airlines.

'See what I mean,' Menzies called through the cockpit frame. 'Strap yourself in. We'll be there in a little less than two hours, depending on wind conditions.' Mackie was the only passenger and had his pick of the eight seats. He could see sunlight glinting on the spires and roofs of St Andrews as the plane taxied, turned and took off effortlessly over Tentsmuir Forest. Looking down, Mackie admired the extent of the sandbars and reefs of the Tay estuary as the plane climbed into the soft clouds. Soon they were cruising over the North Sea which could be glimpsed way below in the gaps between banks of cloud. The noise of the engines wasn't quite as muted as he had been led to believe. He wished he had brought his MP3 player or a book. Still, he felt quite pleased with himself. It was his first solo assignment and marked a new stage in his assimilation to his new unit. He didn't want to fuck it up. The briefing had been short and succinct: Land at Gothenburg City airport, meet NI officer Dahlstrom, use their transport to the Stena Link ferry terminal and meet up with Armoury or Willie Morton as he preferred to call him. He'll be expecting you. Escort him safely back to airport and return to Leuchars. Couldn't be easier. Except for the issue of the man who had called himself Luke Sangster in Clachtoll. 'You know him by sight but that's not his real name.' McLennan had spent a lot of time explaining the niceties of the liaison with MI5 Scotland Station and what he knew or suspected had been going on behind the scenes. 'So if you see this man – and we're working on his real identity – keep a wide berth. Don't let him see you.' Apart from that, the job was a home run. His mind drifted off to all the work he had to do on his cottage at Friockheim and he began to doze.

He woke to find the co-pilot Angus Dunn crawling through the cockpit frame into the cabin. 'How are you doing back here?' he shouted. 'Comfortable isn't it?'

'Not bad,' Mackie said, blinking. 'How are we doing?'

'We're getting there. We're over Denmark now. Not as fast as your average jet. Edinburgh to Gothenburg Landvetter takes around an hour and a half on a 737, we're about two hours.' He checked his watch. Should be descending in around twenty minutes. Okay?'

The plane descended smoothly to the regional airport fifteen kilometres north of the city, the smaller of the city's two airports, which mainly handled internal Scandinavian flights as well as some budget international flights. He liked the small scale of the place at first sight. It looked clean and orderly, what you'd expect from the Swedes.

Menzies shook his hand as he walked away. 'So, we'll see you soon for the return flight,' he said.

'Two hours tops,' Mackie said. 'Thanks.'

As he cleared customs by showing his authorisation he saw his Swedish police contact waiting at the gate. NI Officer Jan Dahlstrom looked quintessentially Swedish; her cropped blonde hair a perfect match for the pale blue and dark blue uniform. She had a holstered Sig-Sauer P226 and her tall, rugged-looking male colleague, Officer Erik Ohlsen, had a sub-nosed Heckler & Koch MP5 sub-machine gun strapped on. Mackie was pleased to see them and took a professional interest in their hardware. The uniforms and guns were going to make his job easier.

'Our vehicle is just outside,' Dahlstrom said.

'Grand.'

As they exited the airport carpark in the four-door blue Volkswagen Transporter T5, Mackie looked at his watch and turned it an hour forward to CET. He noticed they were a little behind schedule. He was due to meet Morton at 3 p.m. local time. It was nearly that now. The plane had been slower than expected. 'I've to meet him at the Stena Line Ferry terminal,' he told Erik Ohlsen who was driving.

'We're in a hurry, so I take the quickest route, yes?' Ohlsen said.

'Please. You know the city. I don't.'

'We get there in fifteen minutes I think.'

'Good.'

Soon the T5 was cruising through what appeared to be industrial wastelands and he glimpsed the river and docks. Then they were on a busy high bridge.

'Nice bridge,' he murmured. 'Looks new.'

'Alvsborgbron,' the driver muttered.

'Right.' Mackie looked upriver and saw the blue and white Stena Line ferry at the quay. 'There,' he said, pointing. 'That's where I need to be.'

'That's the one?'

'Absolutely. We'll only be ten minutes late.'

Morton had felt the pulse of an incoming message on WhatsApp as he tried to find his way back to his B&B. He was feeling tired, the soles of his feet were sore. He had thought he might go back and lie down for a while then go out later for something to eat.

The message was from Emily. It astonished him. *They will fly you home today. Meet your escort in Stena Line Denmark Terminal waiting room this afternoon approx. 3 p.m. your time. Someone you know. See you soon, E xx.* What did it mean? Someone you know? Was Emily coming? He typed a reply: *someone I know? Who?* He waited, standing in the shade of a tree outside a supermarket. And waited. Finally, a reply. *A man you know, that's all they will tell me.* He immediately typed: *Who's they?* And an immediate reply: *Scottish police. Justice Sec authority.* 'Oh, okay,' he said out loud. He looked at his watch. He'd better get moving.

By now, Morton had an inkling of the city streets and recognised the wide road alongside the canal, the lines of trees. Despite his tired soles, his hunch was right and he came out within sight of the ferry terminal. He used a pedestrian crossing and a footbridge that crossed the four-lane E45, with the stern of a big blue and white ferry directly in view. The passenger waiting room would in the main block a few hundred yards south. There were few pedestrians. Most people in this area were in cars. There were large carparks everywhere. Mostly empty. He wasn't noticing anything or anyone in his hurry to get to the terminal. But as he came down the ramp onto the tree-lined pedestrian lane into the terminal buildings, he saw a man up ahead who looked familiar. *Someone you know.* It couldn't be! Even from fifty yards away, he saw it was the man who had pretended to be Luke. He'd been set up! He turned quickly and hurried back up the ramp. From the parapet, he carefully looked back, shielding his face with his hand. The man was still coming. Was he lying in wait for me, he wondered? But the man veered off on the footpath heading upriver. What was going on? The man had passed within twenty feet of Morton who hunched over the parapet of the footbridge, pretending to be talking on his mobile phone. Morton took stock of what he'd seen. In dark trousers and a black raincoat, the man bore little resemblance to the person he had met at Clachtoll who had driven him from Glasgow to Edinburgh, his companion across the North Sea. The man who had tricked him and left him for dead in a deep forest in the middle of nowhere. But there was no doubting it. He knew in his waters. Someone had got hold of Emily's phone. The message he had received from her was fake. Or this man had intercepted it, somehow? At any event, it wasn't safe to stay around. He looked at his mobile. Should he send a message? Was Emily there? He would have to take a chance. He typed: *Set up? You know who was there* and pressed the send arrow. He waited. No answer. He walked on a few paces. Then the phone was buzzing. Emily. He grabbed it and put it to his ear and listened.

'It is you!' he exclaimed. 'I thought I'd been set up.'

'No – you haven't. Look, I'll pass you over...'

'What? Who is this?'

'The name's McLennan,' said the gruff voice in his ear. 'Chief Inspector. You've not, repeat *not*, been set up, Morton. We want to bring you home safe, but if I understand you correctly you saw someone else at the terminal?'

'Yes, the man who...'

'Okay. We think his name is Gerald Hamner. We're working with Swedish Police to get him arrested for attempted murder. Is he still there?'

'Not far away. He didn't see me, I don't think.'

'He must have been tipped off somehow. Look, our man is right there too. He should be with you.'

'I'm not in the terminal building. I'm a hundred yards away.'

'I see. Make contact as planned. Is that possible? And keep well away from Hamner, whatever you do.'

'What if he comes back?'

'Don't worry. Our man will have the Swedish police with him. They will deal with him. Leave it to them. Better go, Morton. Keep in contact. First priority is to get you out safe.'

'Okay.' Morton was reassured, and exhaled noisily and stood there, blinking his eyes, trying to dispel the tension. He retraced his steps, glancing right and left, walking rapidly back along the footpath to the main building of the Terminal. But he was thinking: In all of Sweden – the vast size of it – they had come, by some bizarre homing instinct to the same hundred yards of tarmac and concrete by the side of the mighty river! How could it be a coincidence? But he could test it. If there was no-one in the Terminal building that he knew, then it *was* a set-up and Emily was being conned. And this man, claiming to be Chief Inspector McLennan, was a fake too. What was going on? He had sounded genuine and Emily sounded as if she trusted him, but what if they were putting on an act and she was under duress? He would soon know for sure.

CHAPTER TWENTY-NINE

A slight wind in the trees flickered streetlight into reflecting pools in the wet concrete made brilliant by the lights of the city. Morton had been watching the man for nearly an hour as the sky was drained of natural light and these lights came on, shoals of them on both sides of the mighty Gota River, emerging with the phosphorescent brilliance of a million dead herring. The sprawling Stena Ferry terminal was beyond the footpath and the footbridge leading over the canal. And between the terminal and Morton, the slight figure of the rain-coated Hamner standing under a streetlight. There were few other pedestrians near the river's edge. A sea breeze strengthening from the estuary, Morton was starting to feel cold, wishing again he had warmer clothes, a fleece, gloves, his beanie hat. Idly, he wondered where they were. There had been nobody he knew in the ferry terminal. The only person was this man, Gerald Hamner. Nor had there been any more calls on his mobile. Even more suspicious. He was desperately worried about Emily and what was going on in Edinburgh. McLennan, Hamner – were they in it together, out to get him? Was Brodagh in on it? How wide was the network of spies and agents? He had got to within a hundred yards from Hamner near an urban beach with sand and large colourful umbrellas twisting in the breeze but curiosity or a kind of rage had made him retrace his steps and walk back, keeping his distance from the man. Hamner was unaware of him, standing looking down river towards the ferry terminal and the lights of the distant bridge. What was he waiting for? As Morton watched, a blue and white Stena car ferry backed out of the terminal, great wide stern towards him, its horn blasting five times. Morton could see the flicker of faces up on the decks, the glow of a cigarette here and there. Then it slowed, stopped, engines slammed into forward gear, half-speed and it began to sail down mid-river, the constellation of lights merging quite quickly into the pantheon of lights on all sides in the distance. The whole operation had lasted ten minutes. Morton wondered if it was for Frederickshavn or further afield, perhaps even Harwich. As it passed under the high Alvsborg bridge further down, it seemed to Morton that its upper deck barely cleared the underside of the bridge, the lines of cabin lights fitting into a pattern with the intermittent red tail lights and white headlights of traffic on the bridge. Gothenburg was moving into the night shift and with it cooler breezes from the Kattegat. Without taking his eyes off his quarry, Morton, in the shadows at the edge of the streetlights, zipped his jacket – Hassi's jacket – up to the neck. What was the man doing? He felt a strong urge to rush out; barge him into the river. But he might bungle it and end up in the river himself. The man might have a gun. But why was he hanging around here on the deserted Skeppsbron in the dark? Why was he not in the terminal? Morton was too distant to make out the expression on his face, even before the light had gone, but there was no question it was him: This murderer who must now know that his victim was not dead. These calls he had been getting proved he was under orders to locate Morton and finally obliterate him. There could be no other explanation. Slighter of frame, his hair shorter, he seemed older-looking too. Or maybe it was just the change of clothes giving that impression? Morton knew he was wandering in the realms of the subjective. He recalled seeing him in the shadows outside the Guesthouse at Värnamo. If he had walked away then of course, none of this would be happening. Brodagh had known instinctively that he was a fake. But then she had sent him off to Sweden. Or had she? It seemed an odd volte-face. *Second thoughts.* What was the man's motive? Who did he work for? Silhouetted now against the moving sheen of the water, Hamner was taking yet another call, turning this way and that as he talked. Morton wondered what language he was speaking. Could he get nearer to find out? Between them was open ground, a concrete void with a few benches and metal litterbins, patterned with pools of light from the string of ornate streetlamps near the concrete river barrier. There was nowhere in between to hide. Hamner might finish his call and turn around at any time and see him.

Across the tar-thick river, the lights of the docks and harbours were sporadic and distant. Morton remembered there was a series of benches by the riverfront about two hundred yards downriver, nearer the pedestrian crossing, the footbridge and the footpath to the ferry terminal. Morton realised if he sat there, he might be near enough to overhear part of the conversation, as the man passed. The man would approach him, not the other way around and so would be less wary. If he sat on the middle bench, absorbed in his mobile phone the man would never suspect who he was. After all, he had passed Morton earlier on the path without recognising him. Although he might now know Morton was alive it would surely not occur to him that he could be so near at hand?

Using the shadows at the outer limits of the street lighting, he strode quickly to the bench and made it without being seen. The iron seat was cold under him. He turned sideways to the path, leaning in to the seat back. A slight shift of his head allowed him to observe the footpath to his right. After a minute or two he began to be aware of Hamner coming slowly around the shallow bend towards him, still talking on his phone. Morton pretended to flick through the screen pages on his mobile. It was counter-intuitive to turn his back now he was certain the man was coming past. All his senses screamed for him to turn and see what he was doing. He began to make out the muffled sounds of conversation, the almost imperceptible scuff of shoes on concrete.

And then there he was, sauntering by, unaware or un-interested in the man on the bench. For a couple of raging seconds, Morton had a chance to take him from behind, knock him over. But the mood passed and he kept his head down, warily regarding Hamner under his eyebrows. He'd seen too many of those films where the person attacking was the one who ended up in the river. The roaring river was too wide, too fast, too deep to survive.

But the man stopped, just beyond the third bench and turned nonchalantly to look out again at the river and the lights of the opposite bank. What was he doing? Was he tempting Morton to attack him? Then as he watched, the man put his mobile in his raincoat pocket and turned and looked directly at Morton.

CHAPTER THIRTY

By 3.30 p.m. it was clear to Ross Mackie that something had gone wrong with the arrangements. With officers Dahlstrom and Ohlsen, he had searched every corner of the ferry terminal and finally they stood outside in the afternoon sun, waiting for Morton. McLennan was trying to re-establish contact with Armoury, who, Mackie was assured, was somewhere in the vicinity. He had been spooked by the unexpected presence of the fake Luke Sangster, whose name they had now established was Gerald Hamner, a Swedish national with unspecified military links to several EU countries including the UK.

'What this means, we don't know yet,' McLennan had told him over the phone. 'Most of his connections are dead ends or lead to sites that no longer exist. The man is a bit of a ghost. I've seen this sort of stuff before and it's never good. We're not going to let it drop, but that's for later.'

'Why is Armoury not responding to your calls, sir?' Mackie asked. 'That's my immediate concern. The NI officers are keen to move. They think he's a no-show.'

'Have you explained the situation to them? Armoury's obviously nearby. He just needs coaxing in, reassurance. I'll keep trying his mobile.'

'Right.' And as Mackie put his phone back in his pocket, he turned to look back at the terminal, towards his colleagues and suddenly read *Kiel – Gothenburg* on the stern of the ferry. His heart sank.

'Is there another Stena Line ferry terminal? This one's for Germany.'

Dahlstrom nodded sagely. 'For sure. The Denmark terminal. It is a mile upriver.'

'Damn!' Mackie groaned. 'We're at the wrong bloody terminal. Quick!'

As they piled into the Transporter, he dialled McLennan and explained. Even the NI officers could hear McLennan's reactions. Dahlstrom gave him a withering look.

'Those Swedish police are real dummies yes?'

'It's not your fault,' Mackie said. 'It's mine. I saw a ferry and assumed…'

When they got to the Masthuggstorget and saw the much larger terminal building, Ohlsen drove the Transporter up onto the concrete piazza and parked outside the doors. They rushed in, drawing startled glances from tourists. But there was no Morton.

With an ear to his mobile, Mackie could hear his boss sounding off: 'A simple operation, Mackie and you've blown it! I clearly told you the Denmark terminal…'

'Yes, sir. Sorry sir.'

'So get out and find him! Before they get to him.'

They conferred at the entrance doors. Mackie said: 'This is definitely the right place and he's still around, out there somewhere. He's not answering his mobile because he thinks he's being set up.'

Officer Jan Dahlstrom looked at him. 'This is new. You told us it was a simple job to collect a witness. But there is something you are not telling us?'

'Look, we don't have time… but there is a possibility that

someone who tried to kill him before is here too.'

Erik Ohlsen's forefinger curled around the trigger of his MP5. 'Is this person armed? Do you know who he is?'

'Yes. We think his name is Hamner, Gerald, white male, around thirty-five. I know him by sight. He's five feet eight, that's about one point seven metres, about your height, thin, longish hair. That's all I know. But we must concentrate on finding Morton.' Mackie took out the head and shoulders photo of Morton again and showed it to them under the lights of the entrance.

'Right. One of you stay here. You look over in that direction and I'm going to take a walk up the river a bit. Short circular walks and back here in ten minutes, okay.'

'I'll stay here,' Ohlsen volunteered. 'His name is Morton William, yes. I am pronouncing him right?'

'William Morton. Right, see you in ten minutes.' Mackie walked quickly up the pedestrian footpath. The light was fading fast, the streetlights on. He believed if Morton could see him, he would come forward and realise that he had not been set up. He had to hope so anyway. There were very few people about, and he carefully checked out anyone he saw. It was a bit off the tourist track. Perfect place for a murder, he was thinking. As he crossed the footbridge over a canal, he saw a long stretch of the riverbank, a curving low concrete wall dotted along its length with streetlights separating the dark river from the city. Then he heard a shout somewhere ahead in the distance.

The man shouted: 'Did you think I didn't see you, Morton? I've been waiting for you.'

'Waiting for me?' Morton shouted, standing up. 'But I'm already dead. Didn't you know that? I'm a ghost.'

The man came forward warily, moving from side to side. Morton felt anger and rage, no fear whatsoever. He had the intoxicating taste of adrenaline in his mouth.

'No hard feelings. Morton. Orders.'

'Whose orders? I'm no security threat. You know that.'

'You wouldn't be if you *were* dead, but you're not. How you managed that, Morton, I don't know. You surprise me.'

'You got me to come all the way here. What I want to know is – why? All I ever wanted was to help find a missing person. I'm a journalist, not a spy.'

Hamner was eight feet away. 'For what it's worth, Morton, the original idea was to get you out of the way. But you know how these things go.'

Standing face to face, now only six feet apart, Morton realised something that he had forgotten; he had the advantage of height and weight. 'Hamner your name is, apparently.'

'I'm surprised you know that. But it's not going to do you any good. You've buggered everything up now.'

'Oh dear!' Morton sneered. 'You're going to tell me – *now* – who you work for.'

'I don't think so. Anyway, you know already.'

'MI5?'

'In Sweden?' Hamner laughed abruptly. 'No, no.'

'MI6, then.'

'Make up your mind.'

'One or the other. Whatever – but you've gone way, way beyond any possible remit you could have. Attempted murder? That's what's coming your way.'

'Oh dear, and it was all going so well…'

He was quick. Quicker and more powerful than Morton had anticipated. Morton tried to duck but was caught on the side of the head. The pain maddened him. He should have run then but stood his ground, caught Hamner's swinging fist and wrenched it down. They traded ineffectual blows. He saw the parapet, the shining black river up close, the lights behind, night sky above, stars, the moon half-hidden by cloud. Concrete. He scrambled to his feet, felt the jar of his blow landing solidly on Hamner's skull. But the man pulled away and was scrabbling in his raincoat.

He had a gun.

With a surge of adrenaline, Morton charged him and they fell together against the rough concrete edges of the parapet. He jarred his elbow. The pain of it made him kick out and lash with his fists. In the dim light he couldn't see the gun but was desperate to incapacitate the man before he could use it. He slammed the man's head on the edge. Hamner stumbled but kicked Morton in the stomach. He felt sick, staggered back. Hamner was coming at him, the gun fired. He heard the sounds of people running to help. Hamner was off balance. Somebody rushed in, shouting, punching. He couldn't get to his feet. He was badly winded.

'Jesus, Willie! The scrapes ye get intae.'

He looked up to see Ross Mackie! And a Swedish police-woman. 'Where's he gone?'

'Ah, no sure. In the river, I think.'

'Hamner?'

'Aye, but whether he jumped or was pushed, who can say. This is his gun. Good shot, Officer Dahlstrom. She saved the day, Willie, or you would be strumming your wee harp by now.'

The next hour went by in a blur for Morton. The Swedish Police instituted a search of the river by motor launch, searchlights down river, by the docks, out to the estuary, but nothing or no-one was found. As the night fully descended, someone handed Morton a blanket and despite it, he felt cold and jittery, his teeth chattered. It was the thought of what might have happened, of what nearly had happened. The nausea of spent adrenaline, regurgitated fear.

Mackie accompanied him in the Police T5 which whisked them through lit streets to the airport. Sitting in the back seat, Morton was too tired to complain when he saw the smallness of the Beechcraft King Air waiting for them in the night wind out on the perimeter of the airport. They helped him crawl into the narrow cabin where he couldn't stand upright. He slept most of the way through the uneventful flight which was a blessing as he wasn't a great flyer. It was past midnight before the plane touched down in moonlight at Leuchars. Waiting there was Emily and Chief Inspector McLennan – the voice on his mobile – from Special Branch. Willie slept all the way into Edinburgh in Emily's arms and was still drowsy when they reached the flat at Lochend Grove.

When he awoke the next morning, sunshine was streaming in to the familiar small bedroom over the felt roof of the garden shed. Emily brought him coffee. Propped up on the pillow, he savoured it and tried to count the aches and pains in his legs, neck, trunk and elbow. He was getting old.

'No, I've been up for hours,' Emily told him. 'The usual stuff for the end of semester. How are you feeling?'

'Sore,' Morton said, frowning. 'But thankful.'

'I was very, very worried yesterday. And I didn't know the half of it then. I mean, the forest.'

'I've been lucky, Em. But it was all so pointless, arbitrary. I mean, what did they think? That I was some kind of…?'

'Yes. By the way, the man has been found, in the estuary.'

'Who was he? Who did he work for, that's what I want to

know.'

'Well, you need to get up. We've got a meeting to go to. At Holyrood.'

'Really? I'm not sure I'm up to it.'

'Come on. You're the star of the show.'

When Morton and Emily arrived at the main public entrance of the Scottish Parliament, with the view of Salisbury Craigs, they found Martin Masterson MSP, the serious-faced Justice Secretary, waiting in the foyer flanked by two uniformed security men, big-bellied in navy-blue sweaters.

'You must be Willie Morton?' Masterson said with a thin-lipped smile as they shook hands. 'Funny we've never met before. I know Professor McKechnie of course. Well, I'm delighted to see you and thanks for coming. Apologies for what you've gone through. Here's your day passes. Put them on please.'

The security men ushered them through the body scanners and supervised their bags and personal effects going through the X-ray machines. As they collected their stuff and put on their shoes, Masterson said, quietly: 'There's going to be one hell of a dust up about this, you know.' He shook his head sorrowfully. 'We can't have this nonsense happening in Scotland. We need greater scrutiny of what is going on. You know that Brodagh's messaging account was hacked by persons unknown?' He nodded sorrowfully. 'Yes, those texts you received from her were not real. We'll get to the bottom of it.'

'Goodness me,' Emily frowned. 'Is no-one safe these days?'

Morton tied his laces. 'I'm still not sure what happened, or why?'

Masterson nodded. 'Don't worry, you'll get all that

information. Either today or very soon. I'm demanding – not asking – that the Home Secretary come here in person for a private meeting about this affair.'

'Will she come?' Emily asked, wiping the lenses of her spectacles.

As Masterson turned away, Morton saw the determination on his thin face. 'Oh, yes. She will,' he said. 'Follow me, please.'

Masterson led them through the labyrinth of glass doors and up stone steps to the bottom of the Ministerial lifts. They went up to the third floor.

'The meeting is in my room along here.'

He led them into a boardroom with a magnificent and distracting view of the Craigs and Holyrood Park. It was light and airy with the mix of oak, sycamore and smoked glass typical of the post-modernistic work of the Catalan architect, the late Enric Miralles. A slim female civil servant poured coffee into white mugs. Morton saw Chief Inspector McLennan seated at the table, next to a high-ranking uniformed policeman with yards of gold braid on his shoulders and the hat in front of him. The third man, slim, in his mid-thirties in a shiny grey suit, stood over by the window, his back to the room. When he turned, Morton saw that he had large tortoiseshell spectacles covering a pale, freckled complexion. Clutching a black folder and looking apprehensive, he finally chose a seat on his own at the far end of the table.

Emily sat next to McLennan, Morton beside her. A floppy haired man hovered behind Masterson and passed him a mug of coffee. The meeting came to order.

Masterson was chairing. 'Right, let's get introductions out of the way. This is Willie Morton, a freelance journalist who mostly works for the *Scottish Standard* newspaper. Most of you know Professor Emily McKechnie of Edinburgh University.

Chief Constable Damon Boyle is representing Police Scotland, Chief Inspector McLennan of Special Branch and this gentleman' – he indicated the sallow-complexioned man – 'is Desmond Thorpe, Section Administrator for MI5 Scotland Station. Correct?'

'Thank you, yes,' Thorpe said, re-positioning his spectacles on his nose. Morton thought that he looked nervous. Was it his orders that Hamner had been following? Seen up close, he was hardly the bogeyman Morton had imagined.

'And this is a first, I think,' Masterson said. 'That we have such a meeting here in Holyrood, with senior Scottish police, Special Branch and MI5 all present. But this is a very serious issue and perhaps I may say it is something of the straw that broke the camel's back as far as I am concerned.'

He looked around the table. 'As Chief Inspector McLennan will corroborate, the liaison between MI5 Scotland Station and Scotland's Special Branch has not been working effectively for some time and now we have a situation where an innocent civilian – Morton here – nearly lost his life through the deliberate intent of a person working apparently for the British Security Intelligence Service – note that I do not say MI5...'

Thorpe suddenly became animated, his fingers clutched the table top and he looked as if he was going to leave. 'No, no,' he said, 'this is nonsense, I'm afraid. You have been led astray...' his glance settled on McLennan. 'The information you have is simply untrue. For whatever reason, you suspect us – and let's not mince words here – a Nationalist Minister is always going to want to point the finger. I accept that, but the person you accuse... is simply not connected with us at all.'

The Chief Constable said calmly: 'Police Scotland have been informed that the body found in the Gota River was one Gerald Hamner, Swedish national, whose record shows a number of connections with SIS. He was a contractor who had acted for you on previous occasions in Scotland and in Northern Ireland. The facts are there.'

'This man Hamner has absolutely no connection to us.'

'That's your position is it?' McLennan said sarcastically. 'Deny everything? Nothing ever happened? Morton was in Sweden on *holiday*?'

'Some holiday!' Morton snorted.

'Exactly,' Masterson agreed. 'Swedish police have agreed to check into Hamner's background more deeply for us, his comings and goings, his financial accounts etcetera. I doubt you'll be able to deny your connections with him for long. Also, we are investigating the hack of Brodagh Murdoch's phone. We suspect your organisation may have been involved in that too. Your position is untenable and I intend to demand a face to face meeting with the Home Secretary. It's time to put a stop to this arrogance and high-handed behaviour. The Scottish Police Authority and myself as Justice Secretary need to have complete overview on all operations that could be described as counter-terrorism, if that's how you see this shoddy attempt at entrapment and attempted murder.' He looked directly at Thorpe, frowning. 'In fact,' he added, 'that is my legal right as enshrined in the legislation. There is no provision for MI5 or MI6 to withhold information on operations from me. We have tolerated this too long.'

Thorpe stood up, clutching his folder. 'On that note, you will perhaps allow me to take my leave? I did not come here to listen to a political rant.' He moved around the table and headed out of the room.

Masterson was shaking with anger. 'Political rant… we are the Government…' but Thorpe was gone. 'Good grief, this is ridiculous. Well, you see the problem we face?'

Morton chose his moment. 'So, can I use any of this in a story?'

Everyone looked at him but no-one wanted to pre-empt the Justice Secretary. 'Yes. All of it. Well, not names obviously. No, wait, let's think about it.' He gestured to the floppy haired young man. 'Adrian is my PPS. We'd better have a think about it. You can do a story of course but we want to ensure nothing is said to prevent the Home Secretary from agreeing to meet me on the issue. We want change and maybe, maybe, we have to hold back a little. You heard what Thorpe said. "A political rant." Well, that's what she will say. That'll give her the perfect way out for refusing a meeting. So, let's think very carefully.'

'I'm sure they will authorise a D Notice,' McLennan said. 'Their first instinct. Muzzle the press. Jail the journalists. Shoot the dissidents. That's their style.'

'Maybe,' said Masterson, closing his file. 'But not in Scotland. Not any more. Their day is over.'

However, in the days following on from the Holyrood meeting, it became clear that the incident was unlikely to prove a watershed moment in the reorganisation of security and intelligence overview in Scotland. The Home Secretary refused to discuss the 'Morton affair' as it became privately referred to and backed the Chief of the Joint Intelligence Committee in denying any involvement. Hamner, they repeated, had no connection with the British Security and Intelligence Services. They refused to discuss whether MI5 operatives in Scotland had obtained authority for kicking in Sangster's door in Marchmont. Or why they had allegedly attempted to entrap Brodagh Murdoch, a leading media figure in Scotland and hack her mobile phone. They refused to discuss their attitude or strategy on hackers and media groups supportive of independence. The uneasy liaison in Scotland between MI5 and the Scottish Special Branch continued. The Scottish Justice Secretary took a greater interest in security and intelligence matters in Scotland and met more regularly with Special Branch and senior officers of the Scottish Police Authority – until he was reshuffled six months later.

There was one chink of light and it came, surprisingly, from the efforts of a Scots Tory, a former Edinburgh MP, no less. The Rt Hon Sir Malcolm Rifkind KCMG QC MP had been making dogged efforts to reform the Intelligence Security Committee, of which he had been Chair since 2010. He finally prevailed with the passing of the Justice and Security Act 2013, and the ISC moved from being a committee of Parliament to a full Parliamentary committee, its representatives nominated by Parliament rather than the Prime Minister. This was a big step forward. The Committee's role and remit was enhanced to consider the policies, expenditure, administration and operations of all seven organisations of the UK Intelligence community including MI5, MI6, GCHQ, Defence Intelligence (DI), National Security Secretariat (NSS), Office for Security and Counter-Terrorism (OSCT) and the Joint Intelligence Organisation (JIO). It was even agreed that an annual report by the ISC, albeit heavily redacted, could be debated in Parliament. That step forward was mitigated by a half step back. The establishment were already moving quickly in subtle ways to marginalise the ISC. At any event, their remit cannot at present intrude upon operational matters, which of course is the main business of any secret service. However, Rifkind's heroic attempts to democratise and introduce scrutiny where there had been none led, in late May 2015, to an unprecedented invitation to the leader of the Scottish

National Party group at Westminster. The SNP were now to be represented on the ISC. It was a move that had old buffers of empire gagging on their snifters in the sepulchral gloom of the clubs of Mayfair and upper floor offices of Whitehall. But the SNP had taken fifty-six out of fifty-nine seats in Scotland at the General Election. They had been the Government of the devolved administration since 2007. Their Ministers had been involved in security and intelligence overview for eight years. Democracy must prevail even amongst the shadows and ghosts of the world of British spooks.

It was odd that the 'Morton affair' never reached the newspapers. Even the *Scottish Standard* chose not to print Willie's tale. Instead, they and other papers welcomed the positive story of SNP representation on the ISC. Westminster was responsive, flexible, caring – it seemed. Whether this was because D Notices had been issued and enforced behind the scenes, editorial arms twisted and Knighthoods promised, or whether there simply was no appetite for more cross-border wrangling and finger-pointing. Another story that never made the newspapers was the suspension on full pay of Chief Inspector McLennan, pending a full inquiry into alleged infractions of the rules and claims of misappropriation of expenses.

The group of hackers and media people that used to meet in the basement of the pub in Lyon's Vennel fell apart under its own inertia. People stopped attending, got busy with other issues, a few went on to greater things. And who or what Cerberus was, whether male or female, was never revealed. If Luke Sangster knew, he wasn't saying. There were some who concluded it was all a private joke. Brian Treanor, owner of Viroil, was rumoured to be on the list for a peerage in the next Honour's list and no-one was surprised. The old joke that if you steal ten pounds you'll be put in jail but if you steal a hundred million you'll dine with Prime Ministers and be made a Lord is still true.

Gerald Hamner was not acknowledged by family or country; it seemed he had no known next of kin, no relatives not even a permanent home address. Almost nothing was known about him other than the physical certainties of a body that remained indefinitely in Gothenburg morgue. And some emails that may or may not have been sent to or from him. Morton may have got into and out of Sweden without ID or passports as a kind of ghost, but Hamner, it seemed, had never even existed prior to the embarrassment of his corpse being plucked from the Gota.

The sun shone brightly from a blue sky barely fingerprinted with light fluffy clouds as Morton and Emily clambered from the black and red carriage at the cog railway station on the rocky summit of Schafberg, fifty metres beyond the tunnel. Ahead was the up-tilted slab of rock leading to an awesome pinnacle, mitigated a little by a wooden cafe and sun terrace and below it, tables with colourful sun shades.

'Feels high,' Morton said, extending his Leki walking pole.

'Well, it is quite high,' Emily laughed. 'Nearly six thousand feet. Come on, let's get up to the highest point.'

'Amazing feat of engineering, that railway,' Morton enthused, adjusting his sunglasses. 'Some of the track was practically vertical. Look at that view!' In the distance and all around, the jagged teeth of the Salzkammergut peaks shone in the sunshine. The horizon was crammed with mountain peaks of every shade of lavender as far as the eye could see, and between them, the glistening silver Attersee to the north east and to the north west, the Mondsee and beyond, the haze of

Salzburg.

They approached the Schafberg Spitze, Morton overtly aware of the ominous jagged edges, the fearsome overhang and the inevitable sheer drop beneath, guarded by a sturdy wooden fence all along the edge. He watched nervously as Emily snapped photos and selfies at the edge, and helped others to do the same.

'Let's start down,' he suggested. 'Hopefully the descent will be less steep and rocky. Its half two already, you know.'

They set off down the dusty path, boots kicking loose stones, making careful use of their walking poles. It felt to Morton that they were teetering on the edge although this wasn't even half the height of the highest of the Austrian Alps. It was steeper than the Cairngorms though and in the balmy sunshine much hotter. He wondered if it was because they were, technically, nearer the sun. Was that a real consideration or just a daft notion? He had been wondering if he could detect a thinness of the air due to the altitude. But he knew such ideas were naive. Not at this height. The path flattened out and crossed the cog railway track on a large flat plateau where there was a brick building – a cafe, with people outside sitting at tables drinking beer, a cheerful bare-chested man strumming a guitar by a line of wooden huts.

'Imagine running a cafe up here?' Emily said. 'They must get supplies by helicopter – or maybe brought up on the cog railway?'

They passed through a chorus of friendly greetings and the path turned inwards across the face of the mountain to an area of high pasture, tall wildflower meadows and the first sound of cowbells. And then the thick forest began, so they were sometimes in deep shade, sometimes their steps muffled on leaf litter, or kicking loose gravel on dusty and tricky bends. They walked in companionable silence for much of the way. Morton was thinking all kinds of thoughts, reflecting on his lucky escape; what might have been. Oddly, the face of someone he had known at school came to him, Hugo. It'd been some years since he'd bumped into him at the Royal George Hotel. Hugo had stared blankly so Morton had been reduced to the ignominy of reminding him who he was. And of course, the darling of the metropolitan literati hadn't been terribly interested to learn that Morton was a journalist too, even affected not to have heard of the *Scottish Standard*. He'd 'forgotten Morton was in his class,' and Morton wondered if that was an intentional double-entendre. Not in his class, and of course Hugo's pater had been, by coincidence, *the* top-dog of the Intelligence and Security committee. Morton remembered seeing him at the school gates, a dapper figure, spry and wry with piercing fox-like eyes behind Buddy Holly spectacles and a voice like good sherry flowing over padouk oak. It hadn't been a meeting, just a glimpsing and Hugo's dad then merely an Edinburgh MP. 'You could have been one of us, Morton, you sound like one of us,' Hugo had told him then in the lounge of the Royal George, without any apparent awareness that he was being ironic. Looking and sounding right was so important to the elite. But Morton had remembered that remark and now years later it made him think what might have been. Could he have made a different, more successful life? It was an illuminating comment in another way too. The idea of 'one of us' rather than being one of *them*. Belonging to the elite or not belonging. Of being select or one of the *hoi-polloi*, the anonymous plebs. For people like Hugo and his father, it was the basis of their life system, the main item of their faith, the touchstone and motive of the party they supported. A party that existed to keep the plebs from the gates, to protect the privileges of the elite. Despite his gilded schooldays rubbing shoulders with the sons of the elite, Morton empathised with people of all classes, in the common fraternity of *Jock Tamson's bairns*. He couldn't understand those who sought to maintain class divisions, perpetuate inequality and myths of their own self-importance. Britain and empire and Scotland's sub-servient place in the great project.

After two hours, as they walked, a dark raincloud obscured the sun with mighty rumblings of thunder overhead but passed over without rain. They reached the lower pasture, a fairy-tale world of sun through leaves, swathes of wildflowers, the steady drone of bees, hearing the occasional tinkle of cowbells, all different; trebles and deeper notes in twos and threes. And, below, the glassy pale-blue slash of Wolfgangsee. They could make out the white dot of the paddle steamer *Kaiser Franz Joseph* on its trip from St Gilgen to Ströbl. They had ambled in the small towns at either end of the long lake by terraced cafes and verdant flower gardens overhanging the water. Seen the piers where the ferries tied up, the *Wolfgang Amadeus*, the *Salz Kammergut* and others. It was really two lakes joined together by a narrow channel at the town of St Wolfgang where they were staying. As they descended, an occasional farmhouse could be seen through trees and the white church tower and famous black roofs of the Weissen Rössl hotel on the shore of the lake.

'Hard to believe that just last month I was left for dead in a forest,' Morton mused. 'Seems so long ago, so far away.'

'The past is another country.' Emily smiled sympathetically. 'You've come through it. We've come through it. Funny that you never got a story out of it, for all your troubles.'

Morton deeply inhaled the fragrant warm air. 'Hugh didn't

want to do it. Said the context was too difficult to explain. Even although he'd already done that earlier "abduction" piece. I think he was a bit worried about being the only paper that would run it – given the Home Secretary's denials.'

'Worried about legal action?'

'Perhaps.'

Emily glanced over but he couldn't see her eyes behind her sunglasses. 'He's not usually so timid,' she said.

'I think the lack of evidence in Sweden bothered him.'

'Well, Special Branch had to fly you home.'

'True, but they wouldn't corroborate a media story.' He grinned. 'They'd be worried somebody would accuse them of misusing public funds bringing me back in a private plane.'

'You can understand that. That's what did for Chief Inspector McLennan. I liked him, felt I could trust him.'

'A good man. Kicked out on a trumped-up charge,' Morton said, mopping at the sweat on his forehead with a tissue. 'And of course, it didn't help that I refused to name the old couple in Sweden who saved me. There's no way I'm putting their names into circulation. The financial trail; train ticket, B&B receipt, phone purchase, should have been enough to stand up the story. But of course, they only prove that I was in Sweden, not how I got there or what happened to me in Ogeström forest.'

Emily sipped from her water bottle as they admired the lake and the shining town of St Wolfgang. 'You might be right. At least Luke's come out of it alright, with that cyber-security job with RBS. He's earning a fortune. I think he's planning to buy a flat. Off on holiday to the Netherlands next week.'

'Hugh offered me a fulltime job,' Morton told her. 'I said I'd think about it.'

'Oh, he offered you that again?'

'Four days a week. Steady money though.' He sniffed. 'Not to be sneezed at in this day and age. Not sure if it's quite me.'

As they turned a bend into the long downhill and the houses, they saw a rustic wooden bench on a little platform a few feet above the track. Warmed by the sun, it had a panoramic view of the lake. There was something of a fairy-tale about the scene, Morton thought.

'You know, Emily, I don't think he – Hamner – intended to kill me. Not in the beginning. He simply wanted to probe me for information, particularly on Cerberus. I think the plan changed only when Luke turned up and they realised that I could give the game away. They must have planned to bump him off. In fact, their strategy depended on it. So they decided Luke would live and I would have to die and Hamner would disappear.'

'Yes,' Emily agreed, her eyes inscrutable behind sunglasses. 'But Brodagh would remember seeing you with this other man. Ross Mackie too.'

'Mackie would be bound by the Official Secrets Act as a serving policeman or soldier or whatever he is… couldn't say anything. Yes, Brodagh would remember, and she distrusted him from the start, so it would be a mystery but nothing could be proved. There wouldn't be any useable evidence. I would be a rotting corpse in a remote forest in Sweden.'

'Ugh. Don't.'

'I think he was conflicted. He was instructed to do it, but he wasn't happy about it. In fact, maybe his heart wasn't in it. Maybe that was why he failed on the Skeppsbron? We'd spent four days and nights together and then he had to… well, he just… couldn't.'

'Enough! Come on, I need coffee and cake. I loved the

rhubarbe küchen in that place on the square.'

'You can keep your cake. Cold beer for me,' he said, 'and crisps.'

As they descended, hand-in-hand, into the sunshine and the town on the shining lake, the world seemed to give him every indication that it could be, albeit temporarily, a brighter and a happier place.

Acknowledgements

I would like to thank readers who have taken the trouble to contact me, and reviewers, both in the print media and online, who have also been kind. I'd like to thank my stalwart band of supporters: Jean Lee, Susan Procadair, Iain Sutherland, Alan Woodcock, Fiona Macpherson, Mike Strachan, Andrew Scobie, Mick McCluskey, Alan Mair, David McGovern, Norma McDonald, Julian Rudd, Marlene McBay, Jane Phillips, Rob Gibson, Phil Stewart and a few others who prefer not to be mentioned.

The research material of many authors has been useful in this book and I am grateful in particular to the authors of various chapters of *Security in a Small Nation*: Scotland, Democracy, Politics, edited by Andrew W. Neal, Open Book Publishers, 2017.

Author's Note

All the characters in this book are fictitious although where real persons do appear as themselves, glimpsed in passing, it is intended as a celebration of their existence in the real world. I have been vague about the exact location in Glasgow of MI5's Scotland Station for obvious reasons and activities and conversations inside it are of course, entirely a figment of my own imagination.

ALSO BY ANDREW SCOTT

Available from Twa Corbies Publishing

Deadly Secrecy

Willie Morton investigates the death of anti-nuclear activist Angus McBain and begins to suspect he was killed for what he knew. Is the UK Government implicated in the murder of McBain and the movement of illegal radioactive convoys heading for Dounreay?

Paperback £8.99 | Kindle ebook £1.99

* * *

Scotched Nation

Five months after Scotland's Independence Referendum, Willie Morton's uncanny resemblance to a man let off a drink driving charge on Home Office orders allows him to get inside a secret plot by members of MI5, politicians and senior civil servants. But just how far will they go to frustrate democracy?

Paperback £8.99 | Kindle ebook £2.46
Audible Audiobook (Narrated by David Sillars) £12.99

* * *

Purchase these titles at selected local bookshops or online, or order by email from Twa Corbies Publishing: *twacorbiespublishing@gmail.com*

Willie Morton will be back soon in a new escapade…